So much for stealth

He'd only got halfway to the lights when the man addressed him from a pool of shadows to his left, between a thresher and a skid loader. The lookout spoke in Russian, but his challenge had the tone of "Who in hell are you?"

Bolan let his AK answer back, one Russian to another. Three rounds at a range of six or seven feet, two punching through a plastic cooler the stranger carried, loosing plumes of smoke. His muzzle-flashes lit a startled face before it toppled over backward, out of frame.

He dodged between a swather and a mower, reached a different aisle and pounded toward the bright oasis where the action was. Bolan could hear people scrambling, as a voice called out, "Mikhail? Mikhail!"

Presumably calling the dead guy.

Bolan let the others wonder about the body as he moved in for the kill.

Don Pendleton's Mack Bolan®

Road of Bones

A GOLD EAGLE BOOK FROM

W🦅RLDWIDE®

TORONTO • NEW YORK • LONDON
AMSTERDAM • PARIS • SYDNEY • HAMBURG
STOCKHOLM • ATHENS • TOKYO • MILAN
MADRID • WARSAW • BUDAPEST • AUCKLAND

First edition April 2012

ISBN-13: 978-0-373-61552-0

Special thanks and acknowledgment to
Mike Newton for his contribution to this work.

ROAD OF BONES

Printed in U.S.A.

Russia will not soon become, if it ever becomes, a second copy of the United States or England, where liberal values have deep historic roots.

—Vladimir Putin
1952-

Don't you forget what's divine about the Russian soul—and that's resignation.

—Joseph Conrad
1857-1924

I'm resigned to do this job regardless of the opposition. I'll bet my soul on it.

—Mack Bolan

PROLOGUE

Yakutsk, Sakha Republic, Russian Federation

Yakutsk Airport was small by Western standards. One of its two runways was a parking lot for aircraft, while the other handled both arrivals and departures, moving seven hundred passengers per hour at peak efficiency. The international terminal, built in 1996, was showing signs of age. The domestic terminal, meanwhile, was constructed sixty-five years earlier, in Stalin's time.

Tatyana Anuchin and Sergey Dollezhal were going international, a Ural Airlines flight to Leonardo da Vinci-Fiumicino Airport in Rome with 160 other passengers and crew aboard a Tupolev Tu-154M—Russia's equivalent of the Boeing 727. The aircraft had a cruising range of twenty-seven hundred miles, which meant a stop for fuel in Chelyabinsk before proceeding on to Italy. With time on the ground, that meant nine more hours before they cleared Russian soil.

Before they were safe.

"You need to relax," Dollezhal said.

"I'll relax in Rome," Anuchin replied. "Better yet, in London."

"You give them too much credit," he chided. "We have a good lead."

"Oh, yes? Why not hire a car, then?" she challenged. "We'll make it a holiday."

"All I am saying—"

She cut him off, hissing, "They're not as stupid as you give them credit for. They must know that we're running by now."

And unarmed, since they had left their weapons in the car at long-term parking, to avoid any problems with airport security. Anuchin felt naked without the MP-443 Grach semiauto pistol she had carried with official sanction for the past nine years, used twice in the line of duty.

All that was behind her now that she was running with Dollezhal.

"We board in twenty minutes," he remarked.

"And they could just as well be waiting when we land in Chelyabinsk, with two damned ho°urs to kill."

"It was the best connection we could manage," he reminded her.

"I *know* that, but it isn't good enough."

"You say I give them too much credit for stupidity, Tanni," he said, using her nickname. "I think you make them omniscient when they're not."

"We'll see," she answered, thinking to herself that twenty minutes was a lifetime.

"SPREAD OUT and sweep the terminal. Eyes sharp," Valentin Grushin said.

"And if we spot them?" Pavel Antonov inquired.

"No shooting in the terminal," Grushin replied. "No shooting, period, unless they leave no other choice. Remember they're wanted for questioning."

Mikhail Krylov snorted at that. "They may prefer to be shot."

"It's their choice, then," Grushin said. "Just follow your orders."

They fanned out to cover the terminal, three hunters seeking their prey. Outside the terminal, watching the exits, their fourth man—Fyodor Dushkin—sat at the wheel of a Lada Riva sedan, waiting to signal if the targets slipped past them somehow.

If they were even at the airport now.

Grushin trusted the tip they'd received, but the caller had mentioned no flight in particular, no destination. By now, the targets could have flown the coop on any one of nine airlines, with destinations ranging from China and Thailand to Egypt, Tunisia and most of Europe.

What they would *not* do, if they were sane, was try to hide in Russia. That was tantamount to slow and painful suicide.

Grushin was tasked to find and seize the targets, not pursue them if they managed to fly out of Yakutsk Airport. If he missed them, his part in the hunt was finished.

But his trouble would have just begun.

The people who employed him paid for positive results in cash. Their currency for failure was a very different proposition altogether.

As he moved along the concourse, Grushin watched for uniformed Militsiya officers, acutely conscious of the PP-2000 machine pistol that he wore beneath his long coat on a leather sling. The weapon measured only 13.4 inches with its stock folded and weighed about five pounds with a fully loaded magazine of forty-four 9 mm Parabellum rounds. For this job, Grushin had foregone the 7N31 +P+ armor-piercing loads, but had some in the car, in case the hunt became a chase on wheels.

In which case, he supposed, they likely would have failed.

A crackle from the tiny earbud that he wore almost made Grushin jump. Krylov's voice telling him, "I've found them. Ural Airlines."

Flushed with instantaneous relief, Grushin changed course and walked more rapidly across the terminal.

"SON OF A BITCH!" Dollezhal spit the words as if they tasted foul. "I know that man in the blue windbreaker."

Anuchin found the man he was referring to and felt her heart skip as she realized that *he* was watching *them*.

Five minutes left until their flight was called for boarding, and the chance was lost to them. How many other trackers were there in the terminal, converging on them even now?

"Let's go," Dollezhal said urgently.

"Go where?" she countered. "He's already seen us."

"Seeing's one thing," he replied. "Holding's another."

Fearing that they were already lost, she nonetheless stood and shouldered her carry-on with the laptop inside. There was nothing in it to hang them if she had to ditch it, running. All the details were inside her head and in her companion's, ready for bullets to scramble and wipe out the warning they carried.

Even now, they didn't run, but walked with purpose, swiftly, Anuchin having no idea of Dollezhal's plan or destination. When they missed their flight, as they were bound to do, what avenues remained?

"In here," he said, ducking into a men's restroom without looking back.

Cheeks flaming from childish embarrassment, Anuchin followed, prepared to ask what he was doing when he clutched her arm and pulled her away from the door.

"Find a stall," he commanded. "Lock it. Put your feet up."

As if that would help, when the man had seen them both enter. Still, she followed instructions, chose the middle of nine toilet stalls, closed the door and secured its cheap latch. Then she climbed up on the seat, crouching awkwardly over the bowl.

Anuchin heard the restroom door swing open, followed by a scuffling sound and muttered cursing.

Dollezhal was fighting for his life.

Her first instinct was to rush out and help him, but the *phut* of a silenced weapon stopped her. Teetering on top of the commode, she waited, trembling, as footsteps advanced toward the stalls and their doors began to slam open.

The first touch on hers met resistance. A gruff voice said, "Here," and the scraping of shoe soles converged. Knuckles rapped and a voice like a wood rasp inquired, "Are you there, little traitor?"

Irrationally, she kept silent, then bit her tongue to keep from squealing as another *phut* punched a hole in the cubicle's door and cracked the tile behind her, stinging her neck with splinters.

"Open up!" a second voice commanded her. "We're tired of playing now!"

She stood, unlatched the door, leaving room for herself as it opened, with the commode pressing against her calves. Three faces leered at her, three pistols aiming at her face.

"Surprise!" the middle gunman said. "We're going for a ride."

CHAPTER ONE

Yakutsk, seven hours later

Yakutsk owed its existence to the tide of war and tyranny. Constructed as a fort by Cossack warlord Pyotr Beketov in 1632, within seven years it had become the seat of power for an independent military fiefdom whose commander sent troops ranging to the south and east. Discovery of gold and diamonds in the late nineteenth century turned Yakutsk into a mining boomtown. The Sakha Republic still supplied twenty percent of the world's rough diamonds, but Yakutsk owed its final growth surge to Russia's Man of Steel.

Joseph Stalin was one of those people who chose his own name and made grim history—like Jack the Ripper and the Zodiac killer, but on a grand scale. Born Ioseb Besarionis dze Jughashvili, he didn't like the sound of it, and so renamed himself Joseph Vissarionovich Stalin—Russian for "steel"—after joining the early Bolshevik movement and being convicted of bank robbery. Exile to Siberia couldn't tame him, but it gave him ideas.

Climbing the revolutionary food chain with ruthless cunning, Stalin was Vladimir Lenin's strong right hand in 1917 and beyond. When Lenin died in 1924, Stalin rushed to fill the power vacuum in Moscow, exiling or executing his rivals and consolidating power in a dictatorship that scuttled any dreams of a Communist Utopia on Earth.

And he remembered Siberia. Over the next three decades, an estimated twenty-two million passed through Stalin's Chief Administration of Corrective Labor Camps and Colonies, better known as gulags for short. Based on figures released after communism's collapse in 1991, some 1.6 million internees died in Stalin's camps between 1929 and his own death in 1953.

But killing hadn't ended with the cold war in the Russian Federation. Life and death went on as usual. Mack Bolan was in Yakutsk to prevent one death—and likely to inflict more in the process.

Business as usual for the Executioner.

It was a rush job, with time being of the essence. Bolan drove his GAZ-31105 Volga sedan along the Lena River's waterfront with barges and an island to his right, warehouses on his left, looking for the address where he could—hopefully—collect his package from some people who weren't expecting him.

And there it was.

He drove past, boxed the block and rolled back toward the water with the makings of a plan in mind. He'd keep it simple: hit and git, if that was possible.

If not…well, Bolan played the cards that he was dealt.

And on occasion, he'd been known to throw away the deck.

He parked within a half block of his target, killed the Volga's engine and turned to his tools. First up was an AKS-74U submachine gun, nineteen inches long with its wire stock folded, weighing five and a half pounds unloaded. Size aside, it had the same firepower as its parent weapon, the venerable AK-74 assault rifle in 5.45 mm, with a cyclic rate of 650 rounds per minute. On paper, the little gun's effective range was listed as 350 yards, but with an eight-inch barrel it was used primarily for work up close and personal.

For backup, Bolan wore an MR-444 Baghira semiauto pistol in a fast-draw shoulder rig. The Russian-made side-arm was chambered for 9 mm Parabellum rounds, carry-ing fifteen in a double-column box magazine.

His less-lethal option consisted of four GSZ-33 stun grenades, a flash-bang model equivalent to the U.S.-made M-84 that generated one million candela to blind a target on detonation, while shocking him deaf and nearly un-conscious with 180 decibels of concussive sound inside a five-foot radius. When they were clipped to Bolan's belt and the pockets of his long coat filled with extra maga-zines, he left the sedan and locked it, moving toward the warehouse with the address offered by his contact.

Despite the vote of confidence from Langley, filtered back to Bolan through his friends at Stony Man, there was a chance that his informant could turn out to be a rat. In which case, it was fifty-fifty that Bolan would never have a chance for payback.

Not in this life, anyway.

But there was one thing you could say about the odds on any battlefield.

They shifted when the Executioner arrived.

WHEN THE INTERROGATOR took a break, Valentin Grushin braced him, getting in his face to ask him, "Are you making any progress?"

The pale man regarded Grushin as he might a labora-tory specimen, perhaps a frog or piglet offered for dis-section. Grushin thought, again, how much the creepy bastard looked like Dracula. Not old Lugosi, long before his time, but Christopher Lee in the great Hammer films from the sixties and seventies.

"She's tough," the pale man said. "I give her that."

His name was Ivan Shukov, but inevitably he was known within the dark world he inhabited as Ivan the Terrible. No surprise there, from what Grushin had heard—and now seen—of his work.

"I would have said you're getting nowhere," Grushin said, emboldened by his guns and three companions. "All this time, and nothing."

All that screaming, and the generator humming, Shukov murmuring his questions as he placed the alligator clips for maximum effect. How many volts? Enough to singe the flesh without inflicting death or permanent disfigurement.

So far.

Grushin wasn't unsettled by the screaming. He had made some women scream himself—a few from pleasure, others not so much. Insensitivity to suffering was part of what equipped him for his work, a subset of his general indifference to the fate of other human beings.

No. What made his skin crawl in the presence of a man like Ivan Shukov—and there seemed to be a surfeit of them in the world these days—was the disturbing sense that he, Grushin, might fall into the hands of such a man someday.

And then what would become of him?

It would be easy to transgress and fall from grace. A simple comment in the wrong place, at the wrong time, might betray him. Passed along maliciously, amended and redacted, any casual remark could turn into a death sentence. And while he didn't relish death, Grushin had long since come to terms with personal mortality, accepting that the chances of a long and happy life were slim indeed.

It wasn't dying that he feared, so much as screaming out his final breath while everything that made him human was extracted, sliced and diced or seared with flame, by someone like Ivan the Terrible.

Had he already gone too far in goading the interrogator? Would his criticism get back to the man in charge, be filed away for future reference and used against him somewhere down the line? Perhaps, but now it was too late to take it back.

"I'm thinking of a new approach," Shukov said.

"Oh?" Grushin strived for a noncommittal tone.

"Selective applications, heat and cold," Shukov explained. "You have dry ice?"

"Dry ice? No," Grushin replied.

"But you can find some, yes?"

Grushin considered it. Where would he locate dry ice?

As if reading his mind, Shukov said, "I suggest the ice plant. Kulakovsky Street. You know it?"

"I can find it," Grushin said, determined not to ask Shukov for the address.

"A pound or so should be sufficient," Shukov said. "I have a pair of gloves. And tongs."

Of course he would.

"I'll send Mikhail," Grushin said, wishing he could go himself and get away from Shukov for a while. Ivan the Terrible depressed him, set his teeth on edge and made him feel the need to shower under scalding water.

Too late, Grushin thought. He was already soiled beyond redemption, not that he placed any faith in superstition or the church. Forgiveness, if it mattered, always called for a confession and repentance, whereas Grushin had been raised to keep his mouth shut in the presence of authority.

And truth be told, he wasn't sorry for the things that he had done. Well, maybe one or two of them, but just a little.

Dry ice coming up, he thought, and bustled off to find Mikhail.

BOLAN COULDN'T READ the sign, in Cyrillic, outside the warehouse, but he didn't need to. The address was painted in Arabic numerals, and the numbers didn't lie.

Unless his contact had.

No way to second-guess it now as he approached in darkness. Seven hours had passed since the package had been lifted, and he understood the kind of damage that could be inflicted in that span of time.

A gunshot to the head took, what, a fraction of a second? But the men he had to deal with would be after information, likely skilled in methods of extracting it. How long that took depended on their subject's pain threshold and powers of endurance.

No one was immune to torture. Everybody broke, sooner or later, if they didn't die from shock or blood loss. But would a subject give up what his or her tormentors required, or misdirect them? Would the innocent confess to heinous crimes, while the guilty targeted a fictional accomplice?

Bolan reckoned he had seen the worst of it on more than one occasion. If he'd come too late this time, at least he could avenge the victim and make sure that her interrogators felt a measure of the pain they had dispensed. Or maybe they'd be lucky, and he'd simply kill them where they stood.

But first, he had to get inside.

The large doors on the warehouse loading dock were padlocked, and their rumbling would have been too noisy even if they weren't secured. He sought another way inside and found it at the southeast corner of the big, old building. An employees' entrance, he supposed, although its faded sign was gibberish.

He tried the knob and wasn't surprised to find it locked. No sign of an alarm from where he stood, fishing inside a pocket for a set of picks. Bolan spent sixty seconds on the lock—no dead bolt on the door to make it complicated—and he pocketed the picks again before he crossed the threshold.

The soldier was cautious now, letting the stubby muzzle of his submachine gun lead him through a corridor with concrete underfoot and metal walls on either side. The hallway ran for twenty feet and then turned left at a dead-end partition, granting Bolan access to the warehouse proper.

The building was dark, except at the far end, where two banks of overhead lights blazed his trail. Between Bolan and what he took to be his destination, ranks of agricultural machinery stood silent in the murk. He picked out tractors, cultivators, backhoes, combine harvesters. Moving between them, the soldier homed in on sounds of moaning and a male voice asking questions that he couldn't translate.

They were still at work, then, but he still might be too late. Beyond a certain point there was no rescue, and the only mercy came with death's release from hopeless agony. If it came down to that, Bolan was equal to the task.

When he was halfway to the lights, a voice addressed him from a pool of shadows to his left, between a thresher and a skid loader. The lookout spoke in Russian. "Who the hell are you?"

Bolan let his AK answer back, one Russian to another. Three rounds at a range of six or seven feet, two punching through a plastic cooler that the stranger carried, loosing plumes of smoke. His muzzle-flashes lit a startled face before it toppled over backward, out of frame.

So much for stealth.

He dodged between a swather and a mower, reached a different aisle and pounded toward the bright oasis where the action was. Bolan could hear people scrambling, as a voice called out, "Mikhail? *Mikhail!*"

Presumably the dead guy.

Bolan let the others wonder as he moved in for the kill.

TATYANA ANUCHIN hoped she was dying. She'd heard the pale interrogator asking for dry ice and tried not to imagine how or where he'd use it. After the electric shocks, it hardly seemed to matter, but she understood that pain was both his passion and profession. Since she had resisted his best efforts to the moment, he could only plan on doing something worse.

She hoped to die before she cracked and told her captors everything. Exactly what she knew and how she had acquired that knowledge, naming sources both unwitting and deliberate. Sergey had been the lucky one, compelling them to kill him outright at the airport terminal. In retrospect, Anuchin wished that she possessed the same presence of mind.

Next time, she thought, and almost found it humorous.

That would confuse them, if she burst out laughing. If nothing else, it would insult the ghoul they'd summoned to abuse her. Anuchin wondered if he was a colleague from the *Federal'naya sluzhba bezopasnosti Rossiyskoy*

Federatsii, the FSB, someone whom she might have seen at headquarters and overlooked in passing.

Someone from the Lubyanka's basement? Or an operator from the private sector, peddling his skills and predilection to the highest bidder in a cutthroat marketplace?

It hardly mattered now, when she was duct-taped naked to a wooden chair, her flesh a crazy quilt of superficial burns and bite marks from the alligator clips. The jolting pain still resonated in her muscles, in her teeth and jaws. A migraine headache pulsed behind her eyes.

Was it a sin to pray for death? If so, she didn't care.

Could hell be any worse than this?

Against her will, Anuchin began to imagine the next phase of her live dissection. Dry ice, she knew, was the solid form of carbon dioxide. Its normal temperature hovered around -109 degrees Fahrenheit, cold enough to cause frostbite on contact. Above -70 degrees, it sublimated into frosty-looking gas, the "fog" so often used on movie sets for old-time horror films.

And as a tool of torture, she recognized that it could prove effective. As to whether it was worse than electricity…well, she'd simply have to wait and see.

If she withstood the ghoul's next round of questions, how would he proceed? With scalpels or a blowtorch? Acid? Could she hope for shock to spare her from the worst of it, or was he skilled enough to revive her with drugs?

Holding her breath accomplished nothing, as she'd quickly learned. Innate survival mechanisms wouldn't let her suffocate herself. If her hands were free—

The gunshots startled Anuchin from her fantasy of suicide. Her eyes snapped open, saw her captors facing toward the darkness of the cavernous warehouse. The ghoul was shifting nervously from foot to foot, as one of those who'd snatched her from the airport shouted to the long rows of machinery.

"Mikhail? *Mikhail!*"

No answer from the shadows.

The thought of rescue never entered her mind. Who was there left to help her? No one from the Ministry of Justice that she served. They wished her dead, silenced forever, buried with the secrets she'd uncovered.

As for private parties, Anuchin couldn't think of one who had the means to find her coupled with an interest in helping her survive. Certainly, she had no friends within the Russian Mafia, denizens of the thieves world that infested every level of Russian society from top to bottom.

With Sergey dead, she had no one.

A quarrel between murderers, then, with Anuchin caught in the middle. Better that than more torture. She could always hope for a stray bullet to release her from her world of pain.

Was that so much to ask?

Helpless and totally exposed, she closed her eyes again and mouthed another silent prayer.

WHILE ONE OF BOLAN'S targets shouted for Mikhail, others were fanning out to sweep the warehouse, homing in on the echoes of his first gunshots. He saw one man breaking to his left, another to his right, their mouthpiece fading back to crouch behind a bulky gravity wagon.

That left two figures visible beneath the warehouse lights. A naked woman was fastened to a chair with duct tape at her wrists and ankles, plus a loop around her ribs, slumped with her chin on her chest. Beside her, to her left, a tall man in a raincoat stood and goggled at the shadows with protruding eyes. A glint of stainless steel told Bolan that he held a knife.

Completely useless in a gunfight.

From the tall man's look and his reaction to the shots, Bolan knew he was the inquisitor. Without a second thought, he raised the AKS and stitched the gawker with a rising burst from clavicle to forehead, shattering his face. The guy went down as if someone had cut his strings, and Bolan saw the woman in the chair turn toward him, blink, then look around to find out where the shots had come from.

Wondering if she was next?

The shooter behind the gravity wagon was playing it safe. His cohorts, flanking Bolan, did their best to keep it stealthy, but their style was obviously more attuned to smash-and-grab than creep-and-sneak. They telegraphed their moves with scuffling feet, letting their target track them in the dark.

Bolan fell back from the bright lights and climbed aboard a midsize Caterpillar tractor, crouching with his back against its open cab. He'd let the hunters come to him—the first of them, at least—and see what happened next.

The gunman coming from his left was faster, shuffling toward Bolan from behind a bale wrapper. He didn't check the high ground, though, intent on peering under things, where shadows pooled. When he had closed the gap to twenty feet, a burst from Bolan's SMG ripped into him and dropped him, twitching, on his back.

The dead guy's backup took advantage of the muzzle-flash and banged away at Bolan with a pistol, but the Executioner was already in motion, airborne, dropping to a crouch behind the tractor as incoming rounds cracked through its cab.

The soldier broke to his left, keeping the bulk of the machine and its big engine block between his adversary

and himself. When he was near the tractor's nose, he
knelt, then stretched prone and crawled around beneath
the radiator grille, careful to keep his weapon's magazine
from scraping concrete as he went.

He caught the second shooter scrambling toward the
tractor, pistol out in front of him and ready for a hasty
shot if he was challenged. What he *wasn't* ready for was
half a dozen full-metal-jacket rounds slashing through
his thighs and pelvis, spinning him into the line of fire
and ending it with head shots.

Which left one.

Bolan emerged to find the last man standing with a
pistol pressed against the naked woman's head, half-
crouched to use her as a human shield.

The soldier found a vantage point beyond the ring
of light and stopped there, took a second to unfold his
submachine gun's stock and raise it to his shoulder. As
stubby as it was, the little room-broom hadn't been designed for sniping, but at forty feet he thought the shot
was doable.

His weapon had a flip-up rear sight with a front cylin-
drical post. Its eight-inch barrel produced a muzzle ve-
locity of 2400 feet per second, slower than the full-size
AK-74, but an insignificant difference at what amounted
to point-blank range.

While his target shouted, sounding more agitated
by the moment, Bolan found his mark and held it—just
above the guy's left eyebrow, with the SMG's selector set
for semiauto fire. One shot, and if he missed it…

Crack!

A crimson halo wreathed the gunman's head as he
slumped over backward. Bolan thought the naked woman
gasped but wasn't sure. He crossed the open floor to
reach her, opening a knife in transit. Keeping his eyes

averted as he slit the duct tape at her wrists and ankles, he reached around to cut one side along her rib cage.

Finally, he met her eyes and saw the fear behind them. When she asked him something, Bolan couldn't understand it.

"Slow down or speak English," he suggested.

"*Da*. Yes. Who are you?"

"A friend, sent to get you."

"Friend?" She didn't seem to recognize the term.

He nodded. "We need to go. Do you have any clothes?"

"Shredded," she told him, covering herself belatedly as best she could with slender arms. "They thought I wouldn't need them…after."

Bolan scanned the killing ground and saw a sport coat draped across a second chair, almost outside the ring of light. He collected it and passed it to the woman while he thought about the rest.

The man who'd used her as a shield was several inches taller than the woman, but he had a narrow waist. She'd have to roll the cuffs up on his slacks, but it could work if she cinched up his belt.

"You mind a pair of hand-me-downs?" he asked, his back turned as he began to strip the corpse.

"What do you…oh. No, those will do for now. My shoes are over here somewhere," she told him, moving gingerly toward the rim of shadow. "With my bag, I think."

Bolan kept his head turned as she came to get the slacks. When she was covered, buckling the dead man's belt, she told him, "Don't forget their guns."

CHAPTER TWO

Japan, seven hours earlier

Bolan was in the middle of another operation when the call came. He'd been wreaking havoc on a drug pipeline, tracking the flow of heroin from Yakuza controllers through the Philippines, on to Hawaii, where it spilled into the veins of addicts.

He was up against the Yamaguchi-gumi, Japan's most prosperous Yakuza Family and one of the world's largest criminal organizations, with an estimated forty-five thousand oath-bound members and countless other close associates. Aside from heroin, the syndicate made billions annually from gambling, human trafficking and prostitution, internet pornography, extortion, gunrunning, stock fraud and labor racketeering.

It had been five days since he'd taken on the mission, and the Executioner was close to wrapping up his game. He'd taken out the clan's first and second lieutenants, along with a couple dozen soldiers, and was planning a lethal surprise for the clan leader.

But then he got the call from home.

Drop everything and disengage, for now. We have a Level Four emergency.

Something in Russia, Hal Brognola told him, speaking guardedly despite the scrambled line. There was a job that absolutely couldn't wait, lives hanging in the balance.

One life in particular.

How fast could he get from Kobe to Yakutsk in Sakha Republic? Bolan ran the calculation on his laptop while he had the big Fed on the line. His destination was located nineteen hundred miles northwest of Kobe, travel time dependent on how soon he booked a flight, the aircraft he obtained and when it could take off.

"Charter a plane ASAP," Brognola had instructed him. "My dime. Call back when it's arranged, and you'll be met by someone from the Company. They'll have the details and your basic kit. I'm sending through a file right now."

Bolan opened his email, waited thirty seconds, then said, "Got it."

"Good. I'm here until you call about the flight."

The soldier cut the link and checked his watch. Eight-fifteen on a Saturday night in Kobe meant that it was 6:15 a.m. on Friday morning in Washington, D.C., thanks to the international date line. Brognola was a day and fourteen hours behind, but would be tracking the Russian event in real time.

Whatever it was.

Bolan booked his flight before reading the file. A charter company at Kobe Airport could put him aboard a Learjet 60 in two hours, if he had five grand and change to spare. Confirming that, Bolan was told the flight should take about four hours, which would put him on the ground in Yakutsk somewhere in the neighborhood of two-thirty to three o'clock on Sunday morning.

Fair enough.

He skimmed the file then, hitting the essentials, knowing there'd be ample time to study all its details in the air. Two agents of the FSB—Russia's Federal Security Service, successor to the infamous KGB—had been collaborating with the CIA and Interpol to blow the whistle on a network of corruption that involved the upper echelons of government and commerce in the Russian Federation. The specifics weren't provided, being strictly need-to-know, but Bolan got the picture.

There had always been corruption in the Soviet "worker's paradise" under one-party rule, but the floodgates had opened with Communism's collapse in 1991. Overnight, the world's largest state-controlled economy was jostled into line with what some pundits liked to call the "Washington consensus," adopting the alien concepts of liberalization and privatization.

The net result was economic chaos.

Liberalization meant eliminating price controls, which sparked hyperinflation and near-bankruptcy of Russian industry under President Boris Yeltsin. While Russia's elderly and others living on fixed incomes watched their lifestyle go to hell, shady entrepreneurs and black marketeers spawned under Mikhail Gorbachev's perestroika restructuring movement of 1985-90 rose to the top of the heap like scum on a stagnating pond. The Russian Mafia, formerly an underground network of thugs and swindlers, went public—then global—in an orgy of bribery, extortion and violence.

The result, inevitably, was a backlash of opposition, translated into widespread support for antireform candidates. Yeltsin's campaign to Westernize Russia by fiat, including dissolution of Parliament in September 1993, sparked open rebellion in Moscow. While Spetsnaz troops stormed Parliament, killing 187 dissidents and wounding more than four hundred, separatists in the Chechen Republic were charting a course toward civil war and a new age of domestic terrorism.

Meanwhile, a handful of wealthy oligarchs secured a

stranglehold on Russian banking, industry and the mass media, throwing their weight behind Yeltsin's reelection campaign in exchange for sweeping concessions. Public dissatisfaction with flagrant corruption and the endless war in Chechnya propelled the ex-FSB chief to the presidency in 2000—but what had really changed?

Only the names of those in charge, as far as Bolan could tell. The president ran with the oligarchs as the previous one had, while using his office and their widespread power to muffle dissent. The watchdog agency Human Rights Watch branded the man a "brutal" and "repressive" leader on par with the dictators in Pakistan and Zimbabwe. Rumor linked his backers to the assassinations of several investigative journalists, while Scotland Yard suspected Russian intelligence agents of murdering an ex-FSB whistle-blower in London.

Now, if Brognola's information was correct, another Russian agent's life was on the line for trying to expose corruption at the top. Bolan wasn't sure what he could do to help, but he would try—without expecting any radical reform of a society that had been steeped in mayhem, graft and privilege since Grand Duchy of Moscow was established in the fifteenth century.

And do his best, damn right.

The Yamaguchi-gumi would be waiting when he finished up in Russia. *If* he finished. If he lived.

And after that?

Another pipeline would take up the slack, of course. No victory was ever final in the hellgrounds. Only those who fell were out of action. Their intent and motivation would survive.

Raw greed and malice never died.

As long as Bolan lived, there would be more work for the Executioner.

But at the moment, here and now, he had a plane to catch.

By the time Bolan arrived at Kobe Airport with a small suitcase and laptop in a carry-on, the Learjet 60 was already fueled and waiting. Its two pilots were wrapping up their preflight checklist, while a young receptionist—bright-eyed and fresh-looking despite the hour—signed Bolan in and ran his credit card.

It was a limitless Visa, embossed with the name of "Matthew Cooper," which matched Bolan's passport of the moment, and his California driver's license. In fact, the alias aside, his credit card was perfectly legitimate. Whatever bills he managed to accumulate from month to month were paid in full from Stony Man Farm, in Virginia.

When all the paperwork was done, the receptionist thanked Mr. Cooper for his business and directed him outside to board his flight. Bolan hadn't booked a return flight, since he'd have to judge the situation on the ground once he arrived. Returning to Japan might not be feasible. Indeed, he wasn't sure that any airport service would be open to him once he'd managed to collect his package from the kidnappers who presently had custody. There were too many *ifs* for him to plan that far ahead.

If he was met, as planned, at Yakutsk Airport.

If the contact he had never met before provided proper gear and workable directions to his target.

If he found the agent he was on his way to save still breathing, fit to travel.

If he managed to extract the subject without getting either of them killed.

Then he could think about the quickest, safest way to put Yakutsk behind them and get out of Russia with their skins intact. And in the meantime, if Brognola's fears proved accurate, they'd be running from a dragnet that included both official hunters and whatever private thugs the FSB was able to enlist through its connections to the Russian underworld.

A cakewalk, right.

As if.

They were northbound over the Sea of Japan when Bolan reopened Brognola's file on his laptop. According to what he'd received, there'd been two FSB whistle-blowers. Lieutenant Sergey Dollezhal had fourteen years in harness, starting with the Federal Counterintelligence Service, or FSK, which had become the FSB in 1995. He was a legacy, in fact, the son of a former KGB colonel.

Make that *had been,* since his fatal shooting at the Ya-kutsk Airport several hours earlier.

Dollezhal's partner and accomplice in rattling the powers that be was Sergeant Tatyana Anuchin, nine years on the job and partnered with Dollezhal for the past six. Brognola had no details on the cases they had worked, nor was it relevant. Somewhere along the line, they had grown disaffected against the corrupt shenanigans they'd witnessed on a daily basis and had reached out cautiously to Interpol.

Dramatic works of fiction commonly portrayed Inter-pol—the International Criminal Police Organization—as a gung-ho group of global crime fighters. In fact, from its inception back in 1923, the group has served a single purpose: to facilitate communication and cooperation between law-enforcement agencies of different nations. Its agents didn't make arrests, nor did they prosecute sus-pected felons. They had no police powers at all.

But they liaised, and so it was that Interpol put Dolle-zhal in touch with someone from the CIA, who shared his information with the FBI and U.S. Immigration and Customs Enforcement—ICE. A deal was struck, includ-

ing terms of sanctuary in exchange for information leading to indictments and eventual testimony at trial.

It was a risky bargain overall, considering the countless possibilities of weak links in the chain. As recently
as June 2010, a former president of Interpol had been convicted in South Africa on charges of accepting six-figure
bribes from drug traffickers. That case wasn't unique,
and there was also leak potential with the CIA, the FBI
and ICE.

But Dollezhal and Anuchin had taken the chance. For
thirteen months they'd smuggled evidence and information out of Russia—files and photographs, transcripts of
conversations, various financial records—all their han-
dlers needed for indictments, though it likely wouldn't
stand in court without corroborating testimony from the
two agents themselves.

Which brought them to the final phase: escape.

And it had failed.

Somehow, somewhere, they'd been exposed. A hit
team had surprised them, literally at their exit flight's
departure gate with minutes left till takeoff. Dollezhal
had gone down fighting in the terminal men's room; his
partner had been carried off to who knew where.

Well, someone knew.

The screws were tightened, bribes were likely offered
and the information was secured. An address in Yakutsk,
if it wasn't too late by now.

But who would intervene?

The FBI and ICE were too far out of bounds, would
never get cooperation from Russian authorities if those
authorities had been responsible for murder and kidnap-
ping. That left Langley, but the Company still had to work
with leaders of the FSB, at least in theory, so its chief had
passed the buck.

To Stony Man.

Which put Bolan on the red-eye out of Kobe, winging toward Siberia. At least it wasn't winter, but that wouldn't matter if he failed.

Regardless of geography, all graves were cold.

Yakutsk

YAKUTSK WAS LOCATED 280 miles south of the Arctic Circle. It had some 212,000 inhabitants, but Bolan was only looking for one as he stepped off the plane from Kobe.

Brognola's file had named his contact as Yuri Fedchenko, age twenty-seven, a CIA contract employee presumably unknown to the authorities. He would be waiting with a car for Bolan, rented legally in Matthew Cooper's name, together with some tools that might be useful in extracting Tatyana Anuchin from her life-or-death predicament.

And this was where the plan could fail, before Bolan had walked a dozen yards on Russian soil. There could be shooters waiting, either licensed by the state or hired to do a bit of wet work on the side, and that would be the end of it.

The end of him.

But Bolan didn't step into an ambush when he left the plane. The only person waiting for him was his contact, not quite smiling as he reached for the soldier's hand and pumped it once. Fedchenko's English took some getting used to, but he managed to communicate.

There was a warehouse on the river. He supplied the address and a map of Yakutsk with the shortest route marked with a crimson felt-tipped pen. The car he'd brought for Bolan was a GAZ-31105 Volga four-door with a full tank of gas. In its trunk, examined once the Japanese pilots had made their way into the terminal, the Executioner found hardware waiting for the next phase of his task.

Bolan checked the gear, confirmed as best he could that all of it was functional, the magazines fully loaded. He couldn't test the flash-bangs without wasting them and raising hell outside the airport terminal, but that was life.

Or death, if any of the hardware let him down.

"How many men are guarding her?" he asked Fedchenko.

"Four were seen at the airport. Whether they have more at the warehouse, I can't say."

"What are they? Do you know?"

The Russian looked confused. "Sorry, please?" he said.

"The crew," Bolan said. "Are they FSB? FSO? Mafiya?"

Fedchenko shrugged and said, "It could be anyone."

"Where can I drop you?" Bolan asked as they climbed into the sedan, Bolan behind the steering wheel.

Fedchenko named an all-night coffee shop along the route marked on his map, and Bolan reached it seven minutes later, thanked the man and then continued on his way alone.

The next potential ambush site would be the warehouse. Bolan hadn't smelled a setup yet, but caution kept him breathing. He had known Yuri Fedchenko less than half an hour, hadn't met the men behind him who had dealt with Brognola, and trust could only stretch so far.

There'd been a time when Bolan and Brognola both had faith in Langley, but a brutal act of treachery had changed all that. Today, the big Fed kept the Company at arm's length when he could and triple-checked their information prior to putting agents in the field, if time allowed.

This night, there was no time to spare. No room for judgment by committee. It was either take the job and run with it, or leave a brave agent to die.

Some people Bolan knew would probably have let her go without a second thought. Why help a Russian agent, even if her information might jail felons in the States and drag some of her homeland's dirty laundry into daylight? Russia and the U.S. had been rivals for the best part of a century, with only slight improvement under glasnost, perestroika and the rest of it. One less Russki was good, no matter how you sliced it.

Bolan disagreed.

He honored courage, sacrifice and good intentions—though it was a fact they often paved the road to hell. If he could save Tatyana Anuchin's life and put her on a witness stand back home to land some spies and mobsters in a prison cell, Bolan felt bound to try.

But recognizing sacrifice didn't mean that he planned to offer up himself as one. Bolan had never been a kamikaze warrior prone to suicide. He weighed the odds on every move he made, once battle had been joined, and if some of those moves seemed suicidal to the uninitiated, that was an illusion. He was thinking all the time, six moves ahead.

He did his best, anticipating what an enemy might do in any given situation, but he couldn't *know* exactly what would happen. Not until he pulled a trigger and sent death streaking downrange. At that point, Bolan knew that flesh and blood had to yield to firepower.

His own included, sure.

And if he failed, that was the end of it. There'd be no time for Brognola to find another operative, get him in the air to Yakutsk before Anuchin broke or simply died under interrogation. It was now or never, all or nothing.

He drove along the waterfront, the Lena River on his right and flowing northward toward the Arctic Ocean. On its far side lay the Lena Highway, accessed during spring and summer via ferry, or across the frozen river's ice in winter.

When Bolan spied the address he was seeking, he immediately checked for lookouts on the street and snipers on the rooftops. Finding none, he sketched the outline of a plan and drove once more around the block to verify his first impression of the target.

All that now remained was for the Executioner to act.

He would postpone consideration of the future until he had Anuchin safely in his hands.

CHAPTER THREE

Yakutsk

Bolan drove aimlessly, letting the woman calm down. She was hurting, of course. He'd seen the marks of torture on her flesh before she dressed, and while they all looked superficial, he knew he couldn't judge her pain threshold or personal resilience on such short acquaintance.

"You're safe now," he told her.

"Safe?" She made a little hissing sound that could have been sarcastic laughter filtered through exhaustion. "What is safe?"

"We're getting out of here," he said.

"You think so?"

"That's the plan."

After a silent interval, she said, "I told them nothing. It was close, though. If the dry ice had arrived…"

Bolan recalled the first goon he had met, the plastic cooler leaking smoky vapor as he dropped.

"You showed them how strong you are," Bolan said.

"Then why do I feel weak?"

"You're losing the adrenaline rush."

In fact, it didn't matter if she'd cracked or not, as long as she survived and followed through on testifying when the time came. The opposition had to have a fair idea of what Anuchin and her partner had uncovered, and the use to which it would be put. The torture was to verify her knowledge, prior to silencing the final witness and securing—as they hoped—a free pass on impending charges.

"I am cold, as well."

"That's shock," he said. "You need to rest. Stay warm. I wish we had a place where you could shower, maybe get some better clothes."

"There is a place," she told him, sounding groggy. "Keep on this way, then turn north on Ordzhonikidze Street."

"You'll stay awake and help me spot the sign?" he asked, not teasing her.

"I'll try. If not, you'll see a large Pervaya Pomosch pharmacy located on the northwest corner of the intersection. Let it be your guide."

"And after that?"

"I'll be awake, don't worry. I have too much pain for sleep."

He let that pass, knowing from personal experience that a commiserative stranger couldn't help. Instead, he asked, "Is this a safehouse that we're going to?"

"I hope so," she replied, forcing the vestige of a smile.

"It isn't FSB?" he asked.

"Private," she informed him. "Rented with Sergey so we could meet, collect our evidence, discuss what we had learned without an ear in every corner."

Bolan wondered if there had been more between the partners than idealism and a scheme for cleaning up the agency they served. Maybe the safehouse doubled as a love nest when they felt the need.

And if it had, so what?

If Anuchin and the late Dollezhal were hoping for a long-term cleanup of the FSB—much less the Russian Federation—Bolan pegged them as naive. Assuming they could bring down the top men, clean house beyond the normal game of hanging scapegoats out to dry, what then? Had either one of them imagined that they would be welcomed back as heroes to resume their duties for a grateful state?

Fat chance.

Still, they had tried. And Anuchin might succeed to some extent, if he could get her out of Russia in one piece and safely back to the United States.

Huge *if.*

He saw the pharmacy, turned north and drove another quarter mile before the woman had him turn again, and yet again, running parallel to Ordzhonikidze Street through a residential neighborhood. Six houses down, she had him pull in on the left.

"I have a key to the garage, unless they took it," Anuchin told him, rummaging around inside her bag. "No, here it is."

Bolan accepted it, unlocked the small attached garage and raised its door. No gunmen waited in the glare of headlights. He walked back to the GAZ and nosed it inside. Anuchin got out, found a light switch and stood by waiting until he had closed the door, then turned it on.

"In case someone is watching," she explained unnecessarily.

"I think they would have jumped us," Bolan said.

"You'll think I'm paranoid," she suggested.

"After tonight? Not even close," he promised.

Nodding almost thankfully, she turned and led the way into the house.

Moscow

"WHAT DO YOU mean, 'all dead'?" Eugene Marshak demanded.

"Just what I say, sir," Stephan Levshin replied. "All dead. Our men, that is."

Marshak might have slapped Levshin if they hadn't been separated by three thousand miles and six time zones. As it was, he clenched his teeth and said, "Major, if you cannot express yourself more clearly, I will find another officer who can. Now, would you care to try again?"

"Yes, sir," Levshin said stiffly. Wounded pride be damned. The man was growing arrogant. "Our escorts for the package have been killed, Colonel. Along with the examiner."

"Better," Marshak allowed, although the news was bad—nearly the worst it could have been. "And what about the package?"

"Gone, sir."

So it *was* the very worst scenario.

"Can you explain this?" he asked.

"The mechanics of it only, sir," his second in command replied. "At least one individual surprised them. The casings tell us he was armed with a Kalashnikov, one of the 5.45 millimeter models. Two of the escorts returned fire, with no apparent effect."

"You think one man?" Marshak pressed him.

"Yes, sir. From the appearance of the scene."

"I'll have to tell our friend," Marshak said.

"Yes, sir."

No names, although the line was meant to be secure. Who really knew these days?

"I don't suppose there's any way to find out what they learned, if anything?"

"No, sir. Without the package…" Levshin left the obvious unspoken.

"No." Marshak released a weary breath. "You must retrieve it, Major. At all costs. I will arrange for reinforcements as required."

"Yes, sir. Thank you, sir. I don't believe the package has left the area. There's been little time, and it may have been damaged."

"Ah."

Some hope, at least, if the interrogator's ministrations made it difficult for Tatyana Anuchin to travel. Still, she'd managed to escape, aided by whom? At least one killer and a wild card in the game, unknown to Marshak. If the man—or men—were good enough to sneak up on the capture team and take them down, could he—or they—smuggle the woman out of Yakutsk?

Out of Russia?

That was unacceptable. Unthinkable.

"You understand how bad it is for all of us, unless we put it right," Marshak reminded Levshin.

"Absolutely, sir. Our friend's men failed you. I will not."

"See that you don't," Marshak replied, and cut the link.

Six dead in Yakutsk now, counting the traitor Dollezhal. Digging so many graves in permafrost was tiresome, but there had to be room enough for half a dozen bodies in the Lena, surely. Failing that, Stephan could drop them down a mine shaft.

Out of sight, and who would give a damn?

Grigory Rybakov, of course. Four of the dead were his men, out on loan to help the FSB and cover his own ass at the same time. To plug the leak before it drowned them all.

And how bad would it be if Sergeant Anuchin escaped?

Russia's constitution banned extradition of citizens to stand trial abroad, but in rare cases trial on foreign charges might proceed in Russian courts, with "necessary foreign experts" participating in the prosecution. That wouldn't save Rybakov's men in the States or in Europe, of course, but Marshak cared little for them.

He was concerned about himself, the damage to his reputation, his career—and yes, to his accumulated fortune—if the bitch who had betrayed him wasn't found and silenced. He could deal with an internal inquiry, assisted by superiors who had as much or more to lose than Marshak did.

But if the case went public, he was lost.

A colonel made a nice fat sacrifice for others higher up the chain of rank. A general, perhaps, or someone in the prime minister's cabinet. Maybe the prime minister himself?

Before any of his superiors went down, they would be pleased to let him take the fall, resign in shame, perhaps receive a token prison term. There'd be a pension of some sort when he was finally paroled, of course…unless he had an accident in jail, or even prior to trial. Such things weren't unknown in Russia.

They were commonplace, in fact.

The answer was to find Anuchin and destroy her, with the man or men who cared enough to rescue her. And those who had employed *them,* if he had the opportunity.

And it had to be accomplished soon.

WHILE ANUCHIN showered, Bolan used his cell phone for a call to Yakutsk Airport. The Russian agent had gone through the telephone directory with him and had compiled a short list of three charter airlines operating from the local airport.

Bolan passed on Yakutskiye Avialinii, which Anuchin described as an official airport subsidiary, and tried his luck with the second company in line. Private Jets Charter Service had an English-language website and an operator who agreed that they could fly two passengers to Tokyo aboard a Dassault Falcon 50 or a Hawker 800 on three hours' notice for nine thousand dollars U.S.

The soldier put the nonrefundable deposit on his Visa card, and drifted to the bathroom, knocking hard enough for her to hear him in the shower.

"Almost done," she told him.

"Take your time," he called back through the door. "Our flight takes off at seven-thirty."

She turned the shower off and said, "You've booked a plane?"

"It's set," he answered. "All we have to do is check in with their booking agent at the terminal."

There was silence from Anuchin then, except for sounds of rustling fabric. Bolan guessed a towel, then clothing she had taken from a closet in the safehouse. Feeling like a voyeur, he retreated to the living room.

She joined him moments later, dressed in slacks, a blouse and sweater, with a towel around her head. There was a certain stiffness to her movements, which was no surprise after the ordeal she'd been through.

Still, she declared, "That's better."

"You can rest awhile before we go," Bolan said. "Longer, on the flight."

"They must have asked you questions."

"Just my name, and whether I could pay," Bolan replied.

"Your name. Which is…?"

They hadn't got around to formal introductions yet. "Matt Cooper," Bolan said. "And yours, I know."

"Of course, you must. You're CIA?" she asked.

"A cousin, several times removed."

"You realize the airport will be watched," she said.

"I know it's possible."

"Call it a certainty. They've caught me once already there," she stated. "You have no reinforcements?"

"No," he said. "Just me."

"I fear it's hopeless, then," she told him.

"That's the spirit."

Anuchin sat and began to dry her short hair with the towel.

"There are two ways to reach or leave Yakutsk," she said. "If not by air, then over the Kolyma Highway, which begins at Nizhny Bestyakh, on the east bank of the Lena. We can only reach Nizhny Bestyakh by ferry, which my enemies will also watch."

"Let's try the charter first," Bolan replied, "before we count it out."

"Of course," she said. "But you must be prepared to fail."

"If that's the way you feel," he said, "you should have thought about it at the start, before you put your own neck and your partner's on the chopping block."

That obviously stung her, but she took it, nodding.

"You're correct. We were a pair of fools."

"It's never foolish when you try to do the right thing," Bolan said. "Sometimes it has a price, but that's the way things work."

"A great price, yes?" Anuchin said. "First, Sergey's life. Now yours and mine."

"We're not dead yet," Bolan reminded her. "A little confidence could help you stay alive. But if you're giving up, why don't you tell me now. I don't need any dead-weight on my shoulders while I'm running."

"Confidence, of course," she said. "And weapons, yes?"

"I've got a fair stash from the warehouse," Bolan said.

She tried a smile and said, "Let's see them, then."

NIKOLAY MILESCU SIPPED a cup of bitter coffee he had purchased at a kiosk in the international arrivals and departures terminal, watching the travelers who scurried past him, hoping for a glimpse of a familiar face—the person he'd been sent to capture, or to kill, if all else failed.

Milescu had a photo on his cell phone of the woman he was hunting. She wasn't the type he favored, though he wouldn't kick her out of bed. Too bad for her, she'd never get to know him in that way and learn how he could please a woman.

All the future held in store for her was pain.

The problem: she was hard to hold.

In fact, the woman had been picked up once already, at that very airport, but she had been liberated by a man or men who left the snatch team dead. Milescu's boss said one man was responsible, but why take chances? So he'd sent four other guns along, put Milescu in charge and promised them a fat reward if they secured the fugitives.

Alive or dead.

Milescu personally didn't think it likely that the woman would return to catch another flight, after she had been kidnapped from the terminal the previous night, but people frequently did stupid things. He would remain alert and stay in contact with his soldiers, placed strategically around the airport.

With that in mind, he palmed his Motorola phone, the Tundra model that combined normal calling and web access with push-to-talk service, effectively making the cell phone a small walkie-talkie. Keying the button to contact all four men at once, he commanded, "Report in by number."

"Number two," Vasily Ryumin answered. "Nothing yet in the domestic terminal."

"Three here," Naum Izvolsky said. "Baggage claim is clear."

"Number four," Viktor Gramotkin replied. "Nothing but peasants in the parking lot."

Milescu waited to hear from Gennady Stolypin, stationed on the roof to watch the charter hangars through binoculars. When half a minute passed with no response, he keyed the phone again.

"Waiting for check-in, Number Five."

"Hold on," Stolypin answered him belatedly, ignoring all decorum. "I have someone just arriving... Can't see who it is yet."

"Where?" Milescu asked. "Which hangar?"

"Private Jets," Stolypin answered. "Wait a second, while I... It's a GAZ four-door. Can't say what model from this distance. There, it's stopped. The driver's getting out...a man. And now, a woman. Let me check the photo. Yes! It's her! I can take them down from here!"

Stolypin had a VSK-94 sniper's rifle with him on the roof, the silenced model, semiautomatic, with a 20-round box magazine of 9 mm SPP rounds.

"No!" Milescu snapped over his walkie-talkie, up and moving toward the nearest exit. "Do not fire! You know the order."

"Yes," Stolypin answered back. "Alive or dead."

"With higher pay if she's alive. Just watch and wait, until we get there." To the others then, in case they weren't in motion yet, he said, "All hands to Private Jets, south of the terminal!"

His men confirmed with clicking signals, staying off the air. They would be closing on the target, moving swiftly but without a frantic sprint to draw attention from the terminal's police officers.

Milescu reckoned he should thank the woman, if he got the chance. Her desperate stupidity had saved him from a long day sitting at the airport, wasting time while someone else hogged all the glory.

Now, his task was simple—neutralize the woman's escort, one way or another, and collect her for the boss. Take both alive, if possible.

And deliver them to a fate worse than death.

Private Jets Charter Service

"I DON'T SEE ANYONE," Tatyana said. "Do you?"

"Not yet," Bolan replied.

Which proved precisely nothing. They could be under surveillance from a distance, and he wouldn't know it until bullets from a sniper's rifle dropped them on the tarmac, dead or dying by the time the echo of the shots arrived. The Executioner had done that sort of work himself, times beyond counting, and he knew the risks involved.

But sitting in the sedan, outside the hangar, wouldn't keep them safe.

"Sit tight a minute," Bolan said, and stepped out of the car. He left the key in the ignition for her, just in case, but saw no adversaries as he scanned the runway. No one lurking in the hangar's shadow. No vehicles close enough to box them in.

The problem now: they had to discard their weapons prior to boarding, or they'd run afoul of customs when they got to Tokyo. Japanese law forbade private possession of firearms, except for strictly regulated sporting shotguns and air rifles, with maximum penalties of ten years in prison and a fine of one million yen per offense.

Bolan nodded, alert as Anuchin stepped out of the car. The hangar stood no more than thirty feet away, their Hawker 800 already rolled out and prepared for departure. In profile, it was nearly eight feet shorter than the Learjet 60 Bolan had arrived on, but its wingspan ten feet greater.

Eighteen minutes to boarding, by Bolan's watch, if they got through the sign-in procedure on time. And from there—

Bolan knew a curse in Russian when he heard one. He followed Anuchin's gaze and saw two men approaching at a run from the direction of the airport terminal. As he watched, a third man cleared the exit, laboring to catch the other two.

So much for signing in.

"Come on!" he snapped, turning back toward the car. When he was halfway there, a sharp *crack* on the pavement marked a near-miss from a distant rifle, somewhere high and well beyond the runners.

Bolan dropped into the driver's seat and gunned the sedan's engine. Anuchin was a second later, and she had to slam her door as he was wheeling out of there, tires screeching on concrete. The choice was fight or flight, and Bolan picked the option that would maximize their chances of survival with a long-range shooter in the mix.

He fled.

The runners weren't in range to use whatever weapons they were packing as he roared away from them. The rifleman had no such handicap, however, and his second shot glanced off the roof of their vehicle with a resounding bang!

Still no sound from the piece itself, and since the sedan

couldn't aspire to supersonic speed, that meant the rifle had a sound suppressor. Its shots wouldn't alert police inside the terminal unless he took a hit and crashed the car.

In which case, Bolan figured, they were dead.

Anuchin had retrieved one of the weapons liberated from her captors, a compact PP-19 Bizon submachine gun, but it wouldn't do her any good unless he stopped the car, or someone tried to cut them off before they cleared the airport's ring of access roads.

Which, in the circumstances, was entirely possible.

A last shot from the sniper struck their trunk before Bolan swung left around a cargo terminal, putting its bulk between the shooter and himself. Another moment put them on the highway leading back to Yakutsk, with no evident pursuit.

At least, not yet.

"So, we're not flying out," Anuchin said.

"Not today," Bolan agreed.

"And we cannot hide in Yakutsk."

"I wouldn't like the odds," he said.

She slumped. "In that case, there is nothing left except the Road of Bones."

CHAPTER FOUR

First thing, they ditched the sedan their enemies had seen, however briefly, at the airport. Its replacement was a four-door Lada Priora, stolen from the Kruzhalo shopping center along with a spare set of license plates to complete the short-term disguise. That done, when they were relatively safe, Anuchin briefed Bolan on what lay ahead once they crossed the Lena River.

"They will be watching the ferry," she cautioned. "They know that we have no way out now, except overland, which means the Kolyma Highway."

"I don't fancy a swim with the gear," Bolan told her.

"No, that can't be done. It's too far and too cold, even this time of year. We'll require a small charter to take us across. Leave the car in Yakutsk and make other arrangements in Nizhny Bestyakh."

"What kind of arrangements?" Bolan asked.

"Something rugged, for the road ahead," Anuchin said. "If we had a Lada Niva we could try it, but I think a motorcycle is more suitable. Also much easier to find on such short notice. You can ride on two wheels?"

"Not a problem," Bolan said. "But what's this thing about a road of bones?"

"Officially," she said, "it's the M56 Kolyma Highway, linking Yakutsk and Nizhny Bestyakh to Magadan on the Sea of Okhotsk. The distance is something over two thousand kilometers, close to thirteen hundred miles by your reckoning. Those who live along the highway call it *Trassa*—the Route. They need no other name, since it is literally the only road in the district."

"Where do the bones come in?" Bolan asked.

"Stalin ordered construction of the highway in 1932, using inmates from the *Sevvostlag,* the Northeastern Corrective Labor Camps. Work continued using gulag labor until 1953, when the highway reached Magadan—a labor camp itself, in those days—and Stalin, at last, had the decency to die. We call the highway Road of Bones for those who died while building it and were buried beneath or beside it. How many? Who knows?"

"So, it's a straight shot on this road from Nizhny Bestyakh to Magadan?" Bolan asked.

"Hardly straight," Anuchin replied. "There are rivers to cross, with or without bridges, and parts of the so-called highway are crumbling away. Between us and Magadan there are two villages, Tomtor and Oymyakon. Both claim to be the coldest place on Earth, in winter. This time of year, they're simply…chilly."

"So, aside from special wheels, we'll need new clothes," Bolan observed.

"And camping gear, if we can carry it."

"One bike or two?" Bolan asked.

Looking embarrassed, Anuchin said, "I've never driven one."

"Okay," Bolan replied. "That limits how much we can pack, keeping the weapons."

Bolan tried working on the calculation in his head. A trip of thirteen hundred miles on normal roads, with stops for gas and minimal rest, should take about one day at a steady speed of sixty miles per hour. Slow it down for the terrain that Anuchin had described, however, and the clock went out the window. Add the fact that they would almost certainly be hunted, once her enemies—now Bolan's—found out where they'd gone, and you were looking at a road trip on Route 666.

A little slice of hell on Earth.

The soldier considered it and asked, "When do we start?"

"I'M WONDERING," Stephan Levshin said, "whether any of you need to be alive."

The five men facing him looked nervous, rightly so, since they had failed at what was meant to be a relatively simple task. Although he stood alone before them, and all five of them were armed, Levshin was unafraid. These so-called soldiers were disgraced and dared not lift a hand against the man who pulled their strings.

When his remark produced no comment, only shifting eyes and feet, he said, "You had the targets literally in your sights, but let them slip away. How does that happen? Does anyone care to explain your failure?"

Grudgingly, the leader of the party—Nikolay Milescu—answered. "They went to a charter company," he said. "We spotted them outside the terminal, but not in time. When we moved in, they drove away."

"Alerted by the clumsiness of your approach," Levshin said. "And since you did not have a vehicle nearby, pursuit was hopeless. Right?"

Milescu nodded miserably. "Yes, sir."

"Which one of you was the sniper?" Levshin asked.

A hand went up. Its rat-faced owner said, "I was," remembering to add the "sir" a split second too late.

"What is your name?"

"Stolypin, sir. Gennady."

"Have you practiced with your weapon?" Levshin pressed him.

"I'm familiar with it, sir."

"What was the range from which you fired this morning?"

"Say one hundred meters, sir," the sharpshooter replied.

"Using a telescopic sight?"

"Yes, sir," Stolypin replied.

"And yet, you missed—what was it? Three times?"

"No, sir," Stolypin said.

"No? You didn't miss three times?"

"I missed the man, sir. Once, as he was running."

"And your other two shots? What became of them?"

"I hit the car both times, sir."

"Did it stop?" Levshin asked.

Stolypin swallowed hard. "No, sir."

"Another failure, then," Levshin said. "What shall I tell Moscow, when I am asked if you deserve to be employed? More to the point, if you deserve to live?"

"We can fix it," Milescu said, sounding desperate.

"How will you do that?" Levshin challenged him. "Invent a time machine and go back to the moment when your idiot incompetence spoiled everything?"

"No, sir," the gunman said, "but we can find them. We can bring them in or kill them, as you like."

"So, are you psychic now? If you combine your five pea-brains, can you reach out and tell me where the targets are right now?" Levshin asked.

Milescu swallowed the sarcasm and replied, "They need to get away from Yakutsk, sir. If they can't fly, that means they have to cross the river. Travel east. There are no airstrips. They must drive to Magadan, and either sail from there or fly from Sokol Airport."

"And your plan," Levshin replied, "is…what, exactly?"

"Stop them at the Lena crossing, sir. Or, if we miss them there—"

"Meaning you've failed again," Levshin said, interrupting.

"—then we fly ahead to Magadan and meet them when they get there, sir."

"I think not," Levshin said. "If you can't catch them on the ferry, if that very simple task defeats you, I don't think that you deserve a flight to Magadan. If that happens—if you should *fail* again, and your superiors decide to let you live—you'll follow up and take them on the road. The trip would do you good, I think. Make men of you, perhaps."

Milescu muttered something that was probably, "Yes, sir," while his companions stood slump-shouldered, staring at their shoes.

"Go on now," Levshin ordered. "And if any of you have religion, pray you don't fuck up again."

THE LENA FERRY was a death trap. Bolan knew that if they weren't ambushed on arrival at the dock, or killed on board, they would find shooters waiting for them on arrival in Nizhny Bestyakh. No matter how he broke it down, they had to find another way across the river.

And with no bridge anywhere nearby, that meant a charter boat.

Another problem: if their enemies had any sense at all, they wouldn't just stake out the ferry terminal; they'd also have watchers on the Yakutsk waterfront, to head off any end-runs via private boats. That meant contact with a pilot couldn't happen on the docks.

Where else would they find sailors at that hour of the morning?

"Drinking breakfast," Anuchin offered. "Vodka is the Russian equalizer."

There was no shortage of taverns in Yakutsk, as Bolan soon discovered. Bars catering to river boatmen were located near the waterfront, but not directly on the docks, dispensing food and alcohol around the clock as crews departed or arrived on varied schedules. In winter, when the river froze, Bolan supposed they were a place for stranded sailors to commiserate over the tedium of being stuck on shore.

In any case, he didn't think the hunters seeking Anuchin would be looking for her in saloons at breakfast time.

The first place that they tried had two early customers, both of them obvious holdovers from the previous night, well advanced in pursuit of oblivion. The second bar had better prospects—six in all—and two of them were relatively late arrivals, only warming up their shot glasses.

Anuchin donned a smile and approached the better-looking of the nearly sober pair, a robust forty-something character with gray hair showing underneath a yachtsman's cap that had seen better days. Hell, make it better *years.* Bolan stood by while she confirmed the skipper could speak English, more or less, then led him to a table in the corner nearest to the tavern's door.

"You want to go Nizhny Bestyakh, but not on ferry, eh?" The captain smiled. "Afraid someone will see you, *da?* Maybe a lovers' getaway?"

"I see we can't fool you," she said, flicking a glance toward Bolan that was shy and bawdy, all at once. Some actress. "Naturally, we would expect to pay a premium for causing you such inconvenience."

The skipper beamed. "I still remember love, you

know," he said. "But I must also eat and pay for fuel, eh? So…six thousand rubles?"

Something like two hundred U.S. dollars. Bolan nodded, told him, "Done," and peeled off a dozen 500-ruble notes.

Their new best friend in town—Yevgeny Glushko—made the money disappear into a pocket and asked Anuchin, "So, when did you wish to go?"

"There's no time like the present, eh?" she answered.

"You're in luck!" Glushko declared. "My boat is fueled and ready. We can leave at once."

"You have a car?" Bolan asked.

"Car? No car. I walk from pier."

"Relax," Bolan replied. "I'll drive."

Moscow: 3:22 a.m.

FOR BREAKFAST, Colonel Eugene Marshak had a glass of bacon-flavored vodka. He regretted that he had no eggs to go along with it, but since real food meant waking up his wife, he settled for another glass of bacon.

Waiting for the cursed telephone to ring.

He wasn't drunk, couldn't allow himself that luxury as long as loose ends in Yakutsk were threatening to weave a noose around his neck. Marshak's superiors were watching him—perhaps a few of them were losing sleep, as well—and if he didn't solve the problem soon, that task would pass to other, more capable hands.

Which meant the end of him, for all practical purposes. He likely wouldn't be imprisoned, as was common in the bad old days, but being stripped of rank and influence was tantamount to social death. He would be unemployable, beyond some menial position. He would lose the Moscow flat, his summer dacha on the coast.

Mariska would most certainly abandon him, which might turn out to be the only bright spot in the whole disaster. She could leave with nothing, since there would be nothing left to steal, and Marshak could descend into an alcoholic haze without her shrill, incessant carping to disturb him.

Or he could assert himself, demand more of his soldiers in the field and solve the problem now, before it spun further beyond control.

The phone rang once, and Marshak scooped it up. "Yes!"

"I'm afraid there's been another problem, sir," Stephan Levshin told him.

"Why am I not surprised?" Marshak replied with acid in his voice. "Explain yourself."

"I sent five men to watch the airport," Levshin said. "The targets came, but managed to evade them."

"Five against how many?" Marshak asked.

"Two, sir. The woman and a man."

"Were shots fired?"

"I've contained it, sir," Levshin said.

"Contained it how?"

"A silencer was used. The only damage was to the escaping vehicle."

"So, then, at least this was a *quiet* failure, eh? Unlike the last one," Marshak said.

Levshin had no response to that. The empty phone line hummed and crackled until Marshak spoke again.

"Do you at least have some idea of where they're going? What they hope to do?"

"They must get out of Yakutsk to survive, sir," Levshin said. "They cannot fly, which only leaves the road."

"Which road?" Marshak demanded.

"Sir, there's only one from here."

Marshak considered that and understood. "To Magadan, is it?"

"Yes, sir."

"A cold and lonely road, as I recall," Marshak said.

"No escape, sir. That's a promise."

"Which you should be careful not to break," Marshak advised.

There was more silence on the far end of the line. This time, it brought a smile to Marshak's face. It felt good to intimidate subordinates, remind them of their proper place.

To stress his point, he declared, "I will be following your progress, Stephan. If it seems to me that you require further assistance, it will be provided."

Levshin sounded nervous as he answered, "Sir, I'm confident that I can solve this problem with the staff on hand."

"A staff reduced by careless losses, as it is," Marshak replied. "If I decide to send you help, you'll be advised."

"Yes, sir." A nice hint of dejection was audible in his voice.

"And, Stephan?"

"Yes, sir?"

"You realize that both of us are under scrutiny. If you fail, I am judged a failure."

"Sir—"

"And I will not go down alone."

Marshak replaced the telephone receiver in its cradle, poured himself another shot of bacon and began rehearsing his report to his superiors.

THEIR VESSEL WAS the *Zarya,* which Bolan knew meant "sunrise." It was forty-odd-feet long and might have been a trawler once, before it was converted to river commerce.

Several years had passed since it was painted, and the metal fittings didn't gleam, but it felt solid underfoot and there was power in the engine room, once Glushko got it rumbling.

They'd been doubly cautious on the waterfront, leaving the car a long block from the *Zarya*'s berth and walking in with weapons close at hand. If they were spotted, no one tried to make a move. Bolan allowed himself to hope the hostile forces might be spread too thin to cover every point of exit from Yakutsk, but he and Anuchin were agreed to be prepared for trouble on the other side, when they arrived.

As for the possibility of being hit *before* they got across...well, they would have to wait and see.

When they had cleared the dock, he found some privacy and dialed Brognola's number on his satellite phone. It was fourteen hours earlier in Washington—say, 6:40 p.m.—so he tried the home number and heard it ring twice before the big Fed picked up.

"Are we scrambled?" Bolan asked.

"Wait one." A click on the line told him his old friend had engaged the scrambler, turning their words to gibberish for any eavesdroppers between D.C. and the Sakha Republic. "Okay. Are you clear?"

"Change of plans," Bolan said. "We got blocked at the airport."

"So, now what?" Brognola asked.

"Now we improvise," Bolan replied. "We'll be traveling overland."

The big Fed processed that, maybe called up a map in his mind. "That's a long way to run," he observed, "if they're dogging you."

"Without wings," Bolan told him, "it's all that we've got."

"Roger that. And you're coming out…where?"

"Magadan," Bolan said.

"Okay. Hang on a second." He came back seconds later: "They have an airport, Sokol. You can catch Alaska Airlines there."

"Unless it's covered," Bolan said.

"You're right. They wouldn't be that careless," Brognola agreed. "It's also on the Sea of Okhotsk, so you've got a clear shot out to the Pacific, once you're past the Kuril Islands."

"Quite a swim," Bolan said. "What is that, about five thousand miles to San Francisco?"

"Smart-ass. I was thinking we'd have someone meet you," Brognola replied.

"Sounds better," Bolan admitted, "but they'll likely meet with opposition. Maybe the official kind."

"I'll have a word with someone at the Pentagon and see what they can slip under the radar, so to speak."

"Appreciate it," Bolan said. "I'll try to stay in touch as we proceed."

He didn't need to say what it would mean if there was no callback. The downside of a covert op on hostile ground was understood, a given, and remained unspoken. Bolan wasn't superstitious in the least, but there was nothing to be gained by tempting fate.

"Stay frosty, eh?" Brognola said.

"We may not have a choice," Bolan replied. "Siberia, you know?" He cut the link and found Anuchin watching him. "I'm working on a lift, from Magadan," he said, and thought now all they had to do was make it there.

MARSHAK HAD WAITED as long as he dared. The others wouldn't thank him for letting them sleep, if matters spun out of control in the meantime.

He had arranged a three-way conference call, the lines secure against all outside listeners, although Marshak himself was taping every word. It was a hedge against disaster. Call it life insurance.

His companions on the line were Kliment Gabritschevsky, second deputy director of the Ministry of the Interior, with responsibility for the Public Security Service; and Grigory Rybakov, *pakhan*—"godfather"—of the Izmaylovskaya gang, Moscow's oldest and strongest clan of the Mafiya. Between them, they wielded more power than most elected officials in Russia.

"What news from the East?" Gabritschevsky inquired when they had disposed of the curt salutations.

"A new disappointment, I fear," Marshak said. "The traitor returned to Yakutsk Airport with an accomplice, but Stephan's soldiers were unable to detain them."

A jab at Rybakov, since he'd supplied the man Levshin was using in Yakutsk. The mobster took it silently, while Gabritschevsky said, "That's troubling, Colonel. If you can't even contain two people, what does that say for the state of national security?"

"They *are* contained, Deputy Minister. If they remain in Yakutsk, I will root them out. If they attempt to flee, they have a single avenue remaining."

"Ah. The Road of Bones," Gabritschevsky said.

"That's correct, sir."

"Listen," Rybakov cut in. "If you need more soldiers on the ground out there, just say so."

"Four are dead already," Marshak answered. "Five, with the interrogator. I may need *real* soldiers if you want the job done properly."

"What do you have in mind?" Gabritschevsky asked.

"Spetsnaz," Marshak said, the Russian special purpose regiment, trained in counterterrorist techniques and black ops that included hostage rescue, sabotage and targeted assassination.

"That's a big step," Gabritschevsky cautioned.

"It's a big fall, if they get away," Marshak replied.

Rybakov spoke up to say, "You mentioned an accomplice."

"Yes."

"Is this the man who killed my people?" Rybakov asked.

"I believe so," Marshak told him. "There's no proof, of course, but he is traveling with the woman."

"Proof enough," Rybakov said. "I want his head."

"Talk to your men," Marshak replied. "The ones still living. This makes twice they've let him slip away."

"Perhaps I should send Boris out to supervise," Rybakov said, referring to his second in command, a thug named Boris Struve.

"Send who you like," Marshak said. "But the FSB retains command, unless I hear an order to the contrary from my superiors."

Rybakov remained silent, but Gabritschevsky said, "We'll leave the chain of command intact, for now. Use Spetsnaz sparingly, if you require its services. Nothing to draw attention, eh?"

"I understand, sir," Marshak said.

"And get results!" the deputy minister commanded. "We're all depending on it."

"As you say, sir."

Marshak's hand was steady as the other lines went dead, but there was no mistaking Gabritschevsky's meaning.

He was running out of time.

CHAPTER FIVE

Bolan and Anuchin took turns watching the docks through Captain Glushko's old Zeiss binoculars as the *Zarya* completed its river crossing. There were no uniformed police officers in view, nor any gunmen obviously waiting for a chance to shoot them down before they landed on the river's eastern shore.

Could slipping out of Yakutsk be that easy?

Bolan guessed that it couldn't.

"They may be watching us from hiding," Anuchin said, speaking his thoughts aloud.

He nodded. "It's definitely possible."

Bolan knew next to nothing about law enforcement in the Sakha Republic or Russia's Far Eastern Federal District, but he assumed there had to be some cops assigned to Nizhny Bestyakh. Even if they were bought and paid for by the Mafiya, the FSB, whoever, they would still be placed in an embarrassing position by an open firefight on the waterfront. His enemies, if they were halfway smart, might choose to spot Bolan and Anuchin, trail them into town and choose a spot where they could close the trap without dozens of witnesses.

Or maybe they had dropped the ball again.

In which case, Bolan and the woman had an edge. They couldn't count on any great head start, but if they had even a little time to spare, using it wisely was a must.

"Be ready when we disembark," Bolan advised her. "If someone makes a move—"

"Hit back," she finished for him.

"Right. And otherwise—"

"Head for the motorcycle shop."

Their skipper had informed them of the shop's location, with a hand-drawn map to clarify, noting that cycles could be bought or rented from the owner, who—no great surprise—was one of Glushko's oldest friends.

"Be sure you talk to Ilya," he insisted. "Tell him that I send you. He give you good price."

Bolan had thanked him for the tip and watched the skipper closely to make sure he didn't phone ahead. Their pose as lovers on a hasty getaway was thin, at best, and if the *Zarya*'s captain caught a whiff of bounty money he might sell them out.

Why not? A pair of strangers—one of them a foreigner, at that—meant nothing to him when his bills came due. Glushko was local, had to live in Yakutsk after they were gone. Why borrow trouble from the Mob or the authorities if he could bag a double payday from a single river crossing?

But the skipper didn't make a call.

Which, naturally, didn't mean he wouldn't, once they cleared his deck. A quick heads-up to someone, maybe old friend Ilya at the motorcycle shop, and any soldiers waiting for them in the general vicinity could gather for the kill.

And it would have to be a kill. That much had been agreed. Anuchin was dead set against enduring more interrogation, and surrender ran against the grain for Bolan, going back to schoolyard brawls in childhood. Anyone who tried to stop them now would pay a price in blood.

Bolan could feel the *Zarya* slowing, hear its engines

winding down as Glushko began his docking maneuvers. Nothing fancy for the old tub, just a gentle sidling in against a pier with old tires hanging off the side to serve as bumpers. When the hull and rubber kissed, a teenage boy came running up to help Glushko secure the mooring lines.

The soldier checked out the wharf rats who surrounded them. A motley gang of fishermen, dock hands and sailors, people looking for a bargain at the nearby fish stalls. Any one of them could have a weapon tucked away beneath a coat, a shawl or sweater. Any pair of eyes that swept the *Zarya*'s deck could be comparing Anuchin's face to photographs they'd seen.

Bolan shook hands with Captain Glushko on the pier, knowing they'd never meet again, then followed Anuchin into town.

Aboard the Lena Ferry: 9:19 a.m.

"THIS JOB IS SHIT," Viktor Gramotkin muttered.

"Just be thankful that you have a job," Nikolay Milescu said. "That your tiny brain is still inside your head."

"It's not my fault Stolypin missed his damned shot at the airport," Gramotkin said. "If I'd had the rifle—"

"Yes. You talk a good fight," Milescu said. "Tell Levshin about it, why don't you?"

"That bastard? I'm not scared of him."

"Of course not," Milescu said. "We all saw the way you put him in his place."

"You wait. The next time he—"

"Yes, yes. Shut up and take another turn around the deck downstairs."

"You think we missed them?" Gramotkin asked him. "Nikolay, they missed the goddamn boat!"

"Check, anyway, and stop your bitching."

Gramotkin left him, grumbling as he moved off toward the nearest stairwell.

Thankful for the respite from complaints, Milescu scanned the upper deck once more, confirming what he knew without a second look.

A wasted effort.

They'd been first aboard the ferry when it left Yakutsk, and studied every face that boarded after them. The female sergeant from the FSB wasn't among them, and it therefore made no sense to think her bodyguard was on the boat, either.

But they had orders. They would ride the ferry, watch and wait, until a message came from Yakutsk or from Nizhny Bestyakh to tell them the targets were spotted. Then, depending on the ferry's position, they would either proceed at a snail's pace to join in the hunt, or waste more time while the boat unloaded, then reloaded and retraced its path.

Milescu recognized the need for consequences when they had bungled the job at the airport in Yakutsk. Another boss might have killed them on the spot—or at least killed Stolypin, for missing his shots—but Levshin had given them a second chance of sorts. Milescu only hoped they wouldn't be stuck midriver on the ferry when the targets showed themselves again.

There was, of course, no question that the runners would be caught. Even if they somehow evaded capture in Nizhny Bestyakh, where could they go? One miserable road was their only escape route, and how would they travel? In some junker bought or stolen off the streets? Where did they hope to go, with soldiers behind them and more waiting ahead in Magadan?

Milescu almost felt sorry for the stupid traitor and the

stranger who had volunteered to help her. What a lousy bargain he had made, at any price.

Like Grigory Rybakov, Milescu thought, loaning out his soldiers to the FSB. What did the godfather hope to gain by meddling in the cloak-and-dagger world of secret agents? Wasn't running Moscow's underground economy sufficient challenge?

Still, it was not Milescu's place to question orders. He had come this far from Kapotnya's filthy streets, in the southeastern quarter of Moscow, by following directives from older, vastly richer men. Why would he break the pattern now, when it would only leave him destitute at best—or, far more likely, get him killed?

If he was told to ride the ferry day and night until the river froze, then he would ride the ferry, waiting for the targets to reveal themselves. And he would keep any objections to himself. Let Viktor Gramotkin be the lightning rod, if any word of disaffection found its way to Stephan Levshin or the boss of the Izmaylovskaya clan.

Let the blow fall on him, while Milescu smiled all the way to the bank.

YEVGENY GLUSHKO'S MAP was accurate. It led Bolan and Anuchin to the motorcycle shop, located eight blocks from the waterfront, sandwiched between a restaurant and tannery. The warring smells of spicy food and curing hides combined for an assault on the soldier's nostrils as he watched the cycle shop from half a block away.

Once again, he found no obvious ambush waiting there.

"Ready?" he asked Anuchin.

"Ready," she said, slipping a hand inside the pocket of her long coat where a pistol was concealed. She might have trouble getting to the submachine gun hidden in her heavy shoulder bag, but if it went to hell within the next few seconds, Bolan thought he could take up the slack with his Kalashnikov.

He stepped out of the alley first, with Anuchin covering his back, then felt her take a place beside him as they crossed the street. Pedestrians passed by, ignoring them. Bolan relaxed a little as they reached the shop and stepped across its threshold, but he still remained on full alert.

A scruffy guy in greasy coveralls, his gray hair tied back into a ponytail, approached them. Anuchin mentioned Glushko's name and asked for Ilya, whereupon the man nodded and answered her in what appeared to be a Russian dialect.

Bolan knew he had a choice to make: reveal himself as a foreigner, or let Anuchin make the deal and hope it went all right. Without impugning her ability to rent a motorcycle, Bolan was the one who had to drive it, so the choice was made.

"English?" he asked the shop's proprietor.

"Yes. I speak."

"We're heading east on the Kolyma Highway," Bolan told him. "We need a bike that can handle the road with two people and some gear aboard."

"The Road of Bones, eh?" Ilya answered, looking at the two of them as if they'd lost their minds. "Maybe a helicopter you should rent and fly to Magadan."

"We want to try the scenic route," Bolan replied. "Do you have something suitable in stock?"

"Best bike in shop for what you say is BMW," Ilya advised. "The R1200GS dual-sport model. Come this way, I show."

They followed Ilya to the rear of his shop, past various bikes, until he stopped before a black-and-silver machine with the familiar BMW logo on its fuel tank. Like most

dual-sport bikes—also known as "on-off road" models—
the R1200GS had heavy-duty suspension front and back,
with fenders elevated well above the knobby tires. It had
an oversize eight-gallon tank, feeding an 1170 cc two-cyl-
inder engine. The touring package included dual stainless-steel panniers—the equivalent of saddlebags—and
a rack for a pillion bag or other gear in back. The whole
package measured roughly six feet long, with its swooped
seat for two, three feet off the ground.

"It looks good," Bolan told him, "but I'll need to take
it for a test drive."

"Sure, sure," Ilya said. "Your lady is collateral, okay?"

It had been a while since Bolan went two-wheeling,
but it came back to him in a rush once he was mounted on
the BMW. He rolled out of the shop in first gear, checked
both ways before he nosed into traffic, then opened up the
engine as he circled a couple of blocks and returned. It
shifted smoothly and he had no difficulty with the brakes
or throttle. Bolan estimated that the bike weighed something like 450 pounds with nothing packed in the panniers, and tried to guess how it would handle once it had
been loaded, with a second passenger riding behind him.

There was literally no time like the present to find out.

Returning to the shop, he told Ilya, "I like it. So, how
much?"

Ilya considered Bolan's question, as if it had never
crossed his mind before. At last, he said, "Five hundred
thousand rubles. You call it sixteen grand, U.S."

"I call it sold," Bolan said with a smile.

Washington, D.C.: 7:35 p.m.

HAL BROGNOLA double-checked his time zones from the
World Clock website on his laptop, and confirmed that it

was 3:35 a.m. in Moscow. He felt a certain sense of satisfaction as he dialed the number that had been relayed to him through Stony Man.

If I don't sleep, Brognola thought with pleasure, no one sleeps.

The distant telephone rang three times before someone picked it up. A groggy male voice muttered in French, "Who is this?"

"Harold Brognola, calling from the DOJ in Washington."

"You're working late," the other man replied. "Or is it early there?"

"One or the other," Brognola said. "I'm looking for Gerard Delorme."

"And you have found him, monsieur."

"With Interpol?"

"The very same, but out of uniform just now," Delorme said.

"We need to talk on a secure line," the big Fed advised him.

"I can scramble here," the Frenchman said, now sounding wide-awake. "Give me a moment, *s'il vous plaît.*"

"Sounds fair."

Brognola heard a buzz and humming on the line, resolved a second later as Delorme returned.

"That's better," Delorme advised. "You must be calling about my disaster in Yakutsk, *oui?*"

"Sorry to hear you lost one of your assets," Brognola replied. "We've managed to redeem the other for you, but it's touch and go right now."

"The danger is continuing. *Je comprends.* I understand, of course."

Brognola wasn't comfortable giving details of the planned escape route to a total stranger, but he said, "My agent has an exit strategy in mind. It would be helpful if we knew the other players. Who'll be hunting them? What kind of resources will they commit?"

"The *who,* I am afraid to say, is everyone," Delorme said. "My asset, as you call her, has sufficient evidence to topple—and perhaps imprison—leaders of the FSB, the Russian Mafia and certain persons highly placed in government, together with their friends abroad."

"That big, is it?" the big Fed asked.

"Indeed," Delorme said. "As to resources for the hunt, who knows? I can't predict how brazen they may be. The FSB alone has more than three hundred thousand employees. Most of them clerks, I grant you, but there is the Counterintelligence Service and Border Guard Service. Add the Militsiya and MVD Internal Troops, perhaps the Federal Protective Service…"

"Okay," Brognola said. "I get the picture."

"I regret to say, their chances are not good."

"I don't suppose there's anything that you can do to help, from where you are?"

"The Russian Federation is a member state of Interpol," Delorme said, "which means I have a two-room office at the Lubyanka, with a secretary who makes coffee that tastes like dishwater. My function is advisory. The janitors have more authority."

"But you know things," Brognola said.

"Indeed. I was surprised—and gratified, I must say—when these assets trusted me enough to make contact. I served as their liaison to the FBI's legal attaché here, in Moscow. I'm aware that contact was established with the CIA, as well, but details were withheld from me."

"So, you've had no contact with either of the assets since that time?" Brognola asked.

"The woman called me when they planned to leave,"

Delorme said. "Then I heard about her partner from an officer in the Militsiya. I was afraid that she would simply disappear."

"I'm sure that was the plan," Brognola said. "We've put a crimp in it, but information's hard to come by. If you pick up anything—"

"I'll call immediately," Delorme said.

"I'd appreciated it," the big Fed replied, and rattled off his numbers—office, home and cell. "Time doesn't matter."

"As I see, from looking at my clock," Delorme said. "I wish your agent luck."

He'll need it, Brognola thought as he cut the link.

Yakutsk: 9:58 a.m.

STEPHAN LEVSHIN CHECKED the LED screen on his cell phone, failed to recognize the caller's number, but decided to answer.

"Yes?"

On the other end, an unfamiliar voice said, "I am told you are the man to call about a certain woman and her friend?"

"Who told you that?" Levshin said, not denying it.

"I don't remember," the caller said. "It is either true, or not."

"In that case, it depends upon which woman we're discussing, and which friend."

"I don't have names," the caller said, "but someone had a photograph. The woman hasn't changed since it was taken. And a man was with her. If the person who advised me was mistaken, and there's no reward…"

"You have me at a disadvantage," Levshin said. "A

stranger calls, anonymous, and asks for money? You must understand my skepticism, eh?"

"I understand you only pay for goods collected, yes?" the stranger said. "If I direct you to the ones you seek, it cannot be an act of charity."

"Say this, then," Levshin countered. "If I follow your directions and collect the proper goods, you will be compensated. If you are deceiving me, it would be most unwise."

"No threats, or it is goodbye, eh? We understand each other, without that."

"I hope so," Levshin said.

"All right. You need to look in Nizhny Bestyakh, at a motorcycle shop. The owner's name is Ilya Vitruk. You've already missed them there, but he can tell you where they're going."

"What's the address?"

Levshin's caller rattled off a number and a street name, which he dutifully repeated.

"If your information is correct—"

"I'll call you back," the stranger said. "We can arrange the payment when you're satisfied."

The line went dead, leaving a void of doubt in Levshin's mind. He knew his people had been circulating photographs of Tatyana Anuchin throughout Yakutsk and, more recently, in Nizhny Bestyakh. The photos had his temporary cell phone number printed on the back, for easy contact. Since he had no fear of the police, and would discard the phone as soon as he had found the runners, Levshin saw no risk to the procedure.

And, perhaps, it had paid off.

A motorcycle shop meant they were running. Eastward, since it was the only compass point available. The Lena River blocked them westward, and striking off to north or south meant running overland to nowhere, without highways. Northward lay the Arctic Circle, with perhaps a scattering of villages where they could never hope to hide. Southward lay Mongolia, but only if they crossed the Stanovoy and Yablonovy mountain ranges, with peaks above eight thousand feet and no passable roads.

So, it was Magadan or nothing for the fugitives.

Over the Road of Bones.

Levshin had calls to make, and quickly—to his people on the Lena River, and to others already scouring the streets of Nizhny Bestyakh, in case his targets had managed to cross the river unseen.

Which it seemed that they had.

The call might be a ruse, of course, even someone's idea of a joke. If it was, the prankster would live to regret it, but not very long. Meanwhile, Levshin would treat it as a serious lead and hope for the best.

He'd scramble troops to the target and see what they found. If it paid off, then another call was necessary, to Moscow next time, for a status report to Colonel Marshak. He'd be relieved to know the net was tightening around the peasants who presumed to threaten him and those above him.

Levshin's task was to eliminate that threat, to see that order was preserved. Success was paramount.

And the alternative, he knew, was death.

CHAPTER SIX

With space for packing at a premium, Bolan and Anuchin shopped wisely in Nizhny Bestyakh. They started with new outfits for the road, judging that it was better to perspire a bit by day than freeze at night. Their choices—thermal underwear and socks, insulated gloves, flannel shirts under sweaters, with hunting pants and jackets over all—were chosen with respect for what Anuchin knew about the Road of Bones.

As for the rest, they bought two compact sleeping bags; a two-person tent that folded into a twenty-inch square and weighed under seven pounds; a case of bottled water, half the bottles emptied and refilled with gasoline; and enough MREs—as in "meals, ready to eat"—for a week on the road, if they ate twice a day. Bolan passed on the idea of buying a camp stove, preferring to leave space in the BMW's panniers for extra ammo magazines. Last-minute accessories included a first-aid kit, a small tactical flashlight, an NV-01 survival knife from the Kalashnikov factory and an entrenching tool useful for digging or chopping.

For weapons, they each carried pistols—the MR-444 for Bolan, an MP-443 for Anuchin—but most of the hardware captured when Bolan had rescued Anuchin was left in a garbage bin without firing pins. The soldier kept his short AKS-74U, while Anuchin chose a little PP-2000 SMG.

Thus prepared, they rolled out of Nizhny Bestyakh on

a two-lane blacktop, eastbound. The bike ran smoothly on asphalt, was easy to handle, but Bolan knew they'd have some rough riding ahead of them, between rural villages. How well the motorcycle would handle rough country in practice was anyone's guess.

Likewise, Bolan could only guess how much free time they had before Anuchin's trackers picked up their trail and returned to the chase. In another life, he had eluded and defeated *mafiosi* by the hundreds, in urban jungles spanning the world from Los Angeles, Chicago and New York City to London, Paris and Rome. Always outnumbered and outgunned, he'd learned to play the odds, turn them around and use the overconfidence of his opponents to destroy them.

But a hunt in wide-open country, where the quarry had to move and couldn't go to ground, was an entirely different game. In this case, Bolan's enemies held all the high cards—numbers and weapons, familiarity with the killing ground and the ability to plug both ends of a re-stricted pipeline. Bolan couldn't veer off-course, reverse directions or duck down a rabbit hole into Wonderland.

Still, he and Anuchin had surprised their adversaries twice, with her escape from custody and—Bolan hoped—with their passage from Yakutsk through Nizhny Bestyakh. They had a lead, however slim it might turn out to be, and the Executioner had worked with less.

The men who'd underestimated him were legion. Those who had survived that grave mistake were few and far between, remnants of an endangered species driven to the point of near-extinction.

In the bad old days, the men who'd hunted Bolan knew who they were looking for, what he had done, what he *could* do. They came for him despite all that, driven by greed or rage, a hunger for revenge or fear of their employers' wrath, a few propelled by simple arrogance.

The hunters who would follow him along the Road of Bones were at a disadvantage, then, in that respect. They'd only caught a glimpse of Bolan's style, with five men down. It could have been dumb luck. The home team would be confident.

And they would pay for it in blood.

But whether he'd be able to complete the job remained an open question. Bolan wouldn't know until they got as far as Magadan and found out what was waiting for them there.

How many enemies?

What kind of help from Hal?

One thing was certain, though: it would be one hell of a road trip.

Nizhny Bestyakh: 11:03 a.m.

IT WAS GOOD to be off the damned ferry at last. Nikolay Milescu had begun to get seasick—or would it be riversick?—riding the old tub back and forth across the Lena, scanning faces as they boarded, knowing the return trips to Yakutsk were a mind-numbing waste of his time.

At last they had a lead. His team was back together, five men strong, and closing on the target Stephan Levshin had identified. Milescu hadn't asked the FSB man where he got his information. He didn't care as long as it was accurate and placed them closer to their targets.

They were still running behind, Milescu understood, but if they managed to acquire fresh information here, the traitor and her bodyguard would be on borrowed time.

The target was a motorcycle shop, not much to look at, with no customers in view as they arrived. The five men had packed into a Lada Samara sedan, with Naum Izvolsky at the wheel. Milescu had him park in front of the shop, blocking off pedestrian access, and told the driver to stay with the car while he led the others inside.

Levshin had given them an address, but no names. A long-haired grease monkey approached them at the shop's open threshold, half smiling, and asked how he could help them.

"You sold a motorcycle this morning," Milescu informed him, not asking.

"I sell them all day, every day," the man replied.

"Only one interests me," Milescu said. "A man and a woman came shopping. This woman," he added, producing the photo. "You recognize her."

"This is just a face," the shop's proprietor complained. "With women, you know, it can be distracting. I look more at other things."

Milescu laughed at that, the others joining him, then asked, "What is your name?"

"Ilya," the older man replied. "Ilya Vitruk."

"Ilya," Milescu said, "I don't care if this one walked in naked and you spent the whole time staring at her tits, understand me? You saw money, too. You sold a motorcycle to this woman and a man."

A shrug from Ilya as he answered, "Anything is possible."

"Okay," Milescu said. "We'll do it your way, then. The hard way. Viktor, close the doors, eh? Hang the sign up saying we are closed. Vasily, find the power tools."

He watched the color drain from Ilya Vitruk's face. He blurted out, "No! Wait! I'll tell you anything you need to know."

"That's better," Milescu said. "Now, we start again. The woman and a man were here?"

"Yes. Earlier this morning, as you said," Ilya replied.

"They bought a motorcycle from you?"

Ilya bobbed his head. "My best in stock," he said. "The BMW R1200GS."

"And did they mention where they planned to take this fine machine?" Milescu asked.

"The man said east, over the Road of Bones."

"A destination, idiot!" Stolypin gritted.

"Leave it," Milescu said. "There's only Magadan."

"You see?" Ilya said. "I cooperate. All friends together, eh?"

"If we were friends," Milescu said, "you would have called us when they walked into your shop. We wouldn't have to chase them now."

"Call who? For what?" Ilya replied. "I don't know who you are, or why you want these people. No one told me anything."

"Too bad," Milescu said, then told Stolypin, "Make it quick."

"What quick?" Ilya demanded, wide-eyed. Reading death in the faces around him, he bolted toward the shop's back door, covering half the distance before Gennady Stolypin drew a silenced pistol and shot him twice in the back.

Milescu had his cell phone in hand before he reached the Lada Samara, speed-dialing Stephan Levshin's number. Levshin answered on the first ring, as if he'd been standing by and waiting for Milescu's call.

"Well?" he demanded.

"I have news," Milescu said. "Your information was correct. They bought a motorcycle here and told the dealer they were headed eastward, over the Kolyma Highway."

"Magadan," Levshin said.

"If they weren't lying to throw us off the scent," Milescu said.

"Where else is there for them to go?" Levshin asked. "Even if they caught the weekly plane from Tomtor, it would only bring them back to Yakutsk, eh? Or drop them off on foot at Ust-Nera."

Milescu recognized the name. A gold-mining town located on the Nera River, known for its tiny museum and white-water rafting in season. Nothing to attract a pair of fugitives or aid in their escape.

"All right," he said. "We'll get a better vehicle and follow them."

"I'll send what help I can," Levshin replied, and cut the link.

The FSB man would do more than that, Milescu thought. The traitor and her consort were as good as dead.

Road of Bones

ACCORDING TO THE BMW's odometer, Bolan hit the trip's first river crossing thirty-five miles east of Nizhny Bestyakh. It wasn't much of a river, at that—some thirty yards across, and no more than eight inches deep at its center—but Bolan still had to be cautious in fording the stream. The fully loaded bike weighed right around five hundred pounds, and dumping it in water was a surefire way to compromise its engine.

So he took his time, maintained a cautious walking pace as he drove over mossy stones as slick as oil on asphalt, feeling the river's chill through his waterproof boots as he labored to keep the bike upright. Anuchin did her part by clinging to his waist and staying quiet while they crossed.

Throughout the crossing, Bolan tried to keep his mind clear, focused on the crucial task at hand, without digressing into images of hunters closing on them from the west or gathering to meet them in the east. He'd have to face those threats as they arose, but for the moment it was more important to avoid dropping the bike midstream.

A two-lane road of sorts continued on the far side of the river, picking up where its twin on the west bank dead-ended into rippling water. Seemingly, it had occurred to no one that a bridge might be of any use to travelers along the Road of Bones.

Bolan knew it was too soon to check with Hal Brognola in Washington about the plan to help them get away from Magadan. Twelve hundred twenty-seven miles of aging road and rugged country lay ahead of them, before escape by sea became a plausible reality.

And in the meantime, Bolan had to keep his eye on the fuel gauge. The BMW was supposed to average fifty-five miles per gallon on open highways. Based on that, the bike's 5.3-gallon tank should carry them 292 miles, give or take. They carried nearly two gallons of spare gasoline in plastic water bottles, which should extend their range another hundred miles or so, before they ran dry.

One-third of their trip, more or less.

For the rest, they'd have to buy, beg or steal fuel to keep the bike rolling. That, or find some other mode of transportation that he couldn't yet imagine. There were two main towns along their route, but the first—Tomtor— lay some two hundred miles beyond their fill-up deadline.

Another problem to be solved, while they were being hunted by a force of unknown size across the Russian countryside.

All in a day's work for the Executioner.

Nizhny Bestyakh

AT LAST THEY WERE ready to go. Nikolay Milescu had supervised the packing of their vehicle, a Lada Niva built by AvtoVAZ for off-road driving. The name *niva* meant "crop field" in Russian, leaving no doubt that the five-door, four-wheel-drive SUV was meant to handle rugged country.

That would be the Road of Bones.

Milescu only knew the M56 Kolyma Highway by its fearsome reputation, but he took the stories seriously. Bridges washed away and left in disrepair for months—or years—on end. Wild bears and wolves had been seen on the road and the forests that surrounded it. Bandits who wouldn't hesitate to kill a traveler for pocket change, much less a vehicle that they could sell, roamed the highway.

All that, and two elusive targets, one of whom had proved himself a ruthless killer.

Five strong, they were ready for the hunt, at least in Milescu's opinion. Between them, they had eleven guns: one pistol each, four AK-74 assault rifles in various models, one TOZ-194 tactical shotgun and a Pecheneg light machine gun chambered for 7.6 mm Russian rounds, just in case the other firepower proved insufficient.

If they couldn't stop two people on a motorcycle with all that hardware, then Milescu reckoned they deserved to die.

Of course, they had to find the targets first. But thankfully, the traitor and her man had only one highway to travel. Only one potential destination, if they hoped to make it out of Russia.

Aside from weapons, Milescu's team had laid on food and water, the obligatory vodka and four rack-mounted twenty-liter jerry cans of gasoline. The Lada Niva had a fifteen-gallon fuel tank, and its 1.7-liter engine averaged twenty-eight miles per gallon. Call it three fill-ups minimum before they reached Magadan, if the pursuit took them all the way to the end of the line. The extra twenty-one gallons would carry them more than three-fourths of the way to the coast, replenished by fuel stops at Tomtor or Oymyakon as needed.

But Milescu was hoping for good luck this time. They'd had enough screwups already to make Stephan Levshin suspect they were a crew of incompetent amateurs. Most likely, he'd be reporting back to Boris Struve about their failures, leaving no doubt where the blame lay for the targets being still at large. The only way that they could save themselves, Milescu understood, was to deliver on the contract without any further errors or excuses.

And the sooner, the better.

He had tried to calculate their quarry's head start on the Road of Bones, but found it difficult. The Lada Niva's specifications listed a top speed of eighty miles per hour for stock models, with an average cruising speed of fifty-six miles per hour for maximum fuel efficiency. Meanwhile, the BMW R1200GS topped out around one hundred thirty miles per hour, but you could cut that by half for the Kolyma Highway, even with an experienced driver on board.

Milescu started on the math, inside his head, but quickly gave it up. The bottom line was obvious: his crew needed to push their vehicle without destroying it, and hope their prey hit every roadblock possible along the way to slow them. A crash with damage to the bike and one or both riders would be the best-case scenario. Worst case, he was prepared to shoot them off the road and tell Levshin that there had been no other choice.

Bringing the targets in alive was a priority, but not the *top* priority. If they escaped at last, because Milescu had been shy of using deadly force, the final hours of his life would be one long and hellish scream.

"A little hunting trip," Naum Izvolsky said from his seat behind the Niva's steering wheel.

"Vsesoyuznaya pionerskaya organizatsiya, eh?" Viktor Gramotkin answered from the backseat with a smile, referring to the Young Pioneer Movement that had replaced Russia's Boy Scouts under Soviet rule.

"Less talk, more hunting," Milescu advised them, while keeping his eyes on the highway ahead. "Ten thousand rubles to the man who spots them first."

Moscow

"I NEED A MAN—a team, in fact," Eugene Marshak said, "for a critical short-notice operation."

"It's our specialty, Colonel," Major Maxim Bucharin replied. He spoke for Spetsnaz—more specifically, the special purpose troops assigned to service with the FSB. "I only need to know the place and time."

"The place," Marshak replied, "is presently unknown, somewhere on the Kolyma Highway between Nizhny Bestyakh and Magadan. The time could be immediately. It depends upon my scouts locating the intended target."

"So, the Far Eastern Federal District," Bucharin mused. "Our nearest unit is based in Magadan."

"So, is the unit effective?"

"Absolutely," Bucharin said. "May I ask about the target, sir?"

"Two fugitives whose apprehension is essential," Marshak answered. "They've already killed six contract agents. One of them, an FSB sergeant, is attempting to defect with classified information concerning... Well, just let me say that she must not be allowed to escape."

"And the other target, sir?"

"A man, identity and nationality unknown. So far, no one who's had a chance to speak with him has managed to survive."

Bucharin considered the assignment for a moment, then said, "For a small target like this, two people running, without any resources to speak of, I would recommend a small unit. Three men, no more."

"Do you have candidates in mind?" Marshak asked.

"For the leader, yes. I would allow him to select the others on his own."

"How soon can they be mobilized, Major?"

"Within the hour, sir."

"From Magadan, the far end of the road."

Bucharin nodded. "Yes, sir. It would expedite their movement if air transport was approved."

"They have the necessary aircraft already in place?"

"Yes, sir. The Kamov Ka-60 helicopter."

"The Kasatka."

"That's correct, sir," Bucharin said.

Marshak wondered who had named a military helicopter the "Killer Whale," then told himself it made no difference. The Ka-60 used a two-man crew—which, with the Spetsnaz team, made five more people who had knowledge of his search for human prey along the Road of Bones. Whatever happened next could radically inflate that number, if the hunt spread to involve civilians.

Marshak thought about it, then dismissed the thought. It was a fact of life that rural peasants mattered no more in the Russian Federation than they had under Soviet rule, or back in the days of the czars. They served as laborers, and sometimes cannon fodder, but they didn't make the rules. And no one truly listened when they spoke.

Besides, it would be simple to eliminate unwanted witnesses along the Kolyma Highway. What were a few more shallow graves or body dumps, all things considered? Nothing, in the larger scheme of things.

Eugene Marshak was fighting for his rank, his privilege, perhaps his very life. If he failed, he could expect no mercy from his various superiors. No second chance to get it right.

"Proceed without delay," he told Bucharin. "I leave the logistic details in your hands, but will expect hourly updates."

"Of course, sir," Bucharin said. "The officer I have in mind to lead your team is Captain Pitirim Zelinsky, a veteran of the second Chechen conflict and the South Ossetia War. He will not fail you."

"Major," Marshak said, "we both must have the utmost faith that he does not."

CHAPTER SEVEN

Finding solid pavement on the Road of Bones reminded
Mack Bolan of a strip-tease act. Now you see it; now
you don't.

When Tatyana Anuchin had described a highway built
at the expense of several thousand lives, Bolan had pictured two-lane blacktop winding through the wilderness,
neglected over time and gone to seed between the route's
rare villages, but still a *highway* as the term was normally
defined.

Not even close.

From what he saw before him now, and some of what
already lay behind them, he surmised that some protracted stretches of the road were never paved at all,
unless it was with gravel or some cut-rate kind of mac-
adam. If proper asphalt or concrete had been laid down
by Stalin's slaves, no trace of it remained on various protracted sections of the road. Nature had come back to
devour it somehow, as in a television special he had seen
when at the Farm, depicting how New York would look
a century or two after the passing of humankind.

So, here they were, out in the wild. Instead of cruising over blacktop, cracked and weedy after sixty years
of shoddy maintenance, they wound up jouncing over
rocks and soil that had been bulldozed, once upon a time,
then left to suffer from exposure to Siberia's dramatic
weather. Ruts from flooding marked the way, requiring

special care when Bolan crossed them. Shifting sand defied the BMW's knobby tires as they sought traction. Loose stones pinged beneath the motorcycle's fenders with a sound like bullet ricochets.

And then, just when he felt as if the so-called road might shake the teeth from his head, Bolan would find himself on asphalt once again. The highway seemed to rise from nowhere, tired of playing hide-and-seek for now, permitting Bolan to accelerate and gain some time—albeit while he dodged potholes and watched for darting animals.

So far, they'd seen a weasel, half a dozen chipmunks and a vulture lifting off the carcass of some creature that had once resembled a raccoon. None of them bothered Bolan, but he stayed alert for larger fauna, conscious of the fact that bears inhabited the area, along with endangered Siberian tigers. Either could tackle a human and win, but Bolan worried more about wildlife-related accidents. If they collided with a random moose or elk, they could be badly injured. Even swerving to avoid one might deliver disabling damage to the bike.

And still, their greatest danger came from other humans. Bolan pictured Anuchin's enemies—his, now—going door to door in Nizhny Bestyakh, starting first with shops that sold or rented vehicles. How many could there be in a town of some four thousand people? How long would it take before they found Ilya and bribed him or forced him to talk?

And then what?

If the hunters hadn't brought suitable transport with them on the Lena River ferry, they would have to shop around for wheels before resuming the pursuit. Or would they try another tack: sit tight and bolt the door behind their prey, then phone ahead and have another crew stand ready on the road?

Shooters could fly from Magadan to Tomtor, definitely, but they'd still have some five hundred miles to travel westward if they wanted to meet Anuchin on the road. Unless, of course, they were content to wait, arrange the perfect ambush anywhere they chose along the highway and be done with it.

Bolan supposed that if the situation was reversed, if he was hunting someone on the Road of Bones and had a crew at his disposal, armed and funded by the state, he'd do it both ways. Come along behind the runners *and* arrange a trap in front of them. Why not? If Anuchin's information was as dangerous to the powers that be in Russia as Brognola suggested, wouldn't someone want insurance?

So he watched for moose and elk, tigers and bears. And Bolan watched his mirrors for a chase car, watched the road ahead of him for vehicles approaching and for snipers on the wild land to his left and right.

And when he wasn't doing all of that, he watched the sky, where spotter planes could track them, or a helicopter gunship might come swooping down to splatter them with Shipunov 2A42 autocannon fire, spraying 30 mm armor-piercing rounds at a rate of nine per second. It would be easy from a range of fifteen hundred yards, like hosing ants off your driveway with a power washer.

Tough luck for the insects, of course. But anyone who came to spray these ants would learn that they could sting.

Road of Bones: 1:46 p.m.

IZVOLSKY HESITATED on the west bank of the stream, staring across its steady flow of water toward the other side. The Lada Niva's motor rumbled, as if anxious to proceed.

"What are you waiting for?" Milescu challenged. "Get across."

"We can't be sure how deep it is," Izvolsky said.

"You want to walk across it first? I see the riverbed from here. Move out!"

"I don't know, Nikolay…"

"That's right," Milescu said. "You *don't* know. That's why I'm in charge. You want to call Levshin and say we can't go on because you're frightened you might get your feet wet? If you want to tell him that, by all means make the call. I'll leave you here to wait for him, so we don't have to watch him chop you into pieces."

"All right, I'm going." Grudgingly, Izvolsky eased his left foot off the Lada's clutch, pressed down on the accelerator with his right and eased the SUV's front wheels into the water.

They made it all of twenty feet into the river's flow before Milescu felt the Lada slip, begin to tilt, then lurch and stop with his side canted downward. Cursing bitterly, he powered down his window, leaned out through the opening and saw the Lada's right-front wheel nearly submerged.

"Goddamn it, Naum!" he snarled. "You've driven us into a hole!"

"How am I supposed to see it underwater?" Izvolsky asked.

"Never mind bullshit excuses. Get us out of here!" Milescu ordered.

"Okay."

Muttering curses underneath his breath, Izvolsky gunned the Lada's engine, but it got them nowhere, simply churning mud and silt around them, darkening the stream. Naum had already shifted into four-wheel drive, and now he put the truck into reverse, tried backing out, but all to no avail. More mud spewed up around the tires, and now Milescu felt the Lada's tail end start to drift.

"Stop, damn it!" he demanded. "We'll be ass-deep in the water if you keep that up."

"What else am I supposed to do?" Izvolsky asked him. "Swim across, towing the car behind me?"

"It may come down to that," Milescu said. "But first, we try the winch."

The Lada's front-mounted winch had a twelve-volt motor operated from the SUV's battery, with eighty-eight feet of braided steel cable. It was advertised as capable of hauling 12,500 pounds—more than three times the loaded Niva's standing weight—so Milescu was cautiously hopeful.

If the cable reached the far side of the stream, and if the trees he saw there were as sturdy as they looked from where he sat, they should be fine. It was embarrassing, but they could still survive the clumsy error if it didn't strand them hopelessly.

If they didn't allow the targets to escape.

"Who's getting wet, then?" Stolypin asked, from the backseat.

"Are you volunteering?" Milescu asked.

"Well…"

"Get to it, then. We'll feed the cable out to you."

Ryumin laughed and said, "A volunteer. I love it!"

"Good," Milescu said. "You'll help him, then. Secure the cable to that tree, the spruce, and make damn sure it doesn't slip."

"Da, da."

A moment later, both soldiers were splashing toward the Lada's nose, Viktor Gramotkin taking care to keep his mouth shut as he sat alone in the backseat, holding three guns. Izvolsky pressed a button on the dashboard, and the winch began to hum, spooling out cable as Milescu's men began to ford the stream on foot.

The water rose about midcalf, filling their shoes, and from the curses he could hear, Milescu knew it had to be cold. Fresh out of sympathy, he watched them trudge across, lurch up the eastern bank and wrap the cable tight around the stout Siberian spruce, securing its end with a stainless-steel hook.

"All right," he told his driver. "Get us out of here, or strip to make that swim."

Moscow: 8:49 a.m.

MAJOR MAXIM BUCHARIN sat and listened to the ringing of a telephone in Magadan, more than thirty-six hundred miles to the east. Nearly four o'clock in the afternoon there, but his party was paid and commanded to be within reach of his phone at all times, under pain of severe discipline.

Two rings…three…four…

And the familiar voice was in his ear. "Yes!"

"Major Bucharin here, Captain. Engage your scrambler."

"All right." Another moment, buzzing on the line before it cleared, and then Captain Pitirim Zelinsky returned. "Good afternoon, Major. How may I serve you?"

Straight to the point, as always. As expected, no more and no less.

"I need a three-man team, with you in charge," Bucharin said. "Two targets are en route from Yakutsk—well, they're past Nizhny Bestyakh now—to Magadan. We need to intercept them, hold them for delivery if possible. If not, eliminate them."

"Understood," Zelinsky said. "Are they traveling by land?"

"They are," Bucharin said. "Apparently by motorcycle."

"So, it's the Kolyma Highway."

"Yes. Is that a problem, Captain?"

"Only in logistic terms, sir," Zelinsky said. "I will need an hour, more or less, to have my team prepared. From that point, it comes down to strategy. Where do you want them stopped, and when?"

Bucharin frowned at his reflection in a nearby windowpane. "In answer to your second question," he replied, "they should have been collected yesterday, but idiots involved themselves. We need them taken out of play as soon as possible. As to the place, do you have anything in mind?"

"There are three ways to do it, sir," Zelinsky said. "The slowest and the most haphazard is to start from Magadan by land and meet them on the road. We're sure to find them somewhere, but I can't predict where it may be. And we could waste a day or more."

"Next option," Bucharin said.

"Fly from Magadan to Tomtor, sir," the captain said, "and drive westward from there. We save time, but again, the meeting is arranged by chance. There's no doubt we can stop them, but it might be near a village filled with witnesses."

"And the third way, Captain?"

"Ideally, sir, we ought to track them from the air. Receive updated bulletins on where they are, as we proceed westward from Magadan. That way, we can insert ourselves precisely for an ambush at a place of our selection."

"Ah. Of course." And something clicked inside Bucharin's mind as he replied. Another plan emerging, taking shape, to supplement insertion of the Spetsnaz team. "You'll have the information, Captain. Prep your team and let me do the rest."

"Yes, sir!"

"Good afternoon." Bucharin cut off the link.

There was a risk involved in searching for his targets from the air. He'd need a favor from the air force, which was bound to cost him dearly, but Bucharin saw no other option in the present circumstances. Spetsnaz and the FSB didn't have independent access to reconnaissance aircraft, the Beriev A-50 or Mikoyan-Gurevich MiG-25RBSh that could shadow ground targets without being seen from below.

Once they were spotted, though, Bucharin *did* have other options. While Zelinsky mobilized his team in Magadan, the major could send up one of his unit's Kamov Ka-50 Black Shark helicopters armed with a 30 mm Shipunov 2A42 autocannon and wing-mounted rockets to intercept the FSB's rogue sergeant and her still-unidentified escort. Bucharin could obliterate them on the Road of Bones, and never mind the nonsense about taking them alive.

Dead traitors told no tales.

Road of Bones

TATYANA ANUCHIN'S BACK and legs were stiff from riding on the motorcycle, alternately hunching forward against Matt Cooper or leaning back against the pillion bag behind her. She yearned for a respite from riding, regardless of whether the road was intact or they had to negotiate rough, broken ground with its rocking and jolting. She craved relief but knew that every moment wasted brought death closer, breathing down her neck.

They had agreed to stop at nightfall, when the motorcycle's headlight would betray them on the dark highway and hidden obstacles might bring their journey to a crashing halt. Stopping, in turn, meant picking out a place where they could hide—and build a fire, she hoped, to keep the cold at bay without inviting every predator at large to stop and visit.

Anuchin knew she had been lucky, so far, even though it didn't feel that way. Lucky when Sergey had been killed, but she was left alive to answer questions. Lucky when the tall American arrived to spare her from a screaming death. Lucky the two of them had come this far from Yakutsk and were still alive.

But when she started counting all the reasons why she should be grateful, Anuchin had to think about the things that could go wrong within the next few minutes, hours, days.

By now, the hunters likely knew that she and Cooper had escaped from Nizhny Bestyakh. If they knew how, there could be no mistaking her destination. The only question still remaining, in the minds of those who sought to cage or kill her, would be where to find their target at a given moment on the Road of Bones.

With nothing left to do but ride and watch the road ahead, she had been cursed with ample time to think. And foremost in her mind was a pervasive sense of hopelessness. Each mile they covered—off into another time zone now, seven hours and two thousand miles from Moscow—made it more likely that the next would be their last.

She was oppressed by the idea that they were running out of time, and there was nothing she could do to stop the clock.

How had it come to this? When she and Sergey had approached Interpol at the start, it felt as if they were doing a public service. Anuchin knew, in retrospect, that she'd been foolish. After growing up in Russia, rising to a sergeant's rank within the FSB, she should have known that the corruption in her Motherland was totally impervious to change. Whether the leaders called themselves Communists, Liberal Democrats or campaigned for A Just Russia, they all fed at the same trough, wallowed in the same pervasive slime.

If she escaped from Russia now, which seemed unlikely, not to say impossible, what would her testimony in a Western court accomplish? Probably, some members of the Russian Mafiya would go to prison in America, in Britain or in France. Perhaps some diplomats would be expelled, sent home under a cloud of scandal and replaced by others who would happily accept the same bribes, tell the same lies, cater to the same firms that had bought and sold their predecessors.

Net gain? A feeble blow against the great machine no man or woman could destroy, regardless of the secrets held in store. Even if Anuchin managed to unseat the prime minister, which struck her now as total fantasy, he'd simply be replaced by someone as equally corrupt.

It was a futile exercise in self-destruction, since the FSB didn't forget, didn't forgive. Anywhere on Earth she tried to hide, the agency would find her—with a blade or bullet, poison, a hit-and-run car or a lethal dose of radiation in her groceries. It would save time for all concerned if Anuchin simply killed herself, but she'd been raised a fighter and wouldn't surrender simply out of fear.

How long until the sun set now?

Two hours, maybe three. She trusted Cooper to decide when they should stop, and where. A long night lay ahead of them, and she would be prepared to battle through it, if the hunters came. And if they didn't, then the death watch would resume tomorrow.

One more day of waiting for destruction on the Road of Bones.

THE CABIN APPEARED just as Bolan was starting to wonder where they could lie low overnight. He had to look twice, making sure that it was real, and not a figment of his imagination conjured out of wishful thinking.

The second look showed him that it was real enough, complete with sagging roof and missing shingles, chinking fallen out of place between the weathered logs that formed its walls, with shutters sagging and the door askew. Still, it was shelter, with a chimney made of stone, which meant a fireplace they could use for warmth.

Assuming that the chimney wasn't clogged.

And if the cabin wasn't occupied.

It looked abandoned, more or less a wreck, but Bolan couldn't judge the living standards of Siberians who eked a living from the wild along their district's only highway. The dilapidated structure might be someone's full-time home—or, more likely, a hunting cabin used sporadically by expeditions seeking bear, moose or whatever else they killed around those parts for meat and hides.

But it was worth a look, and Bolan slowed the BMW, turning cautiously to leave the road and climb a narrow rutted track nearly reclaimed by weeds and wildflowers. A moment later, he was parked behind the cabin, automatic carbine in his hands, prepared to answer any challenge from inside, or from the gray surrounding woods.

A minute passed, then two, and nature sounds replaced the rumbling of the engine when he switched if off. Dismounting, he and Anuchin flanked the cabin, circling it in opposite directions, watching out for any sign of recent habitation as they went.

Nothing.

Which left only the dark interior, a place Bolan supposed might prove attractive to a bear or pack of wolves between their hunting forays. Letting Anuchin cover him, he eased up to the door that wind or someone in a rush to leave had left ajar, and called into the shadows, "Anybody home?"

No answer.

Anuchin tried it next, in Russian, shrugged when there was no reply, and left it up to Bolan. Crouching to present a smaller target as the door swung open, the soldier pushed it inward, covering what he supposed would be the living room.

In fact, it proved to be the *only* room. And it was empty, both of furniture and any living thing aside from spiders weaving in the corners, maybe field mice underneath the warped and creaking wooden floor.

It was a dump, but at the moment, Bolan welcomed it as if it were a suite in a five-star hotel. There'd be no room service, but they could heat the place with firewood, if the chimney drew and didn't threaten to betray them with its smoke.

Something to think about.

For now, Bolan was satisfied to have a roof of sorts over his head, and walls around him that would keep the night outside. In a worst-case scenario, those walls were also stout enough to make a halfway decent fort, although he knew that being trapped inside the cabin by determined adversaries would mean almost certain death.

He went back out, retrieved the bike and rolled it through the doorway to a corner of the cabin's single room. No one could spot or sabotage it now, and if surprised, they had a long-shot hope of roaring through the front door to escape.

Make that a *very* long shot, on a par with the last ride of Bonnie and Clyde. Still, it was better than nothing, and riding at night carried perilous risks of its own.

"Relax awhile," he said to Anuchin as he took the Glock *Feldspaten* tool from one of the panniers. "I'll cut some firewood and be back before you miss me."

"I already miss you," she replied, and kept her submachine gun close beside her as she settled down to wait.

CHAPTER EIGHT

Despite the Lada Niva's winch, crossing the river still took time. The silt and stones beneath their tires were treacherous, shifting downstream continuously, while the current tried to pull the SUV along. Naum Izvolsky fought the steering wheel, and might have lost it if the winch's cable hadn't linked them to the eastern shore.

At last, fuming with anger, Nikolay Milescu stood beside the muddy, dripping vehicle and glowered at the river. It ignored him, couldn't feel his furious frustration, which in turn made him more bitter toward his crew.

"The best part of an hour wasted," he reminded them. "And in a few more miles we lose another hour, to the change of time. It will be dark soon, and the targets pull away from us as if we're standing still."

"Maybe because we are," Stolypin said.

Milescu rounded on him. "What was that?"

"Nothing."

"That's right! Nothing is what I want to hear from you, idiot!"

"I don't see how they crossed that on a bike," Ryumin said.

"It is *because* they're on a bike," Gramotkin answered him. "It's lighter, easier to guide across. Also, it's easier to find the shallow spots on two wheels than on four."

"Why's that? If they—"

"Shut up, for Christ's sake!" Milescu raged at them.

"Do you understand we can't go on past nightfall if we haven't found our marks by then?"

The others stared at him until Stolypin asked, "Why not?"

"Because *they* won't go on," Milescu said, as if explaining to someone simpleminded. "The road's too dangerous. They'll find someplace to hide overnight, and we could miss them in the dark."

"You mean we have to spend the night out here?" Ryumin asked him, sounding honestly surprised.

"Tonight and every night, until we find these bastards," Milescu said. "Did you think that we'd be driving back each night, to sleep in a hotel?"

Ryumin shrugged and said, "I never thought about it."

"Right. You never thought," Milescu said. "The story of your life. We have a job to do, and there's no quitting until it's done." He rounded on the rest of them, snarling, "Or is there one of you who'd like to tell Levshin we've failed? If so, you can start walking back right now. The rest of us will stay and shoot ourselves, for mercy's sake."

No answer back to that, except for boots shuffling on sand and gravel at the river's edge. Milescu spent another moment glaring at them, then said, "Okay. Stop playing with the goddamned winch and wrap it up, will you? We need to make a few more miles at least, before we lose the light."

His men seemed to think that he was looking forward to a long night in the Niva, cramped and cold, taking the watch in shifts so that their adversaries didn't double back and kill them while they slept. The quality of soldiers he was forced to work with left Milescu feeling weary and depressed.

And worried, certainly.

If he couldn't deliver as required, it actually might

be better to eliminate the middleman and kill himself, before Levshin or Boris Struve saw fit to impose a more painful punishment for failure. Milescu had witnessed the handling of others who had disappointed the Izmaylovskaya clan's godfather, and he had no desire to be on the receiving end.

How much time still remained to him?

Milescu had no doubt that Levshin would use every means at his disposal to locate and neutralize the targets. That could mean the FSB's reserves, internal troops or any other force available. Instead of calling off Milescu's team, however, Levshin would persist in making it a competition, heedless of the damage suffered by the losers when they were called to account for their failure.

But the bastard couldn't argue with success. Milescu simply had to find the targets, capture or eliminate them, and the honor would be his. Let Levshin's backup soldiers bear the taint of failure when they slunk back to their barracks.

Motivated now, he shouted at his team, "Come on! Get in the truck, will you? You're wasting time!"

DARKNESS CLOAKED the Khabarovsk Krai woodland as Bolan and Anuchin ate their MREs inside the ramshackle cabin. Bolan chose chili and macaroni, while the Russian had beef ravioli, warmed with flameless ration heaters, with crackers and cheese on the side.

Although no fire was necessary for their meals, Bolan had gathered wood to light a small blaze in the cabin's fireplace, after wedging shut the sagging window. They'd agreed to douse the fire before they slept in turns, one or the other keeping watch throughout the night against intruders, but it helped to warm the cabin first. The wood smoke troubled Bolan, but he hoped the gusting wind outside would carry it away without attracting any transient predators.

It was a gamble, lying up until the sun rose, but the Road of Bones was dangerous enough by daylight. He refused to risk trashing the bike and stranding them afoot unless there was no other choice available.

This night, at least, there would be sleep.

"I'm sorry," Anuchin said when she was nearly finished with her meal.

"Sorry for what?" Bolan asked.

"Bringing you into all this," she said. "The risk, so far from home. I should have known better, from the beginning."

Bolan shrugged, peeling the wrapper from the HOOAH! bar his MRE provided as dessert. "You didn't plan on being kidnapped," he replied.

"I don't mean that," she said. "The whole thing, really. Russia. The corruption. Nothing ever changes. I was foolish to believe that we—my partner and myself—could make a difference."

"I have to disagree with you on that," Bolan said. "No one's given me the details, but from what I've heard it sounds like you could have an impact."

"Maybe on the *myelkee reeba*—what you call the small-fry—in America or England. Here in Russia, who cares what I say? No one will be indicted, and they can't be extradited by a foreign court, regardless of the charge."

"Exposure has its own value," Bolan said.

"You believe that?" Without giving him a chance to answer, Anuchin added, "I doubt it. Look at our leaders, will you? Fascism, corruption, terrorizing journalists and playing cozy with the Mafiya. What happens? Nothing."

"We all make choices," Bolan answered. "Some produce results we can't imagine, over time. Meanwhile, we deal with consequences."

"And my partner dies," she said. "You may not know it, but this game was my idea. I talked him into it, and now he's dead."

"You think he was a stupid man?" Bolan asked.

Anuchin flared at that. "You don't insult him! He—"

"Okay, then," Bolan cut her off. "He knew what he was doing and agreed with you. He paid a price for that, but put the blame where it belongs, on those who killed him."

"You've already punished them," she said. "I should have done it."

"Next time," Bolan answered. "You were indisposed."

"You mean naked?"

He smiled and shook his head. "Outnumbered. Overwhelmed. Unable to control the situation."

"Ah. That, too," she said. "It is a strange way to be meeting, yes?"

"A funny way to start a road trip," Bolan granted.

"When they find us—"

"If they find us," Bolan interrupted, guessing that she had it right the first time.

"As you wish," she granted. "*If* and when that time comes, I release you from your duty."

"Sorry," Bolan said. "That's not your call."

"My call?" She frowned.

"Not your decision," Bolan clarified. "I take a job, I see it through."

"But I'm a stranger," Anuchin said.

"Who isn't, when you meet?" Bolan replied. "You need help getting out of Russia, I'll do what I can to make it happen."

"And your own life? Does it count so little? Should I ask about your family?"

"They're mostly gone," he said. "And no, I don't discount my life. I spend the time I have the best way that I can. It's better to be here right now, instead of sitting on a sofa somewhere, watching baseball."

"I appreciate your confidence," she said.

"Speaking of which, it's time for me to scout around," he said, "before we douse the fire and settle in."

Taking his carbine from the floor beside him, Bolan rose and slipped out through the cabin's crooked door, into the night.

Khabarovsk Krai: 5:39 p.m.

OLEG KARALI SNIFFED the night and hissed at his companions, "Do you smell that?"

"It wasn't me," Eldar Gerdt said to make the others laugh.

"Shut up!" Karali ordered. "Can't you smell it? The smoke?"

"Something's burning. So what?" Feodor Bunin asked.

"A campfire, maybe," Dmitri Orlova said.

"Yes. I smell it now," said the Ukrainian, Serhiy Lutsenko.

The five were bandits, living by their wits—such as they were—in one of Russia's least hospitable districts. Deaths outnumbered births in Khabarovsk Krai, thereby accounting for the fact that while it was the fourth largest of the country's eighty-three federal subjects, it ranked thirty-fourth in population. Nearly half of the district's people lived in Khabarovsk, near the Chinese border, but Karali and his cronies weren't welcome there.

In fact, they would be jailed—or maybe shot—on sight by the Militsiya.

Such was the lot of individuals who thumbed their noses at the law, took pride in being truly free and stole anything that wasn't nailed down. When owners of the property they coveted raised tedious objections…well, slitting a throat was easier than serving time and vastly preferable to a bullet in the back of one's head.

Karali led the way through trees and darkness, moving parallel to the Road of Bones without setting foot on the highway itself. He didn't like to be surprised, and while nocturnal travelers were rare on the Kolyma Highway, those he saw were generally armed and sometimes represented the authority that he despised.

Karali's gang was a motley group, armed with mismatched weapons. All five carried knives, but only Karali possessed a pistol. It was one of the old Makarovs, but still serviceable when he could find its special 9 mm Makarov ammunition. Presently, he had three rounds in the handgun's 8-round magazine, with no idea of where he could find more.

All five of the bandits had long guns, which helped them pass as hunters at a glance, though none of them were licensed as required by Russian law. Karali carried a bolt-action Mosin-Nagant Model 1944 carbine, while Bunin had the 1891 Cossack version of the same weapon, both chambered in 7.6 mm. Lutsenko carried a KS-23 pump-action 23 mm shotgun manufactured in the seventies and designated as a carbine for its rifled barrel. Gerdt and Orlova both had Baikal shotguns, a 70 mm side-by-side and a 76 mm single-shot, respectively.

Hardly an army, but they managed to get by.

Ten minutes after he had caught the smell of wood smoke on the wind, Karali saw the cabin. It was old, run-down and could have been abandoned, if it weren't for the short stone chimney's drifting trail of smoke. Karali smelled no food in preparation—maybe they were late, had missed it—but a fire meant people. And people always had something worth stealing.

Even if it was only their lives.

He turned and whispered to his cohorts. "All of you be extra quiet now. Watch where you step, and keep your mouths shut!"

Lutsenko grunted at him, while the others bobbed their heads. Karali felt his palms perspiring, where he clutched the wooden grip and fore-end of his carbine, nearly strangling it, the index finger of his right hand curled inside the trigger guard. Army instructors taught recruits to keep their trigger fingers clear, but what did they know about creeping through the woods at night to rob and kill a solitary camper or a family whose luck had just run out?

Karali reached the cabin, tiptoed to the door like some villainous character from a cartoon and found it had been left slightly ajar. He couldn't see inside, but there was space enough to grip the door's edge with his fingertips and jerk it open, lunging through behind his rifle with a snarl designed to terrify.

A woman sat beside the fireplace, gaping up at him. Karali couldn't keep himself from smiling as he asked, "What have we here?"

ANUCHIN WAS EXPECTING Cooper when the door opened. She thought he had been absent long enough to check the woods and answer any calls of nature while he was about it, but the man who stood before her was a leering stranger with a rifle in his hands. Worse yet, more strangers, armed, were crowding in behind him, whispering and chuckling to themselves.

The woman surveyed their weapons, a mismatched collection of sporting arms and military-surplus pieces from bygone eras, each still fully capable of snuffing out her life. The faces behind the guns were more frightening, though, each distorted by lust the intruders made no attempt to conceal.

She was frightened, no question about it, but part of her mind remained calm. Anuchin wondered if she could reach the Bizon submachine gun that lay inside the sleeping bag she had unrolled next to the hearth. How many of the drooling would-be rapists could she kill before they finished her?

"It's strange to find a woman out here, all alone," one of them said.

"She's not alone," another quickly answered. "See the second sleeping bag?"

Cooper had left it rolled beside his pack, leaning against one of the BMW's wheels, but the apparent leader of the group was more alert than his companions. Anuchin thought that if they let her reach the submachine gun, he should be the first to die.

"So, where's your boyfriend?" another gunman asked.

"Or girlfriend, better yet," another sniggered.

"Eldar, Feodor," the leader snapped. "Instead of asking stupid questions, go and find the other, eh?"

"Why us?" one of the pair asked. "I don't want to miss the party."

"You won't miss it," the goon in charge replied. "There's plenty for the lot of us."

"You take the bitch," the tallest man said. "Let me have the motorcycle."

"We'd never see your ass again," their leader snapped, half turning toward the man who'd spoken last. "I ride the bike until we sell it."

"You ride the bike," another said. "I'll ride the bitch."

"Wait your turn," the self-appointed mouthpiece ordered. "Feodor! Eldar! Stop wasting time and find the other one. We'll search the packs while you do that, and find out what they have for us."

"I know what this one has for me," a balding, scar-faced man said.

Anuchin edged her right hand toward the sleeping bag that hid her submachine gun. "You won't like it," she assured him.

"Would you bet your life on that?"

"I'll bet yours," she answered back as Feodor and Eldar left the cabin to begin their search.

Another foot or less to go before the submachine gun's pistol grip was in her hand. She'd left the safety on, but it would take only a second to release it as she raised the weapon, swinging it across the line of men who faced her.

Was there any hope that she could drop all five? The Bizon's helical magazine held sixty-four 9 mm Makarov rounds, spent in five seconds at the full-auto cyclic rate of 700 rounds per minute, but any one of the three men remaining might kill her before she could trigger a shot. Facing a Mosin-Nagant rifle and two shotguns, Anuchin knew it was a risk she'd have to take.

Because she couldn't live with the alternative. Not after all she'd suffered in the past two days. Better to die outright than let another animal lay hands on her and treat her as his property.

"Last chance to leave," she told the three remaining pigs—and slipped her hand inside the sleeping bag.

BOLAN WAS CIRCLING back toward the cabin when he heard the murmur of voices. Two men, by the sound of it, were arguing in Russian. He couldn't translate the dialect, but he used the muffled squabbling sounds to track them, soon determining that they were moving on a course between himself and Anuchin.

And if there were two outside the cabin...

Bolan had a choice to make. If there were more than two intruders in the woods, he guessed the others would be in the cabin now. He didn't try to picture them with Anuchin, or imagine how she'd cope with unexpected visitors. She hadn't screamed so far, and there had been no gunshots. Without trying to interpret those bare facts, Bolan determined that his best choice of responses, for the moment, was the quietest.

Letting his carbine dangle from its shoulder strap, he reached for the NV-01 survival knife and drew it from its sheath. Confronting two men with a blade, when one or both of them were likely packing guns, was clearly dangerous, but Bolan trusted his experience and the advantage of surprise. If he could close within arm's reach, he could drop one of them, at least, before they could alert any companions close at hand.

And if he couldn't get that close, he still had the Kalashnikov, together with his pistol, primed to level out the odds. If that helped Anuchin in the hut, so much the better. And if not, the Executioner was all about revenge.

He closed in on the prowlers, let their voices cover any sounds he may have made as he advanced. Bolan supposed they had to be trying to find out if Anuchin was alone, but if they had a systematic search pattern in mind, it was eluding him. No more than half-alert, they did a fair job moving through the woods, but sabotaged themselves with whispered cross-talk as they went.

He was behind them in another moment, closing up the final gap, prepared to strike. Being right-handed, Bolan chose the figure on his right and clamped a palm over the prowler's squirming lips, twisting his head before he drove the six-inch spearpoint blade into the hollow where his neck and shoulder met.

It was a killing thrust that ripped the jugular, carotid artery and larynx, all at once. The dying man might live for seconds longer, drowning in his own blood, but he was immediately incapacitated by the shock of violent penetration. He collapsed, slid out of Bolan's grasp and crumpled to the ground, even as the big American turned to slash at his companion.

Number two was quicker than he looked, spinning to face the unexpected threat, but still not fast enough to save himself. Without a heartbeat's hesitation, Bolan stabbed him in the face, twisted the blood-slick blade as it withdrew, then struck again, into the stunned man's chest. The gunman made a gargled croaking sound, but then the blade slipped underneath his chin, pinning his mouth shut as it sheared through the soft palate to his brain.

One final twist, and Bolan let the body drop. He paused to wipe his knife across the second dead man's jacket, then returned it to its scabbard, moving off toward Anuchin and the cabin. He was halfway there when sudden automatic fire erupted from their shelter, interspersed with shouts and single shots.

Arriving at the cabin doorway, Bolan hesitated, crouching in the darkness, cradling his Kalashnikov. He took a chance and called out Anuchin's name. Relief swept over him as she called back, "All clear."

Three men like those he'd dealt with in the woods lay dead or dying on the cabin's floor, shot through with the Russian agent's SMG at point-blank range. Bolan took time to pull the weapons from their limp or twitching hands, for safety's sake. One of the three was breathing, barely, but a clinical examination of his sounds told Bolan that he wouldn't be for long.

"I'll dump these guys outside," Bolan said, adding, "unless you'd rather pack up and move on."

"I'm not afraid of ghosts," Anuchin said. "And I can help you move the trash."

CHAPTER NINE

They rolled out at first light, with the BMW's tank topped off and ready for the road. Bolan had been relieved that Anuchin slept during the night, despite their interruption and the bloodletting that followed. She was holding up all right, as far as he could tell, but Bolan wasn't a psychologist and guessed the strain was working on her nerves, in concert with fatigue, to break her down.

According to the bike's odometer, they had covered 117 miles on their first day of travel. At that rate, the drive to Magadan would take eleven days, but Bolan planned to improve that average.

They had been handicapped their first day out by a late start from Nizhny Bestyakh, a dicey river crossing and the normal problems of a shakedown cruise on rugged, unfamiliar ground. Bolan thought he had learned enough to push the motorcycle and himself a little harder on the Road of Bones, without disabling their only means of transportation. If he could double their first day's mileage from now on, at least, they should reach Magadan in four or five days.

Surely 250 miles per day wasn't too much to ask, on a bike that could top one hundred miles per hour?

Unless Siberia and Anuchin's enemies had other plans.

Bolan knew they'd been lucky so far, but that luck couldn't hold.

Traveling by motorcycle didn't lend itself to conversation on the highway, but he had discussed their risks with Anuchin in detail before they hit the road. She had explained to Bolan that the FSB possessed its own internal troops detachment—in effect, a Spetsnaz unit dedicated to the Federal Security Service. They were the FSB's muscle, employed as needed while the agency performed its various functions.

Anuchin wasn't sure if her superiors—the men and women who wanted her silenced—would risk fielding troops, but Bolan knew he had to treat it as a possibility. What did her masters have to lose if they resorted to a bit of overkill? If locals got wind of the action, Moscow could always explain it away. A field exercise, or a strike against terrorists.

Easy.

But if Spetsnaz came, before they got around to Anuchin, they would have to face the Executioner. Bolan's personal rule against killing or wounding police didn't protect soldiers who were sent against him on a battlefield. A casual observer might not grasp the difference, but it was clear in Bolan's mind. Police, like firefighters and EMTs, existed to *help* people. Soldiers were employed and trained to fight. To kill. He could debate a given nation's use of troops all day, dissecting moral and immoral wars, but none of that had any impact on the bottom line.

When soldiers came for Bolan, they were fair game.

That said, he hoped they wouldn't have to deal with any Spetsnaz troopers on the Road of Bones, simply because they were the best and deadliest in Russia. The equivalent of Delta Force in the United States, perhaps, but highly controversial thanks to its performance in Chechnya, in Georgia and at the Nord-Ost theater siege in Moscow.

Better to avoid them, if he could, but Bolan was prepared if he had no alternative. He had survived this long by being ready for the worst, confronting it and turning it against his enemies. Worst-case scenario, his bones wouldn't be lonely in Siberia.

Khabarovsk Krai: 5:46 a.m.

THE MIKOYAN-GUREVICH MiG-25RBSh, known to NATO forces as "Foxbat," was a high-supersonic interceptor and reconnaissance-bomber aircraft that ranked among the world's fastest military aircraft when it entered service with the Russian air force. That was in 1970, and the world had moved on, but the Foxbat still had its place among Russian warplanes. At its thirty-year mark, it had been refitted and upgraded with new RP-25 Sapfeer/ Saphir look-down/shoot-down radar that permitted detection, tracking and destruction of targets moving below the radar system's horizon. Another addition was an infrared search and track—IRST—system permitting the MiG-25 to pinpoint objects that emit infrared radiation, such as jet planes and helicopters.

So, the MiG was still a killer, but this morning's flight was strictly look-and-see. Its pilot and lone crewman, Captain Franz Rostovsky, was attached to the 11th Air Army in Russia's Far Eastern Military District. That morning, bright and early, he had flown out of Dzemgi Airport, five miles northeast of Komsomolsk-on-Amur, with orders to follow the Kolyma Highway and report on any traffic he observed. In particular, his colonel was concerned about two people on a motorcycle, headed eastward.

It seemed a lot of fuss to Captain Rostovsky, but he wasn't inclined to question orders. If the brass wanted to send him up and burn the fuel required for a search with a maximum radius of 186 miles, Rostovsky was happy to oblige. He loved flying, and wouldn't have minded blasting his earthbound target with a Kh-25ML laser-guided air-to-ground missile in the bargain, but he had strict orders to locate, observe and report, without engaging the hostiles.

Captain Rostovsky supposed they were terrorist scum, like the bombers who had plagued Vladikavkaz with bombings since 2008, or the Chechen scum who bombed the Moscow Metro in March 2010, killing forty innocents and maiming more than a hundred. Well, not *exactly* like those bombers, he supposed, since they had blown themselves to shreds in crazy acts of suicide, but maybe these were on their way to stage some new atrocity.

Rostovsky could become a hero if he stopped them, but the violation of his orders would have a dramatically different effect—as in destroying his career, perhaps.

Besides, he couldn't know that they were terrorists, or any other kind of criminal. With orders coming, as he understood it, through liaison with the FSB, they were as likely to be Russian agents on a mission for the government, facing some danger that required covert surveillance to protect them. Maybe *that* was it, and Rostovsky was their faithful watchdog in the sky.

No glory there, except the satisfaction of a job well done.

He had been airborne for the better part of half an hour when he found the target—or, at least, a motorcycle with two passengers—moving at decent speed on the Kolyma Highway. It was headed east, as Rostovsky had been told, rolling at forty miles per hour, give or take, along a section of the road where pavement was intact.

He marked the target's speed, location and direction,

then reported back to his control at Dzemgi. Rostovsky half expected orders to remain on station at high altitude, tracking the subjects while he still had time and fuel remaining, but the word came back at once for his return. Unquestioning, he issued crisp acknowledgment and turned for home.

NEARLY TWO HOURS from the cabin, Bolan was surprised to find a brown bear standing in the middle of the road. It was a hulking thing—related, Bolan knew, to the North American grizzly and giant Kodiak species, but significantly smaller than the latter. This one looked to be seven feet long on all fours, give or take, and Bolan pegged its weight somewhere around eight hundred pounds.

It was a beauty, and a danger to a pair of fragile humans mounted on a motorcycle, totally exposed to claws and fangs in the event of an attack.

Bolan stopped well back from the bear, giving it ample room to move, and kept the BMW's motor idling in first gear. He had enough range, theoretically, to raise and fire his automatic carbine if the bear should charge, but whether his 7.6 mm rounds would drop the creature outright was a question he preferred to leave unanswered, if he had a choice.

As he watched the bear and scanned the woods to either side for more, hoping he wouldn't see a cub emerging from the undergrowth, Bolan considered tactics. Short of killing the beast or hosing it with pepper spray he didn't have, the soldier knew enough to watch the bear's body language, alert for the warning signs of laid-back ears and "popping" jaws. If it began to charge, he knew, the bear could reach a speed of thirty miles per hour in nothing flat, striking with bulldozer force while it savaged frail flesh with its talons and teeth.

"Hang on," he cautioned Anuchin as he revved the BMW's motor to an angry whine, then blew the horn.

It wasn't an impressive sound, per se, but its high-pitched tone seemed to startle the bear, maybe paining its sensitive ears. The beast shook its head, huffed at Bolan a couple of times, then slowly turned and retreated downslope through the trees. Bolan gave it a twenty-yard lead, then gunned the motorcycle from a standing start and put the animal behind them, covering two hundred yards before allowing himself a sigh of relief.

Anuchin's hands clung tightly to his waist, and he could feel her trembling. One more trauma for the lady who was running for her life.

And Bolan feared the next one might not be so easy to avoid.

Megino-Kangalassky District

A VICIOUS MUSCLE CRAMP woke Nikolay Milescu on the verge of dawn. Muffled in a heavy parka, with a knit cap drawn down almost to his nose, knees hiked up nearly to his chest, Milescu felt like something petrified, perhaps the mummy of a cave dweller who'd died during the last Ice Age.

Except that he hurt.

As he began to move and stretch within the confines of the Lada Niva's shotgun seat, Milescu found that every major muscle in his body, from his neck down to his calves and ankles, was a source of individual, specific pain. Impossibly, it seemed to him that each pain was unique, vying with all the others to compel a squeal that would arouse the others snoring in the SUV's cocoon, its windows misted over with their sour breath.

At first, Milescu fought the urge to curse and moan,

but after several agonizing moments he surrendered to it. Why in hell should anybody sleep, when he couldn't?

"Korovy khuy! Kushite govno y oomyite! Yob tvoiu mat!"

Somehow, the fierce obscenities seemed to relieve a measure of Milescu's pain, as if they helped his aching, burning muscles to relax. Around him, his companions woke in something close to panic, groping for their weapons.

"What's the matter?" Izvolsky demanded, then lapsed into cursing himself as one of his knees struck the Niva's steering wheel.

"Where are they?" Stolypin gasped, twisting in his seat so that the muzzle of his shotgun struck the closest window, nearly cracking it.

"There's no one," Milescu said, calming them.

"So, what the hell was all that noise?" Ryumin asked from the backseat, sandwiched between two other bodies.

"It's almost daylight," Milescu said, peeking at his watch to verify that fact. "It's time that we were up and moving."

"It's still dark," Gramotkin protested. "You were worried about driving in the dark, in case we miss them."

"By the time you piss and bitch some more, we'll have the sun," Milescu said. "Get to it now. I give you half an hour, then we're moving out."

"No breakfast?" Stolypin asked, not quite whining.

"Eat it on the road," Milescu told him, opening his door onto the cold dark, easing stiffly from the vehicle.

As he relieved himself with gratitude, Milescu imagined a weasel leaping out of the shadows and clamping on to his genitals. The image changed at once, his furry attack transformed into a tiger. The Siberian species were rarely man-eaters, he knew, but the mental image hastened Milescu's return to the car.

He waited, nervous, while the others straggled back from various directions, zipping up their trousers, cursing at the early-morning chill. None of them were happy about leaving without coffee in their stomachs, but they sipped vodka instead and dug into their packs for food as Naum Izvolsky got the Niva rolling.

It was hardly gourmet fare, but each of them was packing jerky, protein bars, crackers with potted meat and cheese, candy—in short, the staples of a hunting expedition whose participants didn't intend to spend much time afield. Within five minutes, their complaints were stifled by the sounds of chewing, punctuated by a belch from Gramotkin.

"Open a window!" Ryumin demanded.

"Screw that! It's too cold!" Gramotkin answered.

God help us, Milescu thought. In a few more miles, they would reach Khabarovsk Krai and lose another hour, as the time zones changed. Where were their targets now?

Scowling, he stared along the tunnel of their headlight beams, waiting for dawn.

M56 Kolyma Highway: 7:12 a.m.

SEATED AT THE OPEN side door of the Kamov Ka-50 helicopter, Spetsnaz Lieutenant Semyon Denikin watched the rugged countryside sweep past, three hundred feet below. The Black Shark could cruise at eighteen thousand feet, but for the present mission they were skimming treetops, following the Road of Bones.

Denikin and his four-man team had scrambled in response to a report from a surveillance flight from Dzemgi, following a target over the Kolyma Highway.

Typically, there was no explanation for the sudden call-out, no discussion as to why two strangers traveling by motorcycle from Nizhny Bestyakh to Magadan must be liquidated.

And, in truth, Denikin didn't care.

He was a soldier by profession and enjoyed his work. He offered no whining self-deprecation, no claims that killing enemies of the state was a necessary evil forced upon him by a brooding sense of duty. Why deny that hunting humans was the most invigorating sport ever devised by man?

The helicopter's two-man crew didn't require a Spetsnaz team to do its killing for them. The Kamov Ka-50 had a top speed of 196 miles per hour, its rotors powered by twin Klimov TV3-117VK turboshaft engines, with a hunting range of 339 miles. Once a target was sighted, it could be struck from the air by a twin-barreled Gryazev-Shipunov GSh-23 automatic cannon spewing 23 mm armor-piercing slugs at 1600 rounds per minute, or by 80 mm S-8 rockets fired from wing-mounted pods.

But headquarters wasn't satisfied to have these targets slaughtered from a distance. For this killing, someone at the top desired the human touch, however brutal that might be.

Accordingly, Lieutenant Denikin was armed with a PKP Pecheneg light machine gun, belt fed with 7.62 mm rounds and boasting a cyclic rate of 800 rounds per minute. His four companions carried AK-9 assault rifles, chambered for 9 mm subsonic rounds, but their role was limited to mopping up after Denikin made the kill. They would retrieve the corpses—body bags included in the helicopter's cargo—and torch the motorcycle to prevent it being used by local bandits.

Simple.

With coordinates provided by the MiG-25 spotting plane and a simple calculator, they could chart the progress of their prey on the Kolyma Highway and catch the travelers unawares. The runners would be dead almost before they knew they were in danger.

Denikin had volunteered to capture them alive, if feasible, but the idea was rejected out of hand by his superiors. Whatever the subjects had done to invite execution, implacable enemies wanted their heads.

Denikin's earpiece chirped, the Black Shark's pilot telling him their target had been sighted half a mile ahead. The helicopter's nose dipped as its rotors chopped the air, accelerating in pursuit. Denikin cocked his PKP and leaned farther out of the open side door, his weapon's weight supported by a strap that spanned his chest and looped across his left shoulder.

All ready. He could start the party any moment now.

THEY HAD BEEN MAKING decent time since Bolan dodged the bear, rolling over firm pavement most of the way and weaving around the potholes. His top speed had been fifty miles per hour, give or take, but they were making progress, putting miles behind them.

Bolan had no illusion that they had escaped detection in their flight from Nizhny Bestyakh. Even if a miracle had happened, and the hunters hadn't found the shop where they'd acquired the BMW, it would be obvious to anyone with eyes and half a brain that Tatyana Anuchin had to be fleeing eastward. Steps would have been taken to pursue or intercept them, meaning that their hours of riding unopposed were numbered.

As to where and when the enemy might strike, Bolan could only stay alert, knowing that it could happen anytime and anywhere.

The cabin where they'd killed five men was close to eighty miles behind them now, placing them within four hundred miles of Tomtor and eleven hundred miles from Magadan. It was progress, but Bolan still wished they could make better time.

That thought had barely formed when Anuchin slapped him on the shoulder—not a gentle tap, but a demand for his immediate attention. Slowing, Bolan turned his head as she leaned into him, and heard her voice come muffled through the plastic face screen on her helmet.

"Look behind!" she warned.

He slowed the BMW further, cranked his head around until the muscles in his neck creaked, and his eyes picked out an airborne shape pursuing them. At first glance it resembled a huge prehistoric insect, recognizable immediately as a military attack helicopter, flying at an altitude below two hundred feet.

Bolan couldn't cite the model number of the whirlybird offhand, but that was insignificant. Regardless of the nomenclature, it was faster than the motorcycle, more maneuverable since it wasn't earthbound, and its weaponry would be superior to anything that he and Anuchin carried.

The soldier had a choice to make, and if he didn't make it in a hurry, they were dead.

One option was to give the bike its head and race along the open highway, knowing that the chopper's speed was double theirs or better, and its pilot didn't have to worry about lumps or potholes in the pavement while it lasted. If the blacktop quit on them before the helicopter blasted them to bloody tatters, then the motorcycle's speed would drop or it would crash, leaving the chopper unimpaired and free to pick them off at leisure.

The alternative was taking if off-road, using the woods

for cover while endangering the cycle, Anuchin and himself. Even the least miscalculation would suffice to dump the bike, perhaps to put it permanently out of action. On the other hand, he might just lose control and crash into a tree, breaking his neck and leaving his companion to the wolves, if she survived the crash.

Choices.

One looked like certain death to Bolan, while the other was a gamble with the odds stacked heavily against them, but a possibility they might survive. In other words, no choice at all.

"Hang on!" he shouted, and felt her arms lock tight around his waist. Without another backward glance, Bolan swung to his left and took the bike into the trees, roaring uphill to leave the Road of Bones behind.

CHAPTER TEN

One minute into the pursuit, Bolan thought that he'd blown it. As he left the cracked and aging pavement, nosed the BMW between a pine tree and a spruce, climbing the hillside, he could feel its tires lose traction on a bed of mulch and fallen leaves. He had the choice to power through or dump the bike and flee on foot.

He powered through.

After a few heart-wrenching seconds, Bolan felt the rear tire of the R1200GS dig in and grip the rocky soil of the hillside. It almost leaped away from him then, but he hung on while Anuchin clung to him in desperation.

Bolan heard the chopper closing in behind him, half imagined he could feel its rotor wash, but there was no way it could follow through the trees. Its crew could track him, though, whether they used their naked eyes or infrared technology that registered the heat from human bodies and the BMW's engine.

And the chopper's crew could also kill them from a distance, right.

As proof of that, a burst of automatic fire ripped through the trees behind him, slashing vivid scars on bark and churning up the forest floor. Bolan zigged left, zagged right, as best he could, but looming trees and the uncertain nature of the ground beneath his tires made true evasive driving difficult. The rising landscape shielded and betrayed him, with a fine impartiality, proving that Mother Nature didn't give a damn.

There was a limit to the angle of ascent Bolan could handle with the motorcycle, short of flipping over backward with the bike on top of him. He hadn't reached that point yet, but another drawback of hill-climbing was the fact that it would ultimately put him closer to the warbird that was stalking him. Somewhere above him lay a crest or ridge, above which his pursuers might decide to hover while they rained death on him in the form of bullets, rockets or grenades.

With that in mind, he changed directions, swung around the thick trunk of an elm tree and aimed the bike downhill. There was no point alerting Anuchin, since she couldn't clutch him any tighter if she tried. By now, their second day of travel, she'd adjusted to the BMW's pillion seat, knew when and how to lean on turns.

If she fell off, by any chance...

Bolan put that thought out of mind and concentrated on his driving, heard the chopper pass above their heads, roaring upslope. The pilots hadn't caught his change yet, couldn't turn their aircraft on a dime in any case. Helicopters had better maneuverability than fighter planes, but they were still subject to basic laws of physics. They could hover and reverse, but backing a chopper downhill at treetop level, while crewmen on board tried to shoot a moving target, was a recipe for failure.

Maybe disaster.

More bullets spattered around them, all wasted, but the shooters only had to get lucky with one. A hit on Bolan or the bike would take them down. A hit on Anuchin might have the identical effect, whether her fall obstructed the chain drive or threw the bike off-balance. If she fell,

Bolan would have to stop and check on her, at least confirm the kill before he took steps to escape without her.

And by then, he calculated, any shooter worth his salt would have him slotted for the kill.

So forward movement was the key, as long as he could manage it. And at the moment, it was all downhill.

"Turning around," the helicopter's pilot warned Semyon Denikin as he gunned the Black Shark through a banking turn with treetops nearly close enough to touch. Denikin clutched his PKP machine gun, let the shoulder harness take his weight when he would otherwise have pitched headlong into the rush of wind, crashing a hundred feet or more to crushing impact through a gauntlet of tree limbs.

It would be something, though, Denikin thought, to plummet from this height without a hope of living through it, dying with his eyes wide-open as the ground rushed up to meet him.

But he wasn't supposed to die this morning. It was someone else's turn.

The chopper made its turn and started back downhill, chasing the motorcycle. It was difficult to see his target through the trees, just fleeting glimpses here and there, a waste of ammunition if he tried to drop them now.

Instead, he keyed his microphone and told the pilots, "Get back to the road! I need a field of fire!"

They didn't ask to do Denikin's job for him, unloading on the motorcyclist with their autocannon or the S-8 rocket pod. Their orders were specific and explicit. Denikin would be forced to ask them for assistance if he needed it. Nothing but transportation would be volunteered.

Denikin knew his targets had to be desperate, had to recognize that they were in a lose-lose situation. If they stayed off-road, zigzagging through the forest on a sloping hillside, they were bound to fall or crash sooner or later. If they came back to the open road, they were exposed.

In either case, they were as good as dead.

Denikin's only worry was that they might somehow find a place to hide and wait him out, until the Black Shark needed to refuel. Denikin didn't know the local landscape well, couldn't say whether there were caves or old mine shafts nearby, but would be educated quickly if his targets disappeared.

That would require a change of tactics on his part. He might be forced to leave the helicopter with his men and hunt their enemies on foot.

The road was wide enough, Denikin guessed, to let the Black Shark land without inflicting damage on its forty-seven-foot-wide rotor blades. In the event that he was wrong, if there was danger of the blade tips striking trees along the roadside, then Denikin and his team could scramble down a dangling ladder and proceed, while being shadowed from the air.

If all else failed, he was prepared to let the chopper pilots do his killing for him, but verification would still be required. One way or another, Denikin would have to lay hands on the corpses, retrieve them for delivery to his superiors.

The highway was beneath him now, Denikin watching through the trees as his intended victims rushed to meet him, dodging in and out among the trees. Smiling, he braced the PKP against his hip, angling its muzzle toward the tree line, index finger on the weapon's trigger.

Waiting for the kill.

ANUCHIN FELT AS IF she might be sick at any moment, but she bit her tongue and kept her meager breakfast down by will alone. She clung to Matt Cooper's waist as if breaking that contact meant death.

At first, after they charged off-road, the agent had kept her eyes closed, frightened by the tree trunks rushing past her, but the darkness had intensified her roiling nausea. With eyes open, at least, she might see danger coming if the bike began to swerve. There might be time to leap clear, save herself, before it crashed.

And then what?

She had no illusions about being able to evade the helicopter that was chasing them. She couldn't outrun it, couldn't go to ground while its infrared tracking devices looked down from on high to reveal her. If it came down to a standing fight, she knew their adversaries had the edge with weapons boasting longer range and greater striking power, while the pilots were secure inside a fully armored cockpit.

There were ways to bring the helicopter down, of course, but whether they could manage it was anybody's guess. And it was certain they couldn't inflict sufficient damage while they raced along the hillside, dodging bullets from the air.

They would be forced to stand and fight, which felt like suicide.

Cooper was driving well, for all the turmoil his maneuvers caused in Anuchin's stomach. It felt as if he had been racing motorcycles all his life, though no experience on open tracks would have prepared him for this game of life and death among the trees. Each time the Black Shark's automatic weapons chattered, the woman braced herself for the explosive pain that came before oblivion— but each time, Cooper brought them through intact.

Each time, so far.

They couldn't win this game of cat and mouse, she

realized. A Russian combat helicopter could fly farther, faster, than their BMW could travel on its eight gallons of gasoline. Even if they weren't blasted from the saddle by machine-gun fire, they would run dry eventually and be left on foot, cut off and trapped a thousand miles from anywhere.

Somehow, that thought quelled Anuchin's nausea, replaced the sickly feeling with a grim determination to survive—or, at the very least, to take some of her adversaries with her at the end. She could imagine their pursuers in the helicopter, smug expressions on their faces, toying with their prey like so-called sportsmen who shot elk and wolves from planes. They were cowards who had been sent by other fearful men in Moscow, to protect themselves, their precious reputations and their privileges.

To hell with all of them.

As Cooper turned the BMW back downhill, a spray of bullets chasing them and missing by at least ten feet, Anuchin knew the helicopter would be waiting for them when they reached the highway. They couldn't avoid it, and the open road would be their death trap unless Cooper had another plan in mind. If so, he couldn't brief her on it, busy as he was just keeping them upright and charging down the slope past trees that could destroy them if he brushed against one in their flight.

A few more yards, and she could see the Black Shark waiting for them, hovering twenty feet above the pavement on the Road of Bones. There was a soldier in the open doorway facing them, crouching behind some kind of automatic weapon. Any second now, he would begin to fire.

Anuchin kept her eyes open this time, prepared, if nothing else, to meet her death head-on.

LIEUTENANT DENIKIN welcomed good luck but didn't trust it. If his targets were stupid enough to present themselves for slaughter, so much the better, but he doubted whether that was their intention as the motorcycle raced downhill to meet his hovering Black Shark.

He steered himself to be ready. They were overdue for a mistake.

And as he crouched in the helicopter's open doorway, cradling his machine gun, Denikin couldn't help hoping that the bike would skid and crash, disabling those aboard or slowing them enough, at least, for him to stitch them with a stream of bullets as they struggled to recover. It would end quickly, if not cleanly, and his backup team could haul the leaking mess on board.

As the motorcycle roared closer, gaining momentum on its downhill slalom, Denikin could see the driver, his face obscured by tinted plastic, hunched over the handlebars. Another helmet barely visible across his shoulder had to be worn by the woman, clinging for dear life.

A life about to end.

Denikin stroked the Pecheneg's trigger, tracking its muzzle across the motorcycle's path, but what was this? The driver suddenly swerved sideways, throwing up a spray of soil and fallen leaves that briefly blinded Denikin. The Spetsnaz officer fired into it, cursing, but as the brown-and-gray debris fell back to earth, the bike was gone.

Gone where?

It streaked across the hillside on a course that paralleled the highway thirty yards below it, opening a lead before he shouted at the pilot to give chase.

The driver's skill reminded Denikin of a stunt cyclist he had seen in Zvenigorod when he was ten or eleven years old. Traveling showmen had erected a large wooden vat, perhaps twenty feet deep and equally wide. Inside it, a motorcyclist had driven in circles, faster and faster, until he literally climbed the walls, rising inexorably toward the rim of the vat, where spectators gaped at the laws of physics in action.

Denikin's target might not be that skilled, but he was good enough to give the Black Shark a run for its money. It almost seemed a shame that his destruction was inevitable, a foregone conclusion.

Almost.

Denikin didn't waste sympathy on those he was assigned to kill. But he could still admire an adversary who faced death courageously and made the most of it.

Like now.

Denikin wobbled in his harness as the Black Shark dipped its nose, accelerating in pursuit. The man and woman on the motorcycle were as good as dead. They had postponed death by a few brief moments, but the end result had never been in any doubt.

Seventy yards and closing. Denikin could hose them now or wait a few more seconds for a double kill at point-blank range. This wasn't sport, testing his skill against a woodland animal, so he decided that the best thing was to wait. Be sure. Make no mistakes for anyone to criticize.

He braced the Pecheneg's skeletal stock against his shoulder, focused on its open sights and let his index finger curl around the trigger—just in time to see the motorcycle fishtail and begin to slide.

TIMING WAS CRITICAL. If anything at all went wrong—a slip of any sort beyond Bolan's control, a fraction of a second wasted fumbling for his weapon—they were dead.

The plan had come to Bolan on the fly, full-blown, and

he could only shout the briefest warning back to Anuchin through his mask: "Be ready when I lay it down!"

A squeeze from nervous fingers told him that she understood. Or, anyway, he hoped so. If he was mistaken, then the fall could gravely injure her, and even if he pulled off the maneuver that he had in mind, it could all be for nothing. If he couldn't bring the witness back, he might as well have stayed at home.

Too late to think about that, with the helicopter *whup-whupping* on their right flank, closing fast. Another moment, and they would be under fire, too much to hope the gunner would keep missing at close range.

Bolan was ready when they hit a clearing in the trees, with room to lay the BMW down and still avoid a crash that would destroy the bike. There might be damage, anyway, but when the shooter in the whirlybird got done with them, it wouldn't matter if the motorcycle was intact.

The trick to laying down a speeding bike was getting off it before it dragged and flayed you. Bolan tilted to his left, kicked off from the footpegs and hoped Anuchin was clear as he rolled over once, then came up with the AKS-74U in hand.

The helicopter was almost on top of them, its armored cockpit invincible to .50-caliber rounds and anything smaller, but Bolan wasn't aiming for the pilots. He was angling for the gunner in the open doorway, hoping he was fast enough to score a hit before the heavier machine gun ended him.

Despite a hint of vertigo from Bolan's drop-and-roll, he managed target acquisition with the stubby carbine, triggering a long burst from where he lay cushioned by loam and leaves. The helicopter's gunner had a larger weapon with a higher cyclic rate of fire, but at their present range it hardly mattered. All that counted now was speed and accuracy, with the prize of life awarded to whoever came in first with rounds on target.

Bolan held the AK steady, saw his adversary jerk and jitter as the 5.45 mm slugs ripped into him, slamming him back against his shoulder harness, his long legs flailing. By the time the dying soldier's finger clenched around his weapon's trigger, he had swiveled in the dangling rig so that his muzzle-flashes lit the warbird's cabin, spraying death into the cockpit.

Bolan saw the Black Shark pitch and roll, then tilt into a nose-stand on the Road of Bones. Its contra-rotating coaxial rotor blades, each nearly twenty-four feet long, slammed into the pavement and shattered, one after the other in grim rapid-fire, sending shrapnel off into the woods. Another moment, and the bird flipped over on its back, capsized, twin engines howling as it tore itself apart.

He found Anuchin in the midst of all that racket, rising from the point where she had fallen when the bike went down. He offered her a hand, but she was doing all right on her own.

"The motorcycle," she reminded him.

Next stop, the BMW, still growling in the leaf mulch, lying on its side. Bolan reached down to switch it off, but put the damage check on hold until he finished what he'd started with the Black Shark.

It was down, but Bolan wasn't done.

ANUCHIN WATCHED Cooper running toward the shattered helicopter in a half crouch, covering the wreckage with his automatic carbine. There was someone moving in the aircraft's cabin, as pungent fuel spilled from its ruptured tanks.

How long before it found the superheated turboshaft

engines and burst into flame? Almost before the thought took shape, Anuchin saw a spark beneath the helicopter, where its rotor shaft was crushed beneath some nineteen thousand pounds of steel, plastic and human flesh. Pale flames spread quickly, leaping, driving the big American back as the Black Shark began to flounder in a lake of fire.

Streamers of smoke rose from the fuselage, blown into dark gossamer penants by a fitful breeze. Anuchin smelled the helicopter's fuel and scorching oil, along with something else. Asphalt, she realized. The flames were melting part of the highway, adding one more obstacle for travelers who passed this way after the crash.

She heard people screaming from the center of the fire, saw Cooper raise his weapon, as if he could end their suffering, but with the greasy pall of smoke expanding he couldn't find targets. Grim-faced, he retreated from the pyre and joined her where the motorcycle lay at rest on its left side.

"We need to get away from here," he told her.

They raised the bike together, straining against its deadweight, managing to right it on the second try. Cooper put down the kickstand, crouching to inspect the motor, wiring and chain drive, poking at this and that until he satisfied himself that all the working parts appeared to be intact. He swung into the saddle, started the motor, revved it twice, then listened to it rumble with a note of quiet power.

"Good to go," he told her.

"Are you sure?" she asked.

"If I've missed anything," he said, "we'll find out soon enough."

Less than encouraged, Anuchin took her place behind him on the pillion, gripped his waist and hung on as he steered across the hillside, picking up momentum, nosing down the slope toward pavement when the ruin of the Black Shark was a hundred yards behind them.

When it blew, a crack of heavy-metal thunder that reverberated through the forest and was gone, Anuchin put the burning soldiers out of mind. They'd come to silence her, doubtless on orders from the FSB. Now they were silent, but eliminating them hadn't removed the threat they represented.

Other hunters would be coming, probably were on their way already. When they saw the Black Shark's wreckage and reported back to their superiors, new urgency would energize the hunt.

It was a long way yet to Magadan. And Anuchin knew the worst still lay in front of them.

CHAPTER ELEVEN

Stony Man Farm, Virginia: 4:30 p.m.

"Well?" The tone of Barbara Price's voice left no wiggle room for evasion. "Tell me."

"It was close," Aaron Kurtzman replied, "but they made it."

"Injuries?"

"None obvious," Kurtzman said. "Anyway, they're off and rolling."

"Have you called Hal?" Price inquired.

"Next on my list."

"I'll handle it," she said.

"Suits me."

They had been tracking Bolan's progress via satellite, specifically one of the KH-9 HEXAGON Broad Coverage Photo Reconnaissance satellites commonly known as "Big Bird," built by Lockheed for the U.S. Air Force. The KH-9 followed an elliptical orbit through Earth's thermosphere. Despite its relatively small size—ten feet by four and a half—it weighed close to thirty thousand pounds, chock-full of TV and radio scanners, with high-resolution cameras that could read the headlines of a newspaper from 150 miles overhead.

This afternoon, Big Bird had captured a battle on the far side of the world, between Mack Bolan and the armed crew of a Russian Kamov Ka-50 helicopter gunship. Kurtzman had watched the show, while Barbara Price found busywork to do, removed herself from the proximity of monitors that played the action out in real time. She had waited for the final word, and it was in.

Bolan would live to fight another day, or, at this rate, another hour of the same long, godforsaken day.

"He'll be all right," Kurtzman said as she reached the War Room's elevator.

"Right," she answered, without turning back. "No doubt."

But there *was* doubt. There always would be, every time Bolan went off to put himself in harm's way for some stranger's sake.

Price made her way to her office in the Annex. There, door closed, she sat behind her desk and dialed Hal Brognola's private line at the Justice Department.

The big Fed picked up on the second ring. "Yes?"

"Checking in," she informed him. "It's started."

"'It' being...?"

"The hunt," Price replied. "They sent a Black Shark after Striker, but he reeled it in."

"Air force?" Brognola asked.

"No way to tell for sure," she answered. "Could be army or internal troops."

"The FSB," he said.

"That's my first guess, but it could be FSO or even the Militsiya. If Striker's passenger can deliver the goods advertised, she's got enemies to spare."

"I wish to God we had some kind of pickup procedure in place before Magadan," Brognola said.

"We've worked all the angles," Price replied. "There's no way we can reach that far inside the Federation without touching off a shitstorm."

"Right. I hate it, but you're right."

"Concerning that," she said, "we've got the sub on standby. It's the *Kansas City.*"

"Los Angeles class," Brognola surmised from the name.

"That's affirmative."

All submarines in the U.S. Navy's fast-attack class were named for American cities, except the USS *Hyman G. Rickover,* christened for an admiral whose career had spanned sixty years of service. "Fast-attack" was relative, with a top speed of thirty-eight miles per hour submerged, but there was no question concerning attack capability. Each L.A.-class sub carried twenty-five torpedo-tube-launched weapons, and the latest models also boasted a dozen vertical-launch tubes for BGM-109 Tomahawk cruise missiles.

"Where is it now?" Brognola asked.

"I can't pinpoint it," Price replied, "but it will be in range for pickup by the time Striker hits Magadan."

If he made it that far, was the proviso unspoken between them.

"He'll still have to get offshore somehow, with the package," Brognola said.

"Adapt and improvise," Price replied. "His specialty."

"The day after tomorrow, is it?"

"Maybe, if they make good time," she stated. "Could be longer. They've still got nearly eleven hundred miles to go."

"Right. Jesus. Thanks for updating me."

"We'll stay in touch."

"Okay. Till then," Brognola said, and cut the link.

Two days, if they were lucky. With the FSB and God knew who else hunting Bolan and his passenger on the only highway running west-to-east across the Russian Far

East. They might as well be two mice caged with hawks and weasels, running for their lives.

Except that these mice could fight back, as they'd already proved. How many weasels dead in Yakutsk? And one hawk was down for good.

Brognola had a feeling that it wouldn't be the last.

M56 Kolyma Highway

"WHAT IN HELL IS THIS?" Nikolay Milescu snarled.

"Somebody crashed a helicopter," Naum Izvolsky offered.

"I can *see* that," Milescu said.

"But you asked—"

"Get closer, will you? But be careful."

In the backseat, he heard his men shifting, picking up their weapons. All of them craned forward, peering through the dirty windshield toward the blackened wreckage strewn in front of them.

The helicopter was inverted, resting on its roof with stumps of shattered rotor blades protruding underneath. Its fuselage was charged and crumpled from the crash, resembling some giant alien creature whose spine had been snapped when it fell from the sky. Riding with his window down, Milescu caught the burned-roast smell of human flesh exposed to flame and knew the aircraft's crew hadn't escaped.

"We need to check it out," he said reluctantly.

Already, they'd lost time examining a run-down cabin in the woods a few miles back. Milescu had suspected that his targets might have stopped there, and a look inside revealed bloodstains and bullet holes. Some kind of small-scale massacre had taken place, but who was killed?

More time spent searching in the woods nearby answered his question. They'd found five men, grubby-looking peasant types, all dumped together in a little clearing, fifty yards north of the cabin. Three had died from gunshot wounds, while two apparently were stabbed. Milescu's men had searched their filthy clothes, found nothing to identify the five.

Most likely bandits, he'd decided. Slain by whom?

Milescu's bet was on the agent from the FSB and her companion, given how they'd dealt with other men in Yakutsk. It appeared their luck was holding, but the constant flight and fighting had to wear them down.

Or so Milescu hoped.

The helicopter, now that wasn't a half-assed bandit operation. Clearly, it was military, though he couldn't name the branch. Someone had cared enough to send the very best—and they had failed.

What did that say about Milescu's team?

All right. Someone above him, higher up the food chain, didn't trust him to complete his mission. They were "helping," in the sense of throwing troops and gunships at the targets, likely tracking them long-range from planes or satellites, trying to make the kill before Milescu had his chance.

There was no reason he should care, except that it reflected badly on himself and his companions. Stephan Levshin had assigned Milescu to the hunt, borrowed his services from the boss of the Izmaylovskaya Family—and all for what, if he wasn't allowed to actually do the job?

The problem was perception. If Milescu undertook a mission and let someone else complete it, then his competency might be questioned. Boris Struve might look askance at him. Grigory Rybakov might well decide that he—Milescu—had no further value to the Family.

And that meant he would get the ax. Not in a figurative sense, but literally.

"Stop here," he commanded. "I'll just be a minute."

Moving forward cautiously, mouth-breathing to avoid the worst part of the stench, Milescu made a circuit of the fallen gunship. Crouching to peer inside, he saw the blackened mannequins that once were soldiers, shrunken now into the pugilistic pose charred corpses frequently assumed as living muscles fried.

Returning to the vehicle, he climbed in and told Izvolsky, "Nothing left to see. We'll have to go around."

"Around?" Naum echoed, as if he had never heard the word before.

"Around," Milescu said. "Is there a problem?"

"Not unless you count the rocks, the ditch, the trees—"

"Stop whining. Use the four-wheel drive. Worst case, we have the winch."

"If you say so," Izvolsky replied.

"I say so. Drive on!"

ANUCHIN'S TREMBLING set in when they had left the burned-out helicopter five miles behind them. Until then, Bolan supposed, she'd been too tense and wired up from combat to feel much of anything, with the adrenaline pumping. Now that it was backing off, she could expect the shakes and possible light-headedness. Not necessarily the best condition for a bike ride on the Road of Bones.

She wasn't driving, granted, but he didn't want her going limp and falling off, or even having a reaction that could make him tip the BMW. As soon as Bolan felt the trembling in her hands and arms, around his waist, he started looking for a place to stop the motorcycle. He found it where an overhanging tree shaded the north side of the road and would protect them from an airborne set of prying eyes.

"Keep going, please," she said before he had a chance to speak.

"I need to know that you're all right," Bolan replied.

"I'm fine," she said. "Just…shaky."

"Drink some water," he suggested. "Maybe crack an MRE and have the HOOAH! bar."

She smiled at that, a shaky smile, and asked, "What is this 'hoo-ah'?"

"It's an Army battle cry from basic training," he explained. "The manufacturer caught on to it, then realized that the Marine Corps has its trainees shout *ooo-rah*. That's why you see both names on the wrapper, to keep from insulting one service and losing the millions in sales."

"So, should I say 'hooah' or 'ooo-rah'?" Tatyana asked him, almost teasing.

"Doesn't make a bit of difference to me," Bolan replied. "Just eat the bar to boost your energy, and we'll be on our way."

"It really isn't—"

"Eat!" he said, folding his arms to make it clear they wouldn't move until she had complied.

"All right," she muttered, going through the motions as she peeled one of the bars, ate it and washed it down with bottled water. "There. Satisfied?"

"I'm good to go," Bolan said, as he mounted up again.

Anuchin found her seat behind him, stopped him for a moment with a warm hand on his shoulder. "Thanks," she said. "I'm sorry for the holdup."

"No problem," Bolan said, half meaning it. "We ought

to have some lead time left before they send another bird."

"We can't outrun them all," she said, sounding almost defeated now. "This time we were lucky."

"We make our own luck," Bolan answered, "at least to a certain degree."

"You believe that?" she asked him.

"I know it. I wouldn't be standing here—well, *sitting* here—if I waited for luck to find me in a pinch. Preparation and attitude, instinct and skill. It all factors in."

"You'd be much better off without me," she suggested.

"Not hardly," Bolan said. "The first thing is, I came for you. If I go back without you it's a damned embarrassment." She had begun to smile as he went on. "And second, they've already seen the bike, most likely had an eye upstairs watching what happened to their whirlybird. They wouldn't let me go now if I gave you to them on a platter."

"You've considered it, I see." She masked the smile as best she could.

"Well, maybe for a second there, when Igor tried to blow my head off."

"That was Igor? You were introduced at some point?" Anuchin asked.

"I read it somewhere," Bolan said. "All Russian men are named 'Igor,' except the ones they call 'Nikita.'"

"I forgot," she said, and settled on the pillion seat. "We'd best be going, then, before another Igor or Nikita comes along."

"You said it," Bolan answered as he put the bike in gear and set it rolling over pavement that appeared to last for something like a hundred yards, before it petered out to gravel, dirt and weeds.

Yakutsk

THE WORST PART about calling Moscow with bad news, Stephan Levshin decided, was the difference in time. This call, for instance, would be waking Colonel Marshak shortly after five o'clock, a full two hours prior to his normal time of rising from a warm bed in the capital.

Too bad.

Marshak had ordered Levshin to report any developments at once, and Levshin meant to do as he was told. The news was grim, and likely would infuriate his boss, but Levshin wouldn't make it worse by stalling the report and casting doubts upon his own efficiency.

"Yes," the gruff, familiar voice responded after five long rings.

Levshin dispensed with cheery salutations and announced, "They've failed, sir."

"Failed?" Marshak didn't appear to grasp the concept.

"Yes, sir. With the helicopter. I just got the word myself, from trackers on the road. They've been shot down, with all hands lost."

Levshin kept quiet as the colonel cut loose with a brief tsunami of obscenity.

When the storm had passed, Marshak addressed him in a level tone. "They should be dead by now, Major."

"Yes, sir. I quite agree."

"It is a poor reflection on us all that two gnats torment us so, and can't be squashed."

Gnats? Levshin thought hornets might have been a better choice, since hornets stung like fury, while gnats simply were a harmless nuisance, causing no physical damage. These insects, by whatever name, had proved themselves deadly.

"My men on the ground will continue pursuit, sir,"

Levshin said. "I trust arrangements have been made for interception of the targets well before they enter Magadan."

He didn't phrase it as a question, which would be a challenge to Marshak's efficiency—indeed, his very basic common sense. Levshin didn't expect an answer, but he got one, anyway.

"I have a plan in motion," the colonel said, "though I hoped that it wouldn't be necessary. I will give the order to proceed without delay."

No details offered on the telephone, and Levshin knew that asking went beyond bad form. It was a violation of the basic need-to-know dictum that ruled the FSB, as it had ruled the KGB before it. The less he knew, in fact, the better. If and when another purge occurred, Levshin couldn't be held accountable for things that he was never told, plans that he had no part in hatching.

If the colonel's backup scheme went bad, he would let Marshak bear the heat alone—although the major never doubted that his boss would find some way to spread the misery around. Better if Levshin's men could find the runners and dispose of them, before Marshak's second team had a chance to confront them.

"I will let you know immediately, sir, if there are any new developments," he said.

"Immediately," Marshak echoed, and hung up without a parting word.

Rude bastard, Levshin thought, but he was used to it. Marshak was always curt, abrupt, seemed to have no concept of common courtesy. Perhaps it was a function of his rank, but Levshin didn't take it personally.

Nothing in the FSB was personal, until it came down to a choice that cost you everything.

He thought of Nikolay Milescu and the others, chasing

Sergeant Anuchin and her unidentified cohort along the Road of Bones. Levshin wished that he'd chosen better men, but it had seemed a simple mission at the outset. How was he to know that it would blow up in his face and leave him vulnerable?

There was a saying in the West: If you want a job done properly, do it yourself.

And another from his own country: If there is a person, there's a problem. If there is no person, then there is no problem.

Levshin meant to solve his problem by eliminating two specific people. And it seemed that he would have to supervise the task himself.

Even if that meant traveling the Road of Bones.

Magadan

CAPTAIN PITIRIM ZELINSKY answered his tactical phone on the first ring, as always. It never paid to keep a superior officer waiting, and Major Maxim Bucharin was less forgiving than most.

"Captain Zelinsky!" the major began, as if there could be any doubt.

"Yes, sir." No questions from Zelinsky. Bucharin would come to the point as he always did, offering only the data he wanted Zelinsky to have.

"We are prepared to mobilize your team," Bucharin said. "Are they prepared?"

Zelinsky gave the sole acceptable response. "Ready and waiting, sir."

"Proceed at once to Tomtor, as discussed," Bucharin ordered.

"Yes, sir." Now, regrettably, Zelinsky found himself

compelled to ask a question. "As to the surveillance, sir...?"

Bucharin cleared his throat, as if the answer he must give was physically distasteful. When he spoke, his voice was flat, devoid of all inflection. "We have tried it, Captain. The targets were found and a team was inserted from Yakutsk to stop them. The effort wasn't successful."

Zelinsky frowned at that, but was afraid to press the matter. He couldn't ask who had been sent to do the job. It was beyond his need to know and risked implicit criticism of the officers who had selected ineffective warriors. All that he could do was keep his mouth shut and determine not to make the same mistakes—whatever they had been.

"Your transport is in place, I take it?" Bucharin asked.

"Yes, sir. Ready to depart upon your order."

"Good. The order has been given," Bucharin said, then the line went dead.

So, it was plan B, as discussed the last time they had spoken. Fly to Tomtor and proceed from there on the Kolyma Highway, to a point where it was relatively safe to stop and wait for the approaching enemy. The plan wasn't ideal, but the preferred approach had come to nothing.

Worse, Zelinsky realized. It had to have cost more lives.

He wondered if Bucharin would find some way to blame him for the original suggestion, then decided there was nothing he could do about it either way. The best means of defense right now was finishing the job that had been set before him, with a minimum of sweat for all concerned.

Except, of course, for the intended victims.

They were bound to suffer, but it wouldn't last for long

if Zelinsky had his way. The mission had devolved upon him after others failed, and his superiors would have no patience for protracted efforts to resolve it. Bucharin had abandoned any talk of taking prisoners, which suited Zelinsky completely.

There was less risk to himself and to his men on an assassination job. No whining from a prisoner who claimed that he or she had been abused—as if there was a person in the world who really cared. They could be shot on sight, and then he would report the problem solved.

It meant a black eye for the soldiers who had tried before him, but Zelinsky couldn't worry about that. Most likely, he supposed, they were already dead. Major Bucharin wouldn't call to speak with him if there were others still in play, trying to make amends for some logistical mishap. Zelinsky wouldn't gloat over their graves, but if he profited from someone else's failure, well, where was the harm in that?

Their transport was a Kamov Ka-60 helicopter, the "Killer Whale," named for reasons that Zelinsky couldn't fathom. It would carry him to Tomtor, his three-man team riding in space that would accommodate sixteen, and he would do Major Bucharin's dirty work.

CHAPTER TWELVE

M56 Kolyma Highway

Just my luck, Pyotr Famintsyn thought. I was almost home.

In fact, he had at least two hours of driving still ahead of him, but that was nothing when he'd been away for two days in Yakutsk. The boxed bed of his Ural-375 truck was loaded with supplies that would require unloading when he finally reached home, but even that backbreaking labor paled beside his thoughts of getting off the road, being surrounded by his family once more.

And now this.

It was rare to pass along the rough Kolyma Highway without seeing cars or trucks abandoned at the roadside, broken down and waiting for a tow or simply left to rust and rot away. Famintsyn made a point of driving past them, since they weren't his problem or his property. A man could never tell when he might be accused of stealing something, and Famintsyn didn't wish to run that risk for the pathetic trash normally found in vehicles discarded on the Road of Bones.

But now, it seemed, he had no choice. This vehicle had stopped dead in the middle of the road, left at an angle to obstruct both lanes.

Famintsyn recognized it as an ancient ZIL-130, manufactured in the millions back around the time he was in secondary school. It was a simple box truck, twenty-odd years old, showing its age with chipped and faded paint, scars on its bumper and a long crack snaking halfway up the middle of its windshield. Why it had been slued across both lanes, then left, was anybody's guess.

A riddle with a risk attached.

It seemed deliberate, blocking the road that way in both directions, but if that was the intent, where had the driver gone?

Famintsyn leaned across the inside of his cab to reach the glove compartment, opened it and rummaged underneath a mess of papers for the pistol he kept hidden there. It was an OTs-27 Berdysh model, once proposed to replace the venerable Makarov in military service. The weapon was illegal for civilians, but the risk of fines or jail time was as nothing, compared to the threat posed by bandits along the Kolyma Highway.

Comforted by the feel of the gun in his hands, Famintsyn considered his options. He could try to drive around the ZIL-130, but his truck was slightly larger, which meant putting three wheels off the pavement either way, to left or right, scraping his camouflage paint job with tree limbs. Option number two was pushing the ZIL far enough to one side that Famintsyn could pass on the pavement, a task his ten-thousand-pound truck could most likely accomplish, depending on the other vehicle's cargo.

But first, Famintsyn would be forced to check the ZIL-130's parking brake, release it if it was engaged and put the truck in neutral. That meant crossing open ground on foot, exposed to anyone who might be hiding in the trees or on the far side of the ZIL, waiting to ambush him.

For what?

Famintsyn had his share of enemies, like any modern Russian, but most of the mayhem in Khabarovsk Krai these days sprang from simple greed, vodka or an explosive mixture of both. Bandits roamed freely through the district, hardly troubled as it seemed by the Militsiya.

Which was the reason for the pistol in Famintsyn's glove compartment and the other weapons he kept at home, to deal with any uninvited visitors.

The thought of home—of Akilina and their children waiting for him there—encouraged Famintsyn to hurry. He would take the risk, in lieu of bogging down his truck when there was no prospect of help arriving prior to nightfall.

The decision made, he gripped the handle that would open his door—and then froze. A furtive movement in the wing mirror alerted him to danger, but it was too late.

A tapping on the window opposite demanded Famintsyn's attention. He turned, saw a bearded man smiling with gaps in his discolored teeth, but focused clearly on the old Nagant revolver pointed at his face.

THEY WERE MAKING close to forty miles per hour, Bolan fairly pleased with it under the circumstances, when he came around a curve and spotted two trucks sitting in the middle of the road, about three hundred yards ahead. The closer, newer truck had been proceeding in the same direction he and Anuchin were, eastbound, when it apparently had been obstructed by an older model coming from the east, stopped at an angle, blocking off both lanes.

A trap.

The trucker may have guessed it, but that hadn't helped him. He was caught now, kneeling on the pavement by his cab, with both doors open, people rummaging around inside while one ambusher stood by with a pistol pointed at his head.

Bolan stopped where he was, considering his options.

First, he knew the gunmen on the road weren't Militsiya. If so, they would have been in uniform. Their scruffy look told him they probably weren't military, which left thugs of some kind, seeking—what?

The first answer that came to mind was robbery, reminding Bolan of the prowlers who'd disturbed them at the cabin overnight. As matters stood, however, he couldn't rule out a hunting party searching for himself and Anuchin. This could be a roadblock set up by the Russian Mafiya or independent contractors, trying to take them down by any means available.

Thinking they might have angled for a lift, perhaps? Or someone unaware that they were traveling by motorcycle? That struck Bolan as unlikely, but he couldn't guess how far the need-to-know philosophy might hamper hunters on the ground.

No one downrange had seen them yet. Bolan could turn and double back the way he'd come, hope that it was a simple robbery and find a place to lay up while the bandits finished with their victim. How long could it take to steal a truck and leave its rightful owner in a roadside ditch?

Two problems.

First, in terms of practicality, Bolan couldn't assume that short-term hiding would resolve the threat. The gunmen might maintain a constant watch over this stretch of highway, and if they were seeking Anuchin in the first place, they wouldn't be going anywhere until they found her. There was nothing to suggest that he could *ever* pass this way in safety, while the watchers were in place.

And second, Bolan wasn't sure that he could simply watch a holdup-murder without stepping in to intervene.

Over the years, he'd seen men killed, of course. During his one-man war against the Mafia, for instance, he'd watched mobsters slaughter one another without flinching, thankful for another enemy's demise that didn't cost him any ammunition. It was different with innocents. Watching a stranger being robbed, abused or killed without lifting a hand ran hard against the grain for Bolan.

Granted, he couldn't be certain that the trucker kneeling in the road ahead was truly innocent. For all that Bolan knew, he could be running drugs or other contraband from Yakutsk, east to Magadan. This holdup could be a routine hijacking, an occupational hazard for smugglers.

But he couldn't—wouldn't—take that chance.

Half turning, eyes still on the grim tableau ahead, he told Anuchin, "Get off and up into the trees."

She clutched him tighter. "What are you doing?"

"Stepping in," he said. "With any luck, it won't take long."

"You see that there are five of them?" she asked.

"I make it six," Bolan replied. "There's one more by the second truck."

"Why do this?" she demanded.

"We can't pass unless I deal with them," he answered. "And I'm not a spectator."

She muttered something else in Russian, but dismounted. Bolan saw the Bizon submachine gun in Anuchin's hands as she cleared the tree line.

Charge ahead and risk the bike? No way.

Bolan killed the BMW's motor, put the kickstand down and dismounted, pulling his AKS-74U around on its shoulder strap to hold it before him. Stone-faced behind the tinted visor of his helmet, he began the long walk toward the roadblock.

ANUCHIN THOUGHT Matt Cooper had to have lost his mind. It seemed so easy to retreat before they were observed, and wait until the robbery or whatever it was had run its course, then go ahead. Why would he risk his life and hers to help a stranger now, of all times, when there was so much at stake?

But even as she asked herself that question, Anuchin felt ashamed. When she had joined the FSB, to do her part for state security and law enforcement, there had been no thought of turning a blind eye to any sort of crime. A young idealist, despite her grasp of *realpolitik* and the corruption that was rife throughout Russian society, Anuchin had imagined she could make a difference for the better. In the end, saddened and disillusioned, she had opted for escape and what her masters would regard as rank betrayal.

But at some level, she still believed.

With that in mind, she hurried through the roadside forest on a course that paralleled the highway, tracking Cooper as he moved on foot to meet the gunmen grouped around the trucks parked up ahead. The one guarding their hostage had observed him now, belatedly, and called out to his cronies who were busily searching the Ural-375.

"Look out! We have company!"

The other bandits dropped what they were doing, leaped clear of the Ural-375 and formed a ragged line across the highway, joined by their companion who had hung back with the old ZIL truck. Each of the six was carrying a gun—four pistols she could see, one RMb-93 pump-action shotgun and one Kalashnikov rifle of indeterminate caliber.

Enough to finish Cooper, surely, if they knew what they were doing. But she'd seen him work and knew he wasn't afraid. Besides, Anuchin meant to help him if she could.

"Stop! Drop your weapon!"

The big American did neither. Instead, he leveled his AKS carbine and fired a short burst at the spokesman, whose gun was still aimed at the kneeling truck driver. Anuchin flinched at the suddenness of it, seeing the bandit lurch backward with dark puffs of crimson bursting from his leather jacket and the denim shirt beneath it.

As he fell, the kneeling man lunged to his left, rolling beneath the Ural truck and out of sight, while Cooper broke in the other direction, sprinting for the tree line on the highway's southern shoulder. In a heartbeat, he was out of sight, already gone to ground, while the remaining gunmen fired into the woods without a target.

Now!

Anuchin had extended the PP-19's folding stock as she moved through the trees, pacing Cooper, and she brought it to her shoulder naturally, finger on the trigger, the selector set for 3-round bursts. She sighted on the bandit carrying the shotgun, waited while he pumped its slide to send a spent shell arcing through the air, then fired.

The agent's bullets struck the target in his right side, near the waistline, and they punched him over sideways, sprawling on the pavement. Still alive, he thrashed his legs and screamed in pain, triggered an aimless shotgun blast, then started wriggling like a half-crushed insect toward the cover of the nearest truck.

Anuchin had a choice to make, and so she let him crawl away to die, knowing her time and ammunition would be better spent on others who were still in fighting form. She swung her Bizon toward another mark, but down below the shooters had her spotted now, the four still on their feet unloading with three pistols and the old Kalashnikov.

Ducking the sudden storm of fire, she lurched backward, sprawling in fallen leaves, while bullets flayed the tree trunks overhead.

PYOTR FAMINTSYN wasn't a praying man. He'd been born and raised under Soviet communism, taught from his earliest days the Marxist credo that religion is the opiate of the masses. Still, he knew a miracle when he saw one.

And he knew he was seeing one right now.

The stranger had come out of nowhere, just as Famintsyn heard his would-be killer cock the old long-barreled revolver he held aimed at his head. A few more seconds, he was certain, and the 7.6 mm bullet would strike Famintsyn's skull at 750 feet per second, shattering the bone and sending a hydrostatic shock wave through his brain, exploding from the other side with the concussive force of a grenade.

Famintsyn knew guns, and that knowledge worked against him now, increasing his anxiety in the few heartbeats remaining to him.

But then, everything changed.

He hadn't seen the stranger arrive, had no idea where the man had come from. Famintsyn's back was toward him, so he was approaching from the west, but the Russian had seen no other vehicles so far since leaving Nizhny Bestyakh.

An angel, then?

That would be stretching it, he thought, but when the shooting started and the man who'd been about to kill him dropped like a big sack of laundry, Famintsyn's instinct took over. He lunged for the fallen revolver and, clutching it tightly, rolled under his truck.

So, what next?

All around him was gunfire: two Kalashnikovs, some pistols and a shotgun. When a lighter automatic weapon joined the chorus, it was firing from the roadside trees above the highway, indicating that there was another bandit whom Famintsyn hadn't seen, or else the stranger who had saved his life had help.

And if it cost his life? Despite another vision of his family, Famintsyn thought that he already lived on borrowed time.

Rolling to his right beneath the truck, he saw one of the bandits crouching almost close enough to touch. Famintsyn didn't have to aim the dead man's pistol from that distance, simply straighten out his arm until its muzzle lay within a hand's span of the gunman's hip and thigh.

Braced for the noise and recoil, Famintsyn squeezed the trigger. Instead of his skull, the bandit's pelvis shattered, explosive impact punching Famintsyn's target away from the Ural-375. The wounded gunman shrieked in pain, but still had sense enough to turn through waves of agony and raise his own pistol.

The Nagant was a double-action weapon, so Famintsyn didn't have to pull the hammer back before he fired again. A simple trigger-squeeze advanced the 7-round cylinder and eased it forward, sealing the gap that emits sound and gases from most revolvers, rendering them useless with a silencer.

Not that the pistol in Famintsyn's hand was silent. It was *loud,* numbing his ears with its second shot as the bullet smashed into his target's face and seemed to blur the features beyond recognition as a human visage.

Simple.

Famintsyn had killed before in Chechnya, during his two years of obligatory service with the Russian Ground Forces. He didn't regret his time in uniform, the training he'd received or the experience in combat.

This day, it was saving his life all over again.

Two bandits down and out, that he was sure of, from the six who had waylaid him. If his luck held, and the man—or men—who had arrived to help him weren't killed too quickly by the other scum, Famintsyn thought that he had a chance.

Not much of one, perhaps, but still far better than he'd had short moments earlier, kneeling on asphalt with a gun aimed at his head.

One thing that military service and his life in general had taught Famintsyn: no chance should be wasted. Any opportunity for self-advancement—or, in this case, raw survival—had to be grasped in both hands with a strength akin to desperation.

And if ever he'd been desperate, it was now.

BOLAN SAW the gunman crouched off to his left go down, hip-shot, as he was turning with his AK ready for another burst. Before he had a chance to fire, a second shot from underneath the closer truck ripped through the crippled bandit's face and finished him.

The truck driver, he thought, and left the man to do whatever good he could accomplish from his hiding place beneath the vehicle. Meanwhile, the rattling voice of Anuchin's SMG reached Bolan's ears from somewhere in the woods above him, and he heard a cry of pain suggesting that she'd scored a hit.

The weapons that had tracked him on his short sprint to the trees were firing in the opposite direction now, seeking another target. He couldn't see Anuchin from his vantage point, and that was a relief. If she'd been clearly visible, the bandits still in any shape to fight would drop her where she stood.

Keeping the purpose of his mission foremost in his mind, Bolan knew it was time to wrap up this sideshow and be on his way, without placing Anuchin at any further risk. She'd chosen to assist him, put herself in danger, but the unexpected rescue effort kept them stationary, while their enemies would be advancing for the kill.

He scrambled closer to the tree line, moving in a crouch that minimized his target profile, ready with the AKS next time an adversary showed himself. It was another bandit with a pistol, edging into view from where he'd hidden in the shadow of the older truck, circling around its nose to catch a glimpse of Anuchin on the north side of the highway.

Bolan stopped him with a burst that slammed the gunman up against the truck's grille, pinned him there just long enough to die, then let him crumple to the asphalt in a flaccid sprawl.

The last two shooters lost their nerve then, running for their lives around the older truck and off along the highway, one dropping his handgun as he ran, the other clutching his with no attempt to use it. Bolan could have let them go, but that meant leaving enemies alive and moving in the same direction he was traveling with Anuchin.

Bad idea.

He rose from hiding, shouldered the Kalashnikov and caught the still-armed runner with a short burst to the spine. His target stumbled, wallowed through a clumsy somersault and wound up on his back, staring into the stark blue sky with lifeless eyes.

As Bolan swung around to nail the other fleeing bandit, Anuchin caught him with an SMG burst and the guy went down, skidding a few feet on his face before he came to rest. A final tremor rippled through his body and was gone.

"All done here," Bolan called to her in English. Seconds later, she replied in Russian, and he saw the former captive wriggling out from underneath his truck, placing an old revolver on the ground and standing with his hands raised.

"I'm not one of them," the man called out, then offered something similar in Russian. He was smiling, but it had a shaky look to it, as if he wasn't sure whether to thank his rescuers or turn and run like hell.

"I get that," Bolan told him, lowering his weapon as he stepped out of the woods and back onto the pavement. "You can put your hands down, if you want."

"*Da.* Good. Lucky for me you come along, eh?"

Anuchin joined them then, the trucker visibly astonished at the sight of her. He seemed about to make some comment, then thought better of it, grinning as he bobbed his head, saying, "Thank you! Thank you both!"

"Forget it," Bolan said. "We'll just be on our way."

"But no!" the trucker blurted out. "My life, I owe you! You must come with me to meet my family!"

"Sounds nice," Bolan replied, "but we're a little short of time."

"You travel eastward, *da?*" the trucker asked. "And someone follows you, I think."

"It's not your problem," Bolan said.

"I make it mine! You come with me, we go the same way, put your motorcycle on my truck, eh? And I guarantee no one will trouble you tonight."

He glanced at Anuchin, saw her shrug, thought, What the hell.

"All right. Let's go, before somebody else shows up."

CHAPTER THIRTEEN

"My family and I live near one of the old reeducation camps," Famintsyn said. "It held around two thousand prisoners in Stalin's time."

"You chose the site deliberately?" Bolan asked, hoping he didn't sound too critical.

Famintsyn shrugged and answered, "Land was cheaper there. I also helped myself to some of the materials. For building, *da?*"

"Makes sense," Bolan replied.

They'd had no difficulty with the bike since their new driver's truck came with a sturdy metal ramp for loading awkward cargo. Once the BMW had been wheeled aboard, they covered it with tarp, tied it down and climbed into the Ural's fairly spacious cab. Anuchin winked at Bolan as she took the middle seat, Famintsyn beaming at her from behind the wheel.

He'd told them that his castle, as Famintsyn called it, was located eighty-five miles east of where they'd found him with the bandits, all reposing now, inside their old box truck, which Bolan had maneuvered off the road into a narrow kind of lay-by where it only blocked a portion of one lane. He didn't know when they'd be found, or what condition they'd be in, but it was none of his concern.

Gaining the distance with Famintsyn in his Ural rig had several advantages for Bolan and his passenger. First thing, although the truck's top speed was somewhere in the neighborhood of fifty miles per hour, it was big and tough enough to tackle obstacles that could've stalled the two-wheel travelers for hours. They'd already crossed two rushing streams and miles of broken ground that would have been a major challenge to negotiate by motorcycle.

Second, while they traveled with Famintsyn they were off the grid, at least to some extent. If aerial or satellite surveillance had been used to follow them and spot them for the soldiers in the Black Shark gunship, further peeping from on high would be a wasted effort now. Eyes in the sky would search in vain for Bolan's motorcycle on the Road of Bones, until tomorrow's dawn arrived.

Which brought him to the third advantage. Staying overnight with their new friend, he hoped for several hours of decent rest, in relative security. Of course, there was a chance that FSB teams would be running up and down the highway all night long, after their skirmish with the chopper crew, but that was all the more reason for them to briefly vanish, frustrate their pursuers, leave the hunters wondering how they had pulled off the disappearing act.

The downside, Bolan recognized, was a risk of betrayal. They had saved Famintsyn's life, and while his gratitude struck Bolan as sincere, he also had the look of someone who was used to living by his wits. There was a chance, however slim, that once he'd thought it through, Famintsyn might decide to sell them out.

Unlikely, Bolan thought, based on his reading of the man, but anything was possible. The antidote for being caught off-guard was making damned sure that you never let your guard down in the first place.

So, a night of total rest and relaxation?

Not so much.

"Sometimes I see the ghosts out here, you know?" Famintsyn said. "Maybe the ones who built this highway, or escapees from the camps. Who knows?"

"You sure they're ghosts?" Bolan asked.

"Twice I stop for them," Famintsyn said, "but when I open up the door, nobody there."

The Phantom Hitchhiker. Bolan had heard that story for the first time as a child, and it was old by then. He wore a solemn face and offered no reply.

If any place should have a legacy of ghosts, he thought, it was the Road of Bones.

"SOMEBODY'S STOPPED up there," Izvolsky said.

"I see it, Naum," Milescu answered. "Stop beside it for a minute." Turning to his soldiers in the Lada Niva's backseat, he commanded, "Stay alert."

"It's an old truck," Gramotkin said. "We're looking for a motorcycle."

"Yes," Milescu granted, adding, "It's a shame that you are blind."

"Blind? What the—"

"Bullet holes," Stolypin interjected. "On the left-front fender and the driver's door."

"Bandits," Ryumin offered. "Like the other ones we found."

Milescu guessed that he was probably correct, but they were still required to stop and check it out. If they drove past the people they were looking for, or missed a clue to where they'd gone, it would be his head on the chopping block.

"Right here," he told Izvolsky. "Keep the engine running." He turned toward the backseat: "You three, come with me."

They left the SUV, fanned out to partially surround the bullet-punctured ZIL-130 and advanced with cautious steps, their weapons ready to meet any challenge from the vehicle or from the wall of trees beyond it.

"Blood, here," Stolypin said. "On the pavement."

"More, here," Gramotkin added. "Lots of it."

"Somebody died here," Ryumin said. "More than one."

Milescu stepped up for a peek inside the cab, smelled stale cigar smoke, but found no one there. "Open the back," he ordered as he stepped back to the asphalt.

Ryumin got the big back door, while Gramotkin and Stolypin covered him, Milescu standing off to one side, where a blast of gunfire from the cargo bay was bound to miss him. When he heard Ryumin curse, he stepped around to look inside.

Six corpses, piled haphazardly, comprised the ZIL's cargo. A glance informed Milescu that they'd all been shot repeatedly, their fluids leaking freely after they'd been loaded in the truck. They didn't stink yet, from decomposition, but the other odors wafting from the cargo box revolted him.

Regretting it before he made the move, Milescu reached across the blood-smeared tailgate, careful not to foul his clothes, and clutched the nearest dead man's ankle. He gave the leg a twist and shake, to check for rigor mortis.

"Killed sometime within the past three hours," he announced.

A couple of Milescu's men looked skeptical, but no one challenged him. They were too busy studying the tree line, north and south, for any signs of an impending ambush.

"These weren't killed by bandits," he advised the others.

"Oh? Why do you say that?" Gramotkin asked.

"Look inside the truck again," Milescu said. "They *were* bandits."

Gramotkin peered into the shadows, saw the weapons lying in the farthest corner of the cargo box. "Guns didn't do them any good," he said, sounding a bit unnerved.

"You think the woman and her driver did this?" Stolypin asked.

Milescu frowned. "I can't say that, but we know they passed this way. We would have found them on the roadside, otherwise."

Stolypin counted stiffs inside the truck and said, "That's sixteen dead since they left Nizhny Bestyakh, plus the ones in Yakutsk."

"Are you frightened now?" Milescu asked.

"Hell, no!" Stolypin snapped. "I want to finish this, that's all."

"In that case," Milescu said, "we should get back on the road."

FAMINTSYN'S CASTLE WAS, in fact, a compound that resembled something from America's Old West, surrounded by a stockade fence of upright logs. John Wayne would have looked perfectly at home, peering across the fence to challenge some intruder with his Winchester in hand.

The compound sat a hundred yards back from the highway, accessed by a narrow, unpaved road. A drifting plume of dust announced the truck's arrival, and Famintsyn's family was out in force to meet them at the gate of the stockade. A hasty head count as they entered, with Famintsyn beaming in the driver's seat, revealed nine children ranging in age from four or five years to the early teens. Two women stood behind the kids, one more or less Famintsyn's age, the other easily three decades older.

"My wife," Famintsyn said, with a nod toward the younger woman, "and her mother. Be careful. They'll talk you to death."

"Could be worse," Bolan said.

"This is true. When they hear how you saved me, what heroes you are, they may wish to adopt you!" Famintsyn replied.

"Looks like you have enough kids, as it is," Bolan said.

"But how many are enough, I ask you? When I'm old and frail," Famintsyn said, "I'll need them to take care of me."

The comment brought Bolan's own family to mind, parents and sister lost forever in an act of violence that had launched his lonely war against the underworld, back home. All far behind him now. New faces and new enemies.

"You know," he told Famintsyn, "having us around may put your family at risk."

"*Da, da.* You told me that already," Famintsyn said. "Everyone in Russia is at risk these days. You think I built this fence to keep the chickens in, maybe?"

"Okay," Bolan replied. "Why borrow extra trouble?"

"Why did you help me, a stranger, on the highway?" Famintsyn asked. And he answered his own question, saying, "It's what separates us from the animals."

"I'm just not sure—"

"My friend, enough!" Famintsyn cut him off, feigning severity. "Tonight you dine with us, enjoy yourself and sleep in peace before another day of tribulation. *Da?*"

"Okay," the Executioner replied. "You talked me into it."

"Good, good. Now, come and meet my family."

Famintsyn's brood examined him and Anuchin curiously as they stepped out of the Ural's cab, leaving their weapons on the seat until Famintsyn had a chance to break the ice. He rattled on in Russian for a long five minutes, during which the faces of his loved ones passed through various expressions of surprise, concern and finally relief. When he stopped talking, they were suddenly surrounded, forced into a round of shaking hands with male offspring, accepting hugs and kisses from the females.

One big, happy family, Bolan thought.

Hoping they would be allowed to stay that way.

"Ho-kay!" Famintsyn said. "Now, I must telephone my neighbors. They will hear us, later, and it would be rude to keep them out of the festivities!"

PYOTR FAMINTSYN'S neighbors, some thirty-five in all, arrived in a variety of vehicles ranging from a pair of souped-up SUVs to a sedan that looked homemade, cobbled together out of mismatched parts. They all ran well enough, a testament to rural ingenuity, and there was room for all of them to park inside Famintsyn's compound.

Bolan and Anuchin quickly found themselves besieged by instant friends who pumped their hands and kissed their cheeks, receiving them in every way as if they had been long-lost, best-loved members of the family. Bolan soon got the message that Famintsyn was some kind of local icon, and that their rescue of him elevated them to a position of celebrity.

Okay, so far. But what if one or two among the group of revelers worked out that there was money to be made by tipping the Militsiya, the FSB or someone else to the location of two hunted fugitives?

When they were done with the receiving line, Bolan took their host aside to talk. The air was redolent with laughter and the scent of roasting meat, Famintsyn smiling broadly as they found a corner to themselves.

"You have a troubled look, my friend," he said.

"Call it concern," Bolan replied. "When you said dinner with your family, we didn't reckon on a crowd this size."

Famintsyn nodded, cutting to the heart of it. "You are afraid that one of them may, how you say it, drop a dime?"

Bolan had seen the compound's matched set of satellite dishes. Now he imagined Famintsyn lounging in his recliner and watching cop shows long into the night, absorbing jargon from the faux police.

"It crossed my mind," Bolan admitted. "No offense."

"None taken! You will never find a race on Earth more paranoid than Russians, I assure you," Famintsyn said. "We are born to it. But these people you see are trusted friends. In Khabarovsk Krai, that means that we take one another's secrets to the grave."

"I have some friends like that," Bolan admitted.

"Now, you have this many more! Enjoy their company, and have no fear that they will question you about your business or whoever may be looking for you. That, I promise."

Knowing that it was the best assurance he would get, Bolan relaxed a bit and looked around for Anuchin. He found her with some of the other women, busy at a massive red-brick barbecue positioned near the southwest corner of Famintsyn's rambling two-story house.

Inside, the place was an eclectic blend of styles, something for everyone, from brightly painted *matryoshka* nesting dolls to a Mexican serape and wide-brimmed sombrero mounted on one wall. The furniture was mix-and-match, without regard to any certain style.

And there were guns.

Bolan had been surprised to see so many, gave up counting when he hit a dozen, and decided that his host was either a collector or some kind of closet revolutionary. The arsenal included an AK-47, an Uzi and a venerable PPSh-41 designed initially in 1941, still used by troops in Vietnam, Albania and Guinea. The other weapons included rifles, shotguns and pistols of various styles and calibers, enough to arm a small platoon in an emergency. The Famintsyns, Bolan saw, were clearly not defenseless.

But he wondered who their enemies might be.

WITH TYPICAL Russian perversity, residents of several hamlets scattered across Siberia's Sakha Republic had chosen to call their villages Tomtor. The practice created needless confusion for government officials, and perhaps that was the purpose of the exercise.

The only Tomtor that mattered to Captain Pitirim Zelinsky—the only *real* Tomtor, in his estimation—was located on the Kolyma Highway and boasted a small airport with weekly flights to Yakutsk and Ust-Nera, the administrative center for the Oymyakonsky District. This evening, the airfield would receive a bit of unexpected traffic, in the form of Zelinsky's Kamov Ka-60 helicopter.

Local gawkers might turn out to stare at him and his commandos as they transferred from the aircraft to a waiting Lada Niva SUV. There would be little for the peasants to observe, all of the weapons packed in padded cases, and Zelinsky knew that none of them would try to interfere.

Simply approaching Spetsnaz officers to ask a question

could be dangerous. Obstructing them was tantamount to suicide.

Still half an hour, maybe more, remained before the aircraft touched down at Tomtor. Since takeoff, Zelinsky had received another update on his targets from Major Bucharin. Another team of trackers had found six men killed and stuffed into a truck abandoned on the Road of Bones. They were presumed to be bandits, gunned down while attempting to rob the same people Zelinsky was hunting.

Which made the runners worthy adversaries, at the very least. So far, they'd killed at least a dozen people that he knew of—three of them from Spetsnaz, which demanded retribution. Zelinsky would be happy to perform that function, but he had to find the targets first.

And they would come to him, inevitably, once he and his men were in place on the highway. That was the beauty of the plan. His prey had nowhere else to go.

When he was finished, and the honor of his unit was restored, Zelinsky thought he would be owed a favor by someone higher up the chain of command. Major Bucharin was a hard-nosed officer, but he didn't forget the men below him who performed with special zeal on serious assignments.

First things first, Zelinsky thought. Before collecting a reward, or even guessing what his payoff might involve, he had to find the fugitives he'd been assigned to locate, and destroy them. If he failed at that…well, there would be no commendation from Bucharin or from anybody else.

Based on the fate of his comrades from Yakutsk, he'd be dead.

Which was unthinkable.

Captain Zelinsky had survived combat against the

Chechen savages and ethnic Georgians in the wilds of
South Ossetia. He'd fought pitched battles and prevailed
on covert missions where the combat had been hand to
hand, complete with eye-gouging and throat-slitting. If he
allowed two fugitives to best him, one of them a woman,
what was left for him except a shameful death?

Zelinsky had to smile at that, the very notion that he
could be beaten and humiliated by a pair of common
criminals. It was ridiculous, a joke.

But he would take no chances with them when they
met.

Better a quick, clean kill than muddling about to let
the mission blow up in his face.

ANOTHER EARLY SUNSET in Siberia. Floodlights and tiki
torches held the dusk at bay inside Famintsyn's compound, with the party in full swing. The music piped
through outdoor speakers was a mixture of rock, Russian
hip-hop and Yakut folk tunes. Vodka and beer flowed
freely, and contributed to brisk outbursts of dancing in
the yard.

Bolan nursed a strong Baltika beer and managed to
avoid the dance floor, even when a sexagenarian ad-
mirer tried to draw him from his bench, then wobbled
through an awkward version of a lap dance for his pleasure. Pyotr Famintsyn arrived in the nick of time to lead
her away, cooing something in Russian and steering her
back toward the bar. He returned moments later, shaking
his head in bemusement.

"Poor old Nonna," he said. "She's been widowed so
long, sometimes she seems desperate."

"Sorry about that," Bolan replied.

"Don't worry. She's like that with any man younger

than she is." Famintsyn sipped a glass of vodka, then asked Bolan, "You enjoying yourself?"

"I am," Bolan said honestly. "It makes a nice break from the road and all."

"Tonight, you will be safe, at least," Famintsyn said. "I promise this."

"And I appreciate it," Bolan answered. "But I still think it's a risk for you, and for your family."

"Each day in Russia is a risk," Famintsyn said. "Especially here in Yakutia. The law has little impact here, and what effect it has is mostly bad. The damned police," he snorted. "Many are no more than criminals themselves. As for the bandits...well, you saw."

"Some people may come looking for us," Bolan told his host. "Not bandits, like the ones we met today. Professionals. They won't respond well to evasion."

One more sip of vodka finished his glass. Famintsyn shrugged and said, "I think about that when it happens. They cannot prove you were here."

"Proof won't concern them," Bolan said. "They likely won't have uniforms or badges."

"Only guns, eh?"

"That's more like it," the Executioner said.

"We have guns, too. And we know how to use them."

"That's the very thing I'm hoping to avoid," Bolan replied.

"Don't worry," Famintsyn said. "First thing in the morning, comes my brother—you met Leon?"

Bolan nodded, thinking of the bear hug he'd received from Famintsyn's younger sibling when the man arrived with wife and kids in tow.

"At first light, he comes back and drives you eastward to the river crossing," Famintsyn said. "There was once a highway bridge, but it fell down and no one cares enough to fix it. With the motorcycle, at this time of year, you cannot cross. But Leon's truck will get you to the other side, then he returns."

"We're much obliged," Bolan said.

"As a payment for my life, it's nothing. I should let you have my eldest daughter, at the very least."

Bolan smiled at the offer and replied, "There's no room for her on the bike."

"Something to keep in mind," Famintsyn said, "in case you pass this way again."

"It isn't likely."

It was Famintsyn's turn to nod. "More vodka, then," he said. "Before old Nonna drinks it all!"

CHAPTER FOURTEEN

Stony Man Farm, Virginia

"What am I looking at?" Barbara Price asked.

It could have been the view from any television news chopper in the United States, or any other country that had forests, two-lane highways and a government that sometimes let things slide. Aerial view that picked out objects in the darkness, in this case a boxy-looking SUV chasing its headlight beams along the road, now slowing, pulling over, switching off the lights.

One difference: a TV chopper would have framed the SUV dead center with a million-candlepower spotlight beam. This view was softer, like a glimpse with naked eyes at dusk—but it was coming from a satellite in orbit, peering down through clouds and smog and all the rest of it, from something like a hundred miles straight up.

And it was looking at the Road of Bones.

"Unless I miss my guess," Kurtzman replied, "we're locked on to a hunter-killer team. Same SUV the bird saw yesterday, unless they've got a fleet of them, and headed in the same direction as our runners."

"Stopping for the night," Price said.

"Best guess," Kurtzman said, "they're afraid of missing something in the dark."

"I would be, too."

"Good news for Striker and the lady," Kurtzman told

her, sticking to the standard form of using code names even in their private conversations. Discipline turned into force of habit in no time at all.

"It would be better news for us if we knew where they were," Price replied.

"Still working on it," Kurtzman said. "The bird we're looking through right now is passing east to west. If there's a motorcycle moving anywhere along the highway on this pass, it's turned invisible."

"Which tells us what, exactly?" Price inquired.

She already knew the answer. Nothing. Squat. Not even half of what it took to make jack shit.

"Wish I had something more to tell you," Kurtzman said. "Big Bird can't show us what he's doing if we don't have some idea of where to look. We've programmed it to pick out two-wheeled vehicles on the Kolyma Highway, but there actually has to *be* one, for the satellite to home in on it."

"List of reasons why we're missing him?" Price asked, although she had a fair idea of several on her own.

"This time of day, past 10:00 p.m. their time, they've likely stopped to camp," Kurtzman said. "It's a no-brainer to get the bike off-road, concealed. This far into the game, I'm guessing that they wouldn't bother with a fire."

"Use body heat to keep the chill off," Price suggested.

"Or whatever gear they took along from Nizhny Bestyakh," Kurtzman countered.

"Or that," she admitted. "Other possibilities?"

"The central point of any explanation I might offer," Kurtzman said, "is that they're off the road right now. If they're not camping, well…"

"It's possible that they've been caught," Price said. "Somebody could've picked them off between HEXA-GON overlights."

Kurtzman shrugged, looking glum. "You know that I can't rule it out," he replied. "On the upside, I'm thinking they'd call off the hunters if there was no need for them out on the highway."

"We don't know the SUV people *are* hunters," Price said. "We're just guessing."

"Okay, fair enough," Kurtzman said. "But we picked up a chopper westbound, likely headed for Tomtor. It's a Kamov Ka-60, military bird the Russians call the Killer Whale, NATO designation Hokum C."

"Transporting soldiers?" Price inquired.

"I'm no believer in coincidence," Kurtzman replied. "And Tomtor doesn't have much need for military gear, per se."

"Could be a pickup team," Price said. "For prisoners."

"*Could* be," Kurtzman agreed, "but I don't think so."

"Either way," she said, "I need to update Hal."

M56 Kolyma Highway

ANOTHER COLD NIGHT on the road. Milescu was fed up with sleeping in the Lada Niva, cramped and chilled, clutching a weapon when it should have been a warm and supple woman's body. And he hated standing watch—which, in this case, meant literally standing on the highway, since the stinking breath of four sleeping companions fogged the Niva's windows till they looked like frosted glass.

Damn these people he was hunting. And where in hell had they gone?

After killing the six bandits he'd found in the old ZIL-130, it seemed as if they had evaporated. That was crazy thinking, obviously. They had simply driven on, eluding him once more, leaving Milescu in their dust. But lagging constantly behind them, when he felt he should have overtaken them by now, angered Milescu nearly to the point of lashing out against his comrades.

That would be a foolish move, of course. They feared him now, for the authority he represented, but if pushed too far they would revert to acting like the animals they were. He hadn't chosen them because they were well-disciplined in any normal sense. He'd wanted killers and had gotten them. They were like wolverines who'd undergone a course of basic training, but might snap the leash at any moment if provoked.

So, he pitched in and did his share of lookout duty, ate the shitty food they'd bought and tolerated the complaints about the job they'd taken with their eyes wide-open, knowing it could last for days on end without respite. And all the while, he felt the same things they were feeling, simply kept it to himself in an attempt to lead them by example.

Lead them *where?* Forever eastward, as it seemed, until they either caught the two elusive rabbits they were tracking, or they hit the coast and stared into an icy sea. Which would mean failure, if they came up empty.

And Milescu knew that would be unacceptable to Moscow.

If he failed, there'd be a race to see who killed him first, the FSB or someone sent by Struve and Rybakov. In either case, the end result would be the same.

No good.

The following day, he could only hope, might be their lucky one. Locate the targets, deal with them and go back home.

To claim their just rewards.

But if it took another week, so be it. Every day Milescu saw the sun rise was a good day, more or less. What worried him was the alternative.

Only where mayhem was concerned did he lay claim to a religious attitude. Better to give than to receive.

A rapping on the window near his face recalled Milescu from the verge of sleep. He rubbed a clear spot on the foggy glass and saw Gramotkin peering in at him.

"Your turn," the man announced.

Milescu nodded, stepping from the Niva as Gramotkin took his place. Musical seats was more convenient for the other sleepers in the SUV, not that he truly cared.

"Sounds like a bear close by," Gramotkin warned him, just before he shut the door with a resounding thunk.

Milescu cursed him silently and tucked the AK-74 under his arm, scanning the dark tree line for any sign of movement. He heard nothing in the forest, but the mention of a bear made sure that he wouldn't relax.

Any four-footed prowlers who approached Milescu would be in for a surprise. And he might have a bearskin rug to show for his excursion on the Road of Bones.

But he'd prefer a pair of scalps.

And soon.

THE PARTY AT Famintsyn's compound showed no signs of winding down. Bolan had seen some drinkers in his time, but he was hard-pressed to remember anyone who put the booze away as energetically as Russians with their vodka, or who had as much capacity for alcohol. The crowd was definitely looser than it had been several hours earlier, but there were still no sloppy drunks in evidence, no weepers, no one on the verge of passing out, as far as he could tell.

He'd managed to avoid old Nonna for the most part, ducking her without giving offense, shadowing Anuchin in a way that, hopefully, wouldn't give her the creeps. She needed time away from him, Bolan supposed, after their long days on the BMW, and even though she wasn't from

Siberia, these folks were more akin to her than he could ever be.

Still, Bolan had his reservations about any strangers in the present circumstances, tried to take Famintsyn at his word that all of them were trustworthy, but still gave in to personal experience and instinct in the end. It was better to watch for any twitchy indications of betrayal than to lie back and be taken absolutely by surprise.

He didn't think Famintsyn's family would sell them out, but who could really say how any of the neighbors felt? What they were thinking? What their secret ties might be to the Militsiya, FSB or Russian Mafiya?

A yawn took Bolan by surprise, and he decided it was time to get some sleep. Two guest rooms had been allocated to himself and Anuchin—side by side with a connecting door, Famintsyn pointed out, smiling and winking—and their gear was stowed away before the party had begun. The rooms were upstairs, at the rear of the rambling house, and should afford some insulation from the party noise.

He found Anuchin talking with three other women, interrupted long enough to tell her he was turning in, then left them to it. Something one of her companions said as Bolan left made everybody laugh, likely a question or a comment on their sleeping arrangements.

"Leaving us so soon?" Famintsyn asked him as they passed each other in the spacious kitchen.

"Early morning coming up," Bolan replied. "Another long day on the road."

"Of course," Famintsyn said. "Sleep well, my friend."

Bolan wondered if he would. Long trained in sleeping when and where he could, in combat situations, there were still times when an overactive mind kept him awake. Thinking about the next day on the Road of Bones, for instance, and Famintsyn's brother driving them partway along their route.

A help, of course. Unless they rolled into a trap.

But there was nothing he could do about that possibility this night. The following day would arrive with problems of its own.

And it was almost here.

Washington, D.C.

A MUFFLED BUZZING and a blinking light told Hal Brognola that he had a call incoming on his private line. Barely a dozen people on the planet knew the number, and they never simply called him up to chat. Caller ID told him that it was Stony Man reporting in. The big Fed turned on the scrambler, then picked up on the second ring.

"Good news?" he asked without preamble.

"Don't I wish," Barbara Price stated.

"Okay. Let's hear it."

"We've lost them," Price stated.

Brognola felt his stomach clench. "When you say lost…"

"I mean the Big Bird couldn't find them on its last pass. We got traffic on the highway, here and there, but nothing that resembled Striker and his passenger."

Brognola frowned, swallowed a sense of dread and asked, "So, what conclusion should I draw from that?"

"Unknown," Stony Man's mission controller said. "Loss of visual contact is just that, plain and simple. Trying to explain it, now that's something else."

"Feel free to speculate," Brognola said.

"Best case, Bear says they could be camped off-road without a fire, just lying low," Price answered.

"Right."

Brognola didn't need to ask about the worst case. It was ambush and a swift death if the fugitives were lucky, capture and a slow interrogation if they weren't. And either way, there'd be no cavalry arriving. No last-minute rescue.

"The next pass, west to east, is in four hours," Price informed him. "We'll keep watching."

"Absolutely." That much was a given, understood between them without saying it, but Price was clearly anxious, looking for a graceful way to disengage. Hal let her off the hook, saying, "Okay, then. If there's nothing else…?"

"I'll keep in touch," she said.

"Be looking forward to it," Brognola replied as the line went dead.

The big Fed owed a heads-up to the man from Interpol, in Moscow. He didn't want to make the call, but dodging it seemed cowardly and downright rude. Brognola found the number, checked the time—four-thirty in the afternoon—and placed the call.

"Bonjour," said the familiar voice, not drowsy this time.

"Mr. Delorme."

"Monsieur Brognola. You have news?"

"A bit," Brognola said. "Our people have avoided two significant obstructions to their progress, but we've lost contact for the moment."

"For the moment?" Delorme replied.

"We have a bird's-eye view, sporadically," Brognola said.

"I understand."

"And on the last pass," he continued, "there was nothing."

"Ah." That sounded like grim resignation in the Frenchman's voice.

"I'm hopeful yet," Brognola said, not really feeling it. "Just wanted you to know where matters stand."

"*Oui.* I appreciate the information. If you should learn any more—"

"I'll be in touch, of course."

"*Merci.* Until then, *au revoir.*"

Brognola cut the link, wishing that he had someone else to call, but there was no one. If he knew that Bolan and the FSB agent were dead or had been captured, he could touch base with the Pentagon and have the *Kansas City* turn around. There'd be no point to leaving it in Russian waters if the subjects it was sent to meet weren't coming.

But he wasn't writing Bolan off. Not yet.

The Executioner had managed to surprise him, time and time again throughout their long association, overcoming odds that seemed unbeatable.

Once more, for old times' sake, Brognola thought.

Tomtor

THE KAMOV Ka-60 settled in a cloud of swirling dust and litter, whipped into a flurry by its rotor blades. Captain Pitirim Zelinsky waited for the blades to slow, letting the storm subside, before he opened the helicopter's sliding door and dropped to the pavement below.

The other members of his team, Senior Lieutenant Konstantin Galitzin and Master Sergeant Andrez Petrov, followed Zelinsky, each carrying two duffel bags filled with weapons and other field gear. All three Spetsnaz troopers wore black jumpsuits and boots, unmarked by any vestige of insignia. Each jumpsuit had a tiny GPS tracking device sewn into it, facilitating the retrieval of their corpses if they failed to carry out their mission, but in all other respects they were anonymous.

Two vehicles were waiting for them near the hangar that would house the helicopter in their absence. One, a Lada Niva painted primer gray, was theirs to use until the task at hand had been completed. The other, a black Samara 2 sedan with two men inside—one of them the driver who had brought the Niva for Zelinsky—pulled away and left as the three soldiers reached the SUV.

Zelinsky found the key in the Niva's ignition, as arranged. In back, as Petrov and Galitzin stored the gear, he saw two jerry cans of petrol clamped in place on either side of the tailgate. They could drive about four hundred miles without refueling, but Zelinsky hoped they would locate a decent ambush site before they had to go so far.

But first, to bed.

Zelinsky had considered starting off immediately, but the Road of Bones had far too many pitfalls for nocturnal driving. He could manage it in an emergency, of course, but judging that his targets would be camped somewhere along the way, likely still at least two hundred miles from Tomtor, he felt no great sense of urgency.

They would be ready at first light, begin the westward journey, watching for a likely spot in which to lay their trap. From that point on, it was a waiting game. If no one else waylaid his quarry in the meantime, they would find him at the kill zone he selected and the job would be complete in seconds flat.

Their hotel, four blocks from the airfield, was a flat-roofed concrete box, painted drab brown to match the tundra. Three rooms were reserved, each slightly larger than a walk-in closet of a rich man's dacha, with a washroom at the far end of the hall. Compared to quarters in the Spetsnaz barracks, it was still a low-rent piece of crap.

Never mind. It wasn't meant to be a home.

His men had synchronized their watches with Zelinsky's prior to leaving Magadan. They would be wide-awake by four o'clock and finished with their breakfast in the hotel's restaurant within the hour, ready to depart.

And then, Zelinsky thought as he lay down to sleep, the fun begins.

Khabarovsk Krai

A BLARE OF MUSIC roused Bolan from sleep, shredding the remnants of a dream before he could retrieve them. From the way he felt, lying in darkness, it was just as well.

He'd read somewhere that dreamless sleep was rare—a form of mental illness in itself, or a precursor to insanity. Most people dreamed, whether they could remember any part of it or not, and Bolan's dreams were often dark, fragments of past experience mixed up with apprehension. Nothing in the way of fear, precisely, but successive images of an uncertain future.

In his present circumstance, Bolan was relieved to miss out on an instant replay of his dream, whatever it had been. He lay and listened to the party, winding up to some kind of crescendo in the courtyard of Famintsyn's compound, wondering if any neighbors were excluded from the guest list and might be inclined to file a noise complaint with the Militsiya. He doubted that police would bother rolling out this late to interrupt a rural party, but the less attention drawn to him and Tatyana in their flight, the better.

He considered calling Hal Brognola on his satellite phone, since he was awake, and calculated time zones in his head. It was midmorning, yesterday, in Washington—a creepy kind of *Twilight Zone* experience, as if his meeting with Famintsyn and the firefight on the highway hadn't happened yet. Disorienting, in a way, if you devoted too much time to it.

Since he was wide-awake, Bolan retrieved the phone, punched in the big Fed's private number at the Justice Department and heard Brognola's voice come on the line.

"Brognola?"

"It's me," Bolan replied, in case his old friend's caller ID hadn't logged the sat phone's number.

"Hey, it's good to hear from you." The big Fed's relief was audible. "We lost you with the Big Bird."

"Right. We ran into a situation on the highway," Bolan said.

"Six shooters with a box truck?" Brognola inquired, secure on the scrambled link.

"That's it," Bolan confirmed. "Long story short, we helped somebody out and got a lift to his place. I don't have coordinates, but we made decent mileage. We'll be moving on from here first thing tomorrow."

"I'll advise the Farm. All systems go, then?"

"For the moment," Bolan said.

"Okay. Be advised, I'm told you have a team coming along behind you in some kind of SUV, and we've picked up a military chopper westbound out of Magadan, projected to be landing at…would that be Tomtor?"

"Likely," Bolan said. "We have another day, at least, before we get that far. It could be longer."

"Right, okay. Your lift is waiting when you get there," Brognola replied. "As far as catching it, you'll need to be offshore."

Bolan considered that, had no idea how they would manage it, but answered, "Roger that. Offshore, it is."

"If that's a problem…." Brognola began, but there was nothing else to say.

"We'll deal with it," Bolan assured him, wondering if that was true, or even possible.

"Okay, then. Keep in touch when it's convenient, will you?"

"That's the plan," Bolan replied, and broke the link.

CHAPTER FIFTEEN

Leon Famintsyn's truck was a GAZ-3308 Sadko, overhauled and remodeled from its basic military form to serve civilian needs. He arrived in the rig after breakfast and Bolan trundled the BMW aboard, leaving it tied down and concealed under canvas.

Leave-taking could have been an endlessly protracted ceremony, but Pyotr Famintsyn stepped in to truncate the process, herding his wife and children back from the truck so that Bolan and Anuchin could board it. The soldier's last glimpse of the family, reflected in the Sadko's right-wing mirror, captured all of them in a lineup, arms raised, waving their farewells.

Then, they were gone.

"Some party, eh?" Leon remarked, once they were on the road.

"Some party," Bolan readily agreed.

It had run late, the last guests lurching off at 2:15 a.m., but Bolan didn't need much sleep, and he'd refrained from asking Anuchin whether she had slept at all. She didn't look hung over at the breakfast table, and had put the food away as if she hadn't eaten in a week. It wasn't his job to chastise her if she let her hair down for the evening and tried to put their circumstances out of mind.

"The bridge where we are going," Leon said, "collapsed last June. Or was it May? No matter. Engineers came from the Federal Highway Department to examine

it. They were quite concerned and promised to repair it.
I expect they will begin next year, or possibly the year
after."

"There's no concern for transportation?" Bolan asked
him.

"Oh, *concern*," Leon replied, "we do have in abun-
dance. Moscow is concerned, the politicians here in
Khabarovsk are all concerned. It's getting them to do
something about their great concern that often seems impossible. They are so busy wringing their hands that they
can't sign a check or call the laborers to come and do a
job."

"Sounds typical," Bolan said. "We get that procrasti-
nation in the States, too."

"Ah," Leon said with an index finger raised. "But if
your Brooklyn Bridge fell down, I wager someone could
be found to fix it, eh?"

"Most likely," Bolan admitted. "If the price was right."

"With this—" Leon slapped his steering wheel
"—crossing the river is no problem. You can keep your
feet dry, *da?* And maybe, if you're lucky, those who
follow you will sink, or all be swept away downstream!"

It was the first mention of their pursuers since they'd
reached Pyotr's home the previous night. Bolan didn't
respond directly, but he said, "If Mother Nature wants
to help us out, I wouldn't turn her down. Whatever else,
we're grateful for the ride."

"This? It's nothing," Leon said. "You saved my brother
from the *khuyesosi* who would certainly have murdered
him to pick his pockets. All of us are in your debt, eternally."

"Eternally's a long time," Bolan said.

"Of course, I know you likely won't be here again,"
Leon said. "But if you ever are…"

"You've been very kind," Anuchin said, speaking for the first time since they'd left the compound. "But it's best if you forget that we were ever here."

"Of course, I understand," Leon replied. "We're experts at forgetting, eh, we Russians? All the things I have forgotten for my own good, they could fill a library. What is one more?"

"If someone mentions us, you mustn't be—" she said.

"Upset? Over someone I never met? Of course not!" Leon said, smiling. "But I might still forget and break a nose or two. The vodka, you know, makes me do some funny things sometimes."

M56 Kolyma Highway

ANOTHER MORNING on the damned Road of Bones. Milescu sipped his coffee, burned his tongue and thought that he was doing well indeed to keep the bitter string of curses from escaping.

Naum Izvolsky had requested that somebody else take over driving for the day, so Vasily Ryumin sat behind the Lada Niva's steering wheel, maneuvering around the latest chain of potholes on the highway. Some of them looked deep enough to blow a tire, or even break an axle, and the last thing that Milescu needed was a breakdown that would make him call Stephan Levshin for help.

Better to starve beside the highway and be found a sun-bleached skeleton than to appear inadequate when eyes were following Milescu and his team. Already it was bad enough, with no results to show for all their time and effort.

Somewhere up ahead, the man and woman on their motorcycle had to have stopped when darkness fell. They had to have lost time in their flight, while Nikolay Mi-

Iescu's team drove onward, sacrificing sleep to close the gap. It had been late when, finally, Milescu called a halt and they had settled down to sleep in shifts. That scheme, he hoped, would let them overtake the fugitives this day, or possibly tomorrow.

From the backseat, Viktor Gramotkin asked, "What if we passed them last night?"

"We didn't," Milescu said with more confidence than he felt.

"Say we *did,*" Gramotkin said. "Suppose they're behind us right now.

"Then they'll have a surprise when they catch us," Gennady Stolypin replied. "What's the problem?"

"I'm just saying that they could trail us all the way east and we'd never know it," Gramotkin said.

"They're the ones who've got to hurry, knowing that they're hunted," Stolypin said. "Anyway, you've seen how they take care of opposition. Would they be afraid of us?"

Milescu didn't like that kind of talk, convinced that it could undermine morale, but stifling the conversation wouldn't help. If there was one thing that Milescu needed less than Levshin breathing down his neck, it was a mutiny among his men.

"Maybe bears ate them while they slept," Izvolsky offered. "Maybe they're fertilizer in the woods by now."

"What good is that to us," Milescu asked him, "if we have to go back empty-handed? Offer that idea to Levshin, and he'll have us checking piles of bear shit till the end of time."

"It was a joke," Izvolsky said.

"You make a poor comedian," Milescu told him.

"I still don't understand those bodies in the truck," Gramotkin said. "Why bother packing them away?"

"Maybe to throw off aerial surveillance," Milescu said.

"An old truck beside the road won't draw the same attention as a stack of corpses."

"Still, after the helicopter," Gramotkin said, "they must know they've been detected."

"Have they?" Milescu asked. "Knowing that they're on the highway hasn't helped us find them yet. We're still a thousand miles from Magadan. All of you, keep your eyes wide-open and be ready when we spot that motorcycle."

LEON FAMINTSYN was a storyteller in the old tradition of his people, ready with a yarn for all occasions. As he drove, time passing and the miles slipping away behind them, he regaled Bolan and Anuchin with his own adventures and Pyotr's spanning decades of their lives. Hearing his tales, Bolan was moved to wonder if the Russian ever kept a secret, or if there were other things that he kept to himself, too personal and delicate to talk about.

"We smuggled for a while," Leon was saying, well into their second hour on the road. "Not drugs, you know, but other things the government forbids or taxes until common folk cannot afford to buy it. It was interesting, but I had to settle down at last."

Leon had introduced his wife and children—six of them—to Bolan during previous night's party. Whatever else the Famintsyns might be, they were clearly prolific.

"You've had trouble with police, then?" Anuchin asked their driver in a tone that somehow didn't seem to pry.

"With the Militsiya," Leon replied, "there's no real trouble here in the republic. Their pay is low, and anyone who wishes to avoid them supplements it. If you aren't killing anyone—and sometimes, even if you are—most of them happily ignore you."

"What about the FSB?" she asked him.

Leon snorted, making a dismissive gesture with one hand. "They are concerned with spies and terrorists, not local businessmen."

"I see." If Anuchin was offended, she concealed it well.

"Besides," Leon pressed on, "the government creates and profits from the smuggling trade. When they tax cigarettes, as one example, it's for money, not for people's health. So, someone smuggles cigarettes without the tax stamps, and police collect a toll to look the other way. The state still gets its taste. We just negotiate over the price."

"Did you say *we?*" Anuchin asked.

"Force of habit," Famintsyn said, blushing. "I was speaking in the past tense for Pyotr and myself."

"Of course, I understand," the FSB agent replied.

Bolan wondered if the bandits he'd met yesterday expected Leon's brother to be hauling contraband from Nizhny Bestyakh, or if it had been a random stop. It hardly mattered, either way, since they were out of business, but it put the incident into a new perspective.

Maybe.

Had he saved one criminal from others? Did the firefight, like so much of Bolan's life, boil down to a choice between evils? Should he, on principle, reject Leon Famintsyn's help in getting past their next roadblock?

Ridiculous.

Let armchair moralists say what they liked about others, for whom ends justified the means. Forget about whatever might be printed in some "holy" book or other, handed down through centuries in altered forms, from authors who could never be identified. Each human being made the ultimate decision about right and wrong. Each person finally decided how far he or she would go in the defense of what was decent—call it Justice, Civilized Society, whatever—and the price they would accept to get the job done.

Bolan's price was high, based on his skill and training.

And he wasn't finished running up the tab.

Oymyakonsky District

CAPTAIN PITIRIM ZELINSKY's team had found its ambush site along the highway after traveling a hundred miles due west from Tomtor. On the south side of the road there was a gully deep enough to hide their Lada Niva from the view of passing motorists. Across the two-lane blacktop stood the husk of an abandoned filling station, someone's great idea for making money, swept by fire at some point years ago and left without a roof, doors and windows.

Someone's dream gone up in smoke.

But it would hide Zelinsky's two companions well enough, while he took shelter under camouflage, across the highway, facing to the west. Whoever passed that point would also have to pass inspection, and the ones who failed would die.

Zelinsky had no plan to capture or interrogate the fugitives. From what he understood, that had been tried already and had failed. He wouldn't lose one of his men trying to play policeman on the Road of Bones.

His was a killing mission, what he did best in the world, and there would be no hesitation on Zelinsky's part when he identified his targets.

Anyone riding a motorcycle could expect a rude surprise.

They had selected basic weapons for the ambush. Zelinsky and Andrez Petrov both carried AK-103 rifles, modernized folding-stock versions of the AKM, chambered in 7.62 mm, with Zelinsky's sporting an under-barrel GP-25 "Bonfire" grenade launcher. That weapon's 40 mm caseless rounds featured nitrocellulose propellant inside each grenade, thus speeding the reloading process.

Konstantin Galitzin, meanwhile, was armed with a Saiga-12 semiautomatic shotgun, feeding 12-gauge cartridges from a 10-round detachable box magazine. A skilled operator could empty the gun's magazine within three to four seconds, filling the air with seventy double-00 pellets, each one equivalent to a .33-caliber bullet.

Between them, with their long guns and their sidearms, Zelinsky thought they should be able to stop any targets that arrived without an armored vehicle to shield them from incoming fire. One man and one woman? No problem.

Except that the targets had already dealt with a dozen or more armed contenders, including an airborne team of trained Spetsnaz commandos. It wouldn't do for him to underestimate their capability, much less their willingness to kill.

They had to be stopped on sight, once and for all.

Lying beneath his camouflaged tarpaulin in the roadside ditch, ignoring damp grass underneath his body and the chill it carried to his bones, Zelinsky found that he was looking forward to the challenge. It was another chance to prove himself, impress his various superiors, perhaps to earn another decoration.

Killing two people he'd never met was simply a bonus. It didn't get any better than this.

Khabarovsk Krai

NIKOLAY MILESCU shifted in his seat, stretching his legs as best he could beneath the SUV's dashboard, and grimaced as they hit another pothole in the poorly serviced pavement. He had given up on cursing and simply glared at Vasily Ryumin in the driver's seat.

"Sorry," Ryumin muttered.

"I don't care if you're sorry," Milescu replied. "If you rip a wheel off the axle, your 'sorry' won't fix it."

"I just didn't see it," Ryumin complained.

"So, pay more attention!" Milescu demanded.

It was a toss-up between making decent time and risking damage to the Lada Niva, all the while watching for signs along the way that might suggest their targets had gone off-road, seeking to deceive them. Milescu was a city boy at heart, accustomed to stalking his prey through alleys and tenements, rather than searching the forests and fens. Someone should have considered that before they chose him for the job, but it was too late now for them to reconsider.

He imagined Stephan Levshin, chafing at the bit for every hour wasted, every day that passed without some word of contact, passing word along to Boris Struve, who would in turn alert their boss, Rybakov, that there was still no progress on the hunt. It looked bad for Milescu, and he couldn't even offer the excuse that he was cast out of his element. Complaints would only make him seem a whining, incompetent fool.

A kiss of death in the Izmaylovskaya gang.

Each soldier was only as good as his last completed mission. A hundred jobs well done were canceled, forgotten, after one failure. There was no room for error in a world where the survival of the fittest literally meant the difference between life and death.

"What's that?" Ryumin asked.

Milescu brought his eyes and mind back into focus on the highway, picking out an access road ahead of them, branching off to the left, or north of the highway.

A hundred yards beyond the intersection stood a stockade fence, with rooftops visible above it.

"Looks like someone's built a fort," Gramotkin said from the backseat.

"They must have something to protect," Stolypin added.

"Slow a bit," Milescu told their driver.

"Are we going up there?" Ryumin asked.

If there was a chance, however slight, that someone in the isolated compound had observed his quarry, then Milescu had to know. If nothing else, it would confirm that he was still on the right track. Perhaps they would have noticed when the motorcycle passed, giving Milescu some idea of how long it might be before he overtook his prey.

"They could be in there, watching us right now," Izvolsky said.

"Not likely," Gramotkin stated.

"Turn in," Milescu ordered. Reaching down between his knees, he found his weapon, checked the safety to make sure that he could reach it instantly.

Ryumin turned off-road and nosed the SUV along the unpaved track that led to the stockade. Before they covered half the distance to its gate, Milescu saw heads popping up along the fence top, tracking the vehicle's progress.

"Be ready," Milescu said as they pulled up to the gates and stopped, roughly thirty feet from contact. When he stepped out of the SUV, he left his automatic rifle in the car. Less threatening that way. He'd seem a reasonable man, and courteous.

"What do you want?" a stern-faced man called down to him.

"We're looking for two friends of ours," Milescu said.

"They're traveling by motorcycle from Yakutsk, all the way to Magadan, while we pack the supplies. We lost them yesterday when we stopped to fix a puncture."

"You say a motorcycle?" asked the man atop the fence.

"That's right. A BMW," Milescu answered, "with a man and woman riding it."

"We haven't seen them," the stockade's spokesman replied.

Pausing to compose himself, Milescu asked the stranger, "Are you sure?"

"I've said so. Now, if that's all," the lookout said, "we're all busy, with work to do."

"Just one more thing," Milescu answered, leaning back inside the Niva.

He had almost reached his rifle when a bullet struck the windshield, inches from his face.

M56 Kolyma Highway

THE BRIDGE HAD BEEN substantial in its day, but it hadn't been able to withstand Siberia. Bolan couldn't have said what caused it to collapse, specifically, but its arcing span had fallen into rubble, leaving only remnants at each end. Viewing it from ground level, he was reminded of a stunt ramp built for jumping motorbikes.

Evel Knievel would have loved it.

Bolan, not so much.

Around the tumbled fragments of the former bridge, swift water rushed and filled the air with spray. Bolan guessed that it had to be knee-deep, maybe deeper— deep enough, in any case, to drown the BMW's motor if they tried to cross unaided. Leon's Sadko, by contrast, stood high off the ground and sported a Safari Snorkel to keep its engine running through water or in choking duststorms.

"Here we go!" Leon said as he shifted the truck into first gear and gave it some gas. There was a dip as they nosed down the riverbank, and then the back wheels leveled off as they submerged.

The river, Bolan quickly learned, was deeper than he'd thought. In moments, Anuchin gasped and raised her feet, dripping from water that had found its way inside the Sadko's cab.

"Don't worry!" Leon told her, grinning. "It is just a little damp."

"A little damp? We're flooding!"

"It's nothing! This I promise you!"

And having said that, their chauffeur began to sing. Something in Russian, a lot of it incomprehensible to Bolan, but it had a rousing rhythm to it, and it kept the smile on Leon's face while he was grappling with the wheel to keep his truck from being drawn downstream.

The truck lurched, made a groaning noise and settled deeper on the driver's side, as if the left-front tire had sunk into a hole. Anuchin gasped again, clutched Bolan's hand and showed him worried eyes.

"It's nothing!" Leon said again, ending his song. "We put our faith in four-wheel drive!"

More groaning as the truck rocked back and forth. Bolan could hear the silt and gravel churning underneath it, rattling along the Sadko's undercarriage. If Leon dug the pit much deeper, they would have to swim for it and leave the motorcycle where it was, useless.

With a grinding lurch, the truck broke free and powered toward the eastern shore.

"You see!" Famintsyn beamed. "I told you it was nothing! Ye of little faith!"

CHAPTER SIXTEEN

Khabarovsk Krai

Pyotr Famintsyn regretted firing the first shot, but he'd been sure that the stranger was reaching inside his Lada Niva for a weapon. And, as it turned out, he'd been correct. Outside the compound's fence, he counted five guns firing now, spread out along a skirmish line that had Famintsyn and his loved ones trapped inside.

Of course, the stockade had been built precisely for a day like this, when they might be compelled to fend off people bent on harming one or all of them. The walls were stout, they had supplies enough to last a week or two—including ammunition—but Famintsyn didn't think these strangers planned on a protracted siege.

They had come looking for Matt Cooper and the woman, Tatyana. They had to know that every moment wasted on Famintsyn and his family would put their quarry that much farther out of reach. Famintsyn owed the pair his life, but it had never crossed his mind that he'd be challenged to repay the debt so soon.

Famintsyn held the PPSh-41 submachine gun. Its drum magazine held seventy-one rounds of 7.62 mm Tokarev ammunition, but Famintsyn had fired some two dozen of those already, peppering his enemies' SUV before they pulled back out of range. His wife carried the family's black-market Uzi, while their eldest son had the AK-47 and Famintsyn's other children were armed according to their size and skill.

All told, not a bad little army.

But they were clearly dealing with professionals.

After withdrawing from the compound's gate, weaving erratically to dodge Famintsyn's fire, the hunters had parked out of range and returned to the battle on foot, all armed to the teeth. Just now, one of them was strafing the stockade walls with a light machine gun, probably a Pecheneg, firing measured bursts to conserve ammunition.

Famintsyn recognized the tactic. He had learned it during military service and couldn't mistake its purpose. While one shooter kept their heads down, others would be creeping closer, probing for a point where they could breach the compound. Once inside, if they could find a means of access, there'd be hell to pay.

Defeatist thinking ran against Famintsyn's grain. Counting his offspring who were old and strong enough to fight, their adversaries were outnumbered nearly two to one. Still, in the face of armed professionals who harbored no compunction about killing women, children, they would be outclassed. Famintsyn knew that they had to hold the wall, or else risk losing everything.

How could the stockade walls be breached?

He ruled out ramming with the SUV, since the attackers obviously wanted to preserve it without further damage. Digging underneath the fence would take a fair amount of time, with proper tools, and anyone attempting it would certainly be shot the moment that his head poked into view. The smallest of Famintsyn's children could maintain a roving foot patrol and call out if they saw or heard the enemy at work on tunneling.

Which still left fire or demolition.

The stockade would burn, of course. Its fence was made of logs, the perfect fuel. Famintsyn hadn't treated them with any flame-retardant chemicals. Molotov cocktails could ignite the fence at any point—or several at once—if their opponents had the gasoline to spare, and some way to deliver it. The run up to the fence would be their greatest risk, of course. The same was true for any effort to approach with an explosive charge or hand grenades.

But it could still be done.

Worried, Famintsyn settled in to wait and find out what the hunters would try next.

M56 Kolyma Highway

"So, THAT IS EVERYTHING, I think," Leon Famintsyn said.

Bolan had checked the BMW after they'd unloaded it, kick-started it and listened to the engine rumbling. Prior to setting off from the Famintsyn compound, Leon's brother had insisted that they top off the gas tank from his reserve, along with the plastic bottles they used for refills. As far as Bolan could determine, they were ready to resume their journey eastward.

"You'll be careful, won't you?" Anuchin asked Leon. "The people who are looking for us can be dangerous."

Famintsyn laughed at that. "Who isn't, in this place?" he asked. "Strangers from outside who come sniffing here may get a rude surprise."

"I say again, be careful." Anuchin leaned in for a peck on Leon's cheek that made him blush.

"If I were not a family man," he said, then shook his head and let it go. "Be safe, the two of you. Remember that Siberia forgives no one. It doesn't tolerate mistakes."

Leon shook hands with Bolan, said, "No kiss from

you, I think," and then retreated to his truck. He'd left the engine running, and a moment later he was turning, starting back across the river.

Bolan waited until he was safely on the other bank, then mounted up. "We've got a lead," he said. "Let's take advantage of it."

When she'd settled on the pillion, hands on Bolan's hips, he eased the motorcycle off its kickstand, aimed it eastward and accelerated from their standing start.

With luck, and if they didn't lose the blacktop altogether, he thought they could put two hundred miles behind them before stopping at nightfall. Three hundred wouldn't lie outside the realm of possibility, but that was stretching it.

Bolan had misgivings about leaving the Famintsyn family in harm's way, knowing there were stalkers rolling down the Road of Bones behind himself and Anuchin, but he couldn't focus on that now. Their paths had crossed coincidentally; they'd helped Pyotr out of a tight spot, and he'd repaid the favor in full knowledge that the pair of them were hunted fugitives. Bolan couldn't stand guard over the tribe perpetually, and they wouldn't welcome the attempt if he should try.

Forget it, then.

As if he could.

The Executioner's long road was littered with remains of friends and helpful strangers who had lent a hand along the way. That road was getting longer by the moment, stretching eastward through a landscape fertilized by death. Bolan devoutly hoped that no more innocents would suffer for his sake, but it was possible.

And in the end, he'd likely never even know.

He fixed his thoughts on Tomtor, and on Magadan

beyond it. On a pickup waiting for them somewhere off the coastline, in the Sea of Okhotsk.

One more challenge. But before he faced it, they would have to cover the remainder of their journey more or less intact. And there was no doubt Anuchin's enemies would have more tricks in store waiting along the way.

Khabarovsk Krai

NIKOLAY MILESCU had washed out of military service after basic training, cashiered for repeated acts of insubordination that had cost him six months in a military jail before he was expelled with a dishonorable discharge. Still, he could remember crawling through the mud, beneath coils of concertina wire, while some asshole of a sergeant filled the air above his head with bullets.

He'd despised the exercise as practice, and Milescu didn't like it any better now, when it was life or death.

At least, this time, when he shot back it was for real.

Ryumin had them covered with the Pecheneg machine gun, knocking divots in the stockade fence and keeping those inside from laying down return fire. In the no-man's-land outside the fort, Milescu and his other men were creeping forward, fanning out in hopes that they could find another way inside. Milescu, Izvolsky and Gramotkin carried AK-74 assault rifles, while Stolypin had the TOZ-194 shotgun.

If any of the peasants in the compound raised a head above the wall, it would be blasted from his shoulders. But as long as they were safe inside...

It seemed peculiar, but Milescu had already crawled halfway around the stockade without finding any other entrance. It was only common sense to leave a back door for emergency evacuation, but the obvious precaution was a weakness in disguise—and it had obviously been omitted in this case. When he met Gramotkin crawling lizardlike to meet him from the opposite direction, it was finally confirmed.

"No other way inside," Gramotkin said.

"All right, then," Milescu stated. "We go back and fetch the jerry cans."

Not all of them, he thought. A pair should do it. All they had to do was torch a section of the fence. It might flush out their enemies—or, at the very least, open the fortress to attack. If they could only find a way inside, Milescu reckoned that his soldiers could deal swiftly with the yokels who opposed them.

Leaving one alive for the time being to interrogate.

The fuel was precious, but a family existing in this wilderness, with floodlights on their fence and dish antennas on their roof, had to have a generator. That meant there'd be gasoline inside, likely enough to keep Milescu's Lada Niva running all the way to Magadan. He only needed access to it.

The crawl back to the car seemed longer than the journey from it, now that he had hatched a plan. Milescu's eagerness to see it executed raised his blood pressure, produced a strident ringing in his ears, already echoing from the staccato jabber of the Pecheneg.

One more round-trip and he would have them. Once the stockade was in flames, no matter what provisions his opponents had for fighting fires, it would distract them from defending their perimeter. And that distraction should be all he needed to defeat them.

If the bastards didn't kill him first.

THE FIRE REVEALED a crucial flaw in strategy. When he'd designed the compound with defense in mind, Pyotr Famintsyn had considered that someone, someday, might try to burn him out. He'd reasoned that the stout logs chosen for the stockade fence would give him time to fight the flames. And he was right...up to a point.

But what he hadn't thought about was that a fire set on the outside of the fence could only be extinguished from the outside. Hosing down the inside of the fence might slow the fire's advance, but wouldn't ultimately stop the logs from burning to the point where they were fragile, vulnerable.

Any attempt to douse flames on the outside of the fence permitted those who'd set the fire to shoot whichever member of Famintsyn's family tried to extinguish it. Or, failing that, the firefighters were still distracted from their main job—that of keeping any hostiles well outside the compound.

Now, after he'd cursed himself as seven kinds of fool, Famintsyn stood and watched smoke rising from the north and east walls of his fortress. Somehow, even with himself, his wife and all their children watching, the intruders had crept close enough to douse the fence with gasoline and ignite it, not on one side, but on two. The better to divide his forces, cunning bastards that they were, and maybe leave the front gate undermanned.

A fatalist, like most Russians, Famintsyn wasted no time worrying about how matters had degenerated to their present state. He had to do something about it, but on that point he was stalled. His thoughts were tangled, spiked with unfamiliar fear, disorganized beyond fomenting a coherent plan.

He wished Leon was there to counsel him, or at the very least to lend a helping hand, but that was selfishness. His brother would return home to his own brood after dropping off his passengers across the river. There was no reason for him to come back here, and it was just as well. He'd simply drive into a trap, be taken by surprise and killed.

At least, this way, there would be someone to avenge Pyotr's family if he couldn't rescue them himself. Leon wouldn't forget whatever happened to his kinfolk, nor would he forgive it. Someday, maybe years from now, each of the men responsible would find a smiling stranger on his doorstep.

With a knife or pistol in his hand.

Famintsyn stopped, scolding himself for his distraction and his morbid turn of thought. He wasn't finished yet, nor was his family. They still had weapons, ammunition and their grim determination to survive.

Their enemies might think they'd won the fight, but they were wrong.

In fact, it had only begun.

NIKOLAY MILESCU HADN'T lingered once the fires were set along the north and east walls of the rural family's stockade. He'd left Naum Izvolsky positioned to cover both sides with his Kalashnikov, in case some of the compound residents were brave enough to venture out and fight the flames, then doubled back around in front, where Ryumin still had them pinned down with the light machine gun.

It was falling into place. They'd spent more time than he'd intended on this sideshow, but the armed reaction of the compound's tenants told Milescu they had information he could use. And once he had been challenged, he couldn't admit defeat by peasants, even if it seemed they'd managed to collect an arsenal of military weapons for themselves.

He'd let the fence burn a little while longer, drawing

some of the defenders from their posts, before he made another move. It hurt, not knowing how many opponents he faced with his four men behind him, but Milescu was a battle-tested professional, not some yokel to cringe and turn tail at the first sign of danger. He would persevere, not only from his fear of Stephan Levshin and the men behind him, but as a matter of personal pride.

And when the peasants fell into his clutches finally, he'd make them suffer. That would be a present to himself.

A little entertainment for his men.

How best to crack the fortress, then? The burning walls would weaken, but there would be reinforcements standing by to guard them now. The gate would still be covered, too, though possibly by fewer guns. A safe path would lie somewhere in between the two.

When he was safe—outside the line of fire, Ryumin covering his run back to the SUV—Milescu rose and sprinted to the vehicle. Inside it, mixed up with the other gear they'd packed before they left Nizhny Bestyakh, he found a coil of sturdy nylon rope. He'd brought it as a backup for the Lada Niva's winch, in case they got bogged down, but now Milescu saw that it could serve him in another way.

Taking the rope, leaving Ryumin on the Pecheneg, he scurried off to collect Stolypin and Gramotkin. They were stationed well apart, to cover the stockade and stop its inmates from escaping, so Milescu had to run the gauntlet, braced for hostile fire at any second. No one shot at him, however, making him conclude that they were either busy with the fire, or saving ammunition for a last-ditch stand.

He reached Gramotkin first, told him to come along, and then the pair of them went off to join Izvolsky. Huddled together, moments later, Milescu explained his plan and asked for any questions.

"We just walk up there and throw the rope over their fence?" Izvolsky asked.

"We'll run," Milescu said. "Vasily has us covered."

"And climb over," Gramotkin said. "While we're doing that, we can't defend ourselves."

"Two of us on the ground cover the first man climbing," Milescu said. "Once he's on the other side, he covers those remaining."

"Right," Izvolsky said. "Who's going first, then?"

"I will," Milescu said, dry-mouthed at the thought of it. "Decide between yourselves who follows next."

"And if you're shot?" Gramotkin asked. "What then?"

"I'll know you didn't cover me." Milescu sneered at him. "You can run off and hide like rabbits in the brush, praying that no one ever finds out how you failed."

He didn't have to mention any names. Levshin or Struve, their godfather himself. There'd be no sanctuary for them if they failed.

"All right, then," Gramotkin said. "Let's get on with it."

Izvolsky nodded, looking miserable but resigned.

Milescu tied a noose in one end of the rope, using a slip knot that would cinch it tight around the sharpened tip of one log in the stockade's stout fence. The run up to the wall was thirty yards or so, all open ground. Slipping his left arm through the sling of his Kalashnikov, he rose and sprinted toward the fence, the others moving in behind him, weapons leveled.

Fortune smiled on Nikolay Milescu as he made his toss. The noose found purchase on his first try, tightened as he gave the rope a tug, then he was scrambling upward, panting as he climbed, expecting any moment for a gunman to rise up before him, firing straight into his face.

CHAPTER SEVENTEEN

M56 Kolyma Highway

The marvel of the road was that no two successive miles appeared the same to Bolan's eye. Granted, he saw the same trees in the woods when they pressed close against the highway's berm. He felt the same chill when they crossed a stream and water splashed his legs. He felt the same shocks ripple through the BMW and his body as he navigated fractured pavement. But it all seemed *different*, somehow, as if he were a spectator to Russia's gloomy history unfolding in a 3-D panorama, surrounded by killer special effects.

And *killer* was the word he had to keep in mind as they proceeded. Somewhere in his rearview mirror, though he couldn't see them yet, a team of hunters would be burning up the road—well, trying to, as best they could—in hot pursuit. Some of the trackers might be airborne, though that angle hadn't fared too well for them last time.

And up ahead? What else was waiting for them on their way to Magadan?

Two towns, of course—Tomtor and Oymyakon— where gunmen could be waiting for them on the streets or tucked inside of shops and houses. Otherwise, the road was open to their destination, yet another city with at least a hundred thousand residents, where Bolan was required to find some means of rendezvousing with their ride, somewhere offshore. And in between those settlements lay empty highway, where he knew that damn near anything could happen unobserved.

According to the BMW's odometer and Bolan's calculations, the Famintsyn compound lay roughly three hundred miles due east of where they'd started from, in Nizhny Bestyakh. Leon Famintsyn had driven them another hundred miles or so, before he left them on the river's bank with his best wishes. Do the math, and they still had the best part of nine hundred miles to go, before they glimpsed the Sea of Okhotsk. Call it 860 miles, if you were feeling generous.

And they could still be hit by hostiles anywhere along the way, repeatedly, if that was what it took to bring them down. Arrayed against them were the full resources of the Russian state—or, at the very least, whatever could be mustered by the men whom Anuchin's testimony placed in jeopardy. They'd stop at nothing to prevent her going public, and they still had ample time to stop her cold.

But they would have to reckon with the Executioner.

A quarter mile or so ahead of them, a moose with massive antlers stepped into the roadway. Bolan blew the BMW's horn and got a blank look from the creature in return. It might have been a big-game hunter's dream, but all he wanted at the moment was an open passing lane.

He braked, a hundred yards between the cycle and the moose, in case it charged and he was forced to make a U-turn for a swift retreat. Bolan hated the thought of losing ground, but a collision with an animal that tipped the scales somewhere between eight hundred and a thousand pounds could finish them right there.

No contest.

As it was, the moose regarded them with high disdain for several seconds more, then ambled back in the direction it had come from, taking its sweet time. When it was out of sight, and Bolan felt it safe to go ahead, he gunned the bike and put the moose-crossing behind him in a flash.

One more experience he'd never had before.

And Bolan hoped he'd live to reminisce about it, somewhere down the line.

Khabarovsk Krai

EIGHT SURVIVORS OF THE BATTLE, unarmed, stood in front of Nikolay Milescu, ringed by weapons in the hands of Naum Izvolsky, Vasily Ryumin and Gennady Stolypin. Viktor Gramotkin, killed during the final storming of the compound, lay beside the open gate, his arms folded tidily across his blood-soaked chest. The hostile body count so far: one woman, one teenager and one small child dead. The stockade's patriarch was wounded in the left side, leaning on one of his sons to keep himself upright.

"All right," Milescu told the vanquished. "You have suffered loss, and so have we. There was no reason for it, other than your foolish stubbornness. I asked a simple question and you tried to kill us. This is the result you've brought upon yourself."

Silence from the assembled losers, other than some weeping from the younger children, now half orphans.

"It was stupid of you to attack us," Milescu said, "and it's doubly stupid to invite more suffering on the behalf of strangers who've abandoned you, and who are traitors to your homeland. You may salvage something from this tragedy—your lives, at least—by giving us the information we require."

"Liar." The wounded man bent forward, spit into

the dust. "You will kill us, anyway. We're witnesses to murder."

Milescu cut a quick glance toward Stolypin, standing closest on his left, and smiled. "A country lawyer, eh?" he said. "You're right, of course. I stand corrected. But you still have an important choice to make. *How* will you die? And who dies first?"

The wounded man—Pyotr Something was his name; Milescu didn't give a damn—stared back at him, frowning.

"Am I not clear?" Milescu asked. "What father would elect to see his children killed before his eyes? Would you enjoy watching while we amuse ourselves with the young ladies in your family?"

"Fuck yourself, you filth!" Pyotr Something hissed.

Milescu fired his rifle from the hip, not really aiming, hardly caring who the bullets struck, as long as someone fell. A boy of nine or ten flopped over backward, twitching in the dust, blood pumping from a pair of chest wounds.

Anguished cries went up along the line of stricken prisoners. One of the younger girls gave out a shriek that would have pierced Milescu's soul, if he had still possessed one.

"It's horrible, I grant you, what you're forcing me to do," Milescu said. "How long must it go on? We *know* the people we are looking for were here, with you. Why else would you behave this way, except from some misguided sense of loyalty?"

Silence, except for weeping from the lot of them.

"Oh, I suppose you think they saved your life," he told Pyotr. "From the bandits on the highway? Yes, we found their carcasses. Myself, I think you'd have been better off to let them kill you. Then, at least, your family would be alive to mourn you."

Famintsyn swore vehemently.

Milescu smiled at the obscenities, then shook his head. "You still doubt my resolve," he said. "Have it your own way, then. Which one do you prefer that I kill next? The choice is yours."

M56 Kolyma Highway

LEON FAMINTSYN was exhausted. Did it mean that he was getting old? He could remember when an all-night party followed by an early-morning drive left him unfazed, but now all he could think about was crawling into bed and dropping off to sleep. Or maybe not immediately, if he could persuade Darya to join him.

Yes, he just might have sufficient energy for that.

Driving westward, the river and its fallen bridge already miles behind him now, he thought about Pyotr and his family. They'd had a close call with disaster yesterday, rescued by strangers at the last minute, and to repay that favor they had put themselves at further risk. It worried Leon, seeing kinfolk getting mixed up with the government, its spies and killers, but he knew it would have been a waste of breath to argue.

Leon and Pyotr had been raised to pay their debts of honor without flinching or considering the cost. Their father had worked both sides of the law to make ends meet, though he had never graduated to the status of a full-fledged thief. He'd never joined one of the syndicates, preferring to pay tribute as required for certain shipments of forbidden merchandise and retain a measure of autonomy.

But had they crossed another line this day?

Pyotr claimed he hadn't asked his guests—his saviors—who was hunting them, or why. He'd told Leon, without explaining, that the government was seeking them, or possibly the Mafiya. To Leon, as to most Russians, the two were indivisible. It wasn't simply that the state had pockets of corruption. Rather, it appeared to anyone with clear eyes and a brain behind them that the gangsters and the politicians were identical.

Which spelled danger for whoever posed an obstacle to their collective will.

Still, a debt had been incurred and had been paid. Whether the matter ended there, or whether there'd be repercussions in the future, Leon couldn't say. It was a comfort, either way, to have his gun on the seat beside him, just in case. The pistol wouldn't stop a bear if he encountered one along the way, but men were something else entirely.

Men were dangerous sometimes, whether you threatened them or not.

Despite his weariness, Leon enjoyed the drive. Riding alone permitted him to think without distractions from the other members of his family. Although he loved them deeply, unconditionally, there were times—more frequent as he aged—when Leon craved a bit of privacy, escaping childish questions and adult demands that he participate in this or that decision on the home front. Darya and their brood were priceless to him, but sometimes he simply had to get away.

Another hour, more or less, remained before he pulled into the gravel driveway of his home, three-quarters of a mile from where Pyotr lived. Leon considered stopping by to see his brother first, then pushed the notion out of mind. There would be time enough for talking later, when they'd all had ample opportunity to rest.

If there were plans to make, they could discuss it then. Surely there had to be time for weary men to sleep.

KILLING INEVITABLY energized Milescu's soldiers. Some of them enjoyed it on a primal level, anytime and anywhere, but in the present case Milescu knew that all of them had needed the release of violence. The long, frustrating hunt in which they'd been engaged had frayed their tempers, made them short with one another and with him, which also undercut his discipline. Now that they'd blown off steam and had a target in their sights, Milescu thought it should be better.

They were one man down, Gramotkin dead, but it would still be four against the two runners they were pursuing. On Milescu's orders they had put Gramotkin's body with the others, in the peasant's house, before they torched it. The Militsiya would simply find a mass of charred flesh, calcined bones and ash. If they could make something of that, good luck to them.

Meanwhile, Milescu had another name. Before the peasant patriarch had died, in an attempt to save his family, he had admitted that his brother helped the fugitives escape. He'd driven them eastward, to cross another of the highway's endless rivers, where a bridge had fallen years ago. A two-hour drive one way, they were told. Counting the time they'd spent cracking the compound and interrogating its inhabitants, the brother—Leon— should be on his way back home by now.

Milescu planned to meet him on the way and have a little chat.

Leon would tell them where he'd left the fugitives, what kind of head start they'd obtained and how long it should take Milescu's men to overtake them. He would probably resist at first, being a stubborn peasant like his brother, but Milescu had no doubt that he would crack.

They always did.

Milescu checked his wing mirror and saw the stain of smoke the burning house and outbuildings had smeared across the Siberian sky. How long would that take to draw the late family's neighbors, then bring out police?

Long enough, Milescu hoped, for him to do his job.

He missed Moscow, the traffic and the relatively normal people crowding busy streets. The skies that never truly darkened, day or night. Access to gas stations, decent food, endless supplies of liquor.

Women.

In the world he knew, Milescu was renowned as something of a ladies' man. If he desired a different partner every night, they were available. Out here, though, he was moved to wonder how the peasants ever got together. Small wonder he had heard so many jokes about Siberians and livestock.

"So, now we're looking for a bridge that isn't there," Stolypin said, taking his turn behind the Lada Niva's wheel.

"We'll know it when we see it," Milescu said.

"Hard to miss," Izvolsky offered from the backseat, "since you can't get off the damn road."

"Just concentrate on catching up to these bastards, eh?" Milescu said. "We're all sick of the road. It's not just you."

"Da, da," Izvolsky answered.

"Not bad hunting, though," Ryumin said from the rear, where they had more room with Gramotkin gone. "Better than shooting bears."

"Bears don't shoot back," Izvolsky said.

"That's half the fun," Ryumin replied.

"Three more to deal with," Milescu said. "First the brother, then the prey we were sent for in the first place. Wrap them up, and we can all go home."

THERE WERE BLACK BEARS in the woods. Bolan had seen two of them since they'd said goodbye to Leon and proceeded on their own. The BMW didn't seem to frighten them. Instead, they stood and watched it pass, a curiosity that might provoke them into mayhem if it stopped within their reach.

So, don't stop, Bolan warned himself. But they would need a rest break in another hour, maybe less, with the rough road hammering their bodies. Even though he missed the worst potholes, there was no way to make the ride a smooth one, nothing close to comfort as he put more miles behind them, focused on the goal of Magadan.

The real goal was survival, though. And Bolan knew they had a long way still to go before it was achieved.

Another bear appeared on Bolan's left, much closer to the road than those he'd seen before. He thought it had a surly, more pugnacious look, not simply curious about the humans who'd intruded on its habitat. When the bear rose on its hind legs, standing close to seven feet in height, he half expected it to charge the motorcycle, but it only pawed the air between them with its talons, open mouth displaying yellow teeth.

Bolan felt Anuchin's grip tighten around his waist as they rolled past the bear. The soldier swerved around a pothole and accelerated, left the bruin staring after them and wondered if it would regret lost opportunity.

Too late.

A predator who hesitated missed his chance. Bolan had learned that lesson when he was a young man, still in uniform, and it had served him well through all his wars. Given a chance to strike, he took it without second thoughts or any vestige of regret.

It was the way a warrior stayed alive.

Behind him, Anuchin said something. He didn't catch it, both of them in helmets with their visors down, the BMW growling underneath them. Bolan slowed enough that he could turn his head slightly and call back to her.

"What was that?"

"I said, 'I'm tired of seeing bears.'"

He smiled, invisible behind his tinted mask, and said, "I feel the same way."

"This is like a damned safari ride," Anuchin said, "without guides or security."

"We're doing all right," he stated, and faced forward, twisting the throttle to put on more speed.

He felt the woman settle back onto the pillion, her Bizon SMG no longer nudging Bolan's kidneys. She was right about their shortage of security, but Bolan thought they probably could stop a bear, if necessary.

As for other predators who might be waiting for them down the road, or coming on behind them, they would have to wait and see.

LEON FAMINTSYN SANG along with Epidemia, belting out "Angel of Twilight" from the rock band's *Road Home* album on his dashboard CD player. Radio was hopeless in the hinterlands of Khabarovsk Krai, except for short-wave chatter from truckers and members of the Russian Amateur Radio Union. Leon had a two-way outfit in his truck for dire emergencies, but left it turned off most of the time, bored by the normal traffic, even as he felt guilty for eavesdropping.

Another thirty minutes, more or less, and he would be at home. He could relax, enjoy a meal, postpone consideration of his next trip on the Road of Bones for several days, at least.

A shipment of tobacco was arriving in Yakutsk on Saturday, would cross the river to Nizhny Bestyakh on Monday or Tuesday, all things being equal, and Leon could make the pickup. He hoped to take Pyotr with him this time, bearing in mind the results of his brother's last solo trip on the cursed highway.

Leon didn't regard himself as superstitious—certainly no one could rightfully accuse him of professing a religion—but he *did* believe in curses and bad luck. He knew there were places on the planet where the crimes of man had blighted nature. Take Chernobyl, for example, or the death camps erected by Nazis in Poland during the Great Patriotic War. Those places had seen so much death and misery, Leon suspected that the very soil and trees were now insane.

Same for the Road of Bones.

In fact, if he was forced to say—

He saw the SUV approaching him from westward, braking as it edged into the middle of the highway and denied him room to pass. At first, he thought the driver might be dozing at the wheel, then Leon counted heads inside the vehicle and saw four occupants, all staring straight ahead.

At him.

Leon braked, rolled to a halt when they were still a hundred yards away and found his pistol on the seat beside him. He eased off the safety and thumbed it to the semiautomatic fire position.

Now, he was as ready as he'd ever be.

The SUV—a Lada Niva, he now recognized—came to a halt some thirty feet in front of Leon's truck. The driver kept his seat, while three men opened doors and rose to stand behind them, partly shielded. Leon thought it was a move they had rehearsed for an occasion such as this.

He powered down the driver's window, but made no attempt to leave his vehicle. It wouldn't hurt to hear them out, at least, although he worried that their hands remained concealed.

The man who rode beside the Lada's driver called out to him, "Leon? You're Leon Famintsyn, yes?"

"I don't know you," Leon called back to him, still seated at the Sadko's wheel.

"Your brother told us where to find you," the stranger said.

"Oh?" Leon feigned casual disinterest. "How is Grigory?"

"I couldn't say," the stranger answered, "since the brother we spoke to was named Pyotr."

Was named? Had he heard it right?

"What is it that you want?" Leon asked.

"Just a friendly word. Or, I should say, a word about your friends."

"What friends?" Leon demanded, cradling the pistol in his lap, his index finger on its trigger.

"Those you've just delivered to the far side of the river."

So. He saw it all within the span of time it took a life to crumble, knew Pyotr wouldn't have betrayed the new acquaintances who'd saved his life—much less his own brother—except in dire extremity.

Unless his wife and children had been threatened by a fate only betrayal could avert.

And it had failed to save them, even so. Leon could read that on the faces of these strangers, gunmen, killers. He could see his own death in their eyes.

So be it.

"Right, then," he replied while opening his door, keeping his death grip on the pistol. "So, let's talk."

CHAPTER EIGHTEEN

Khabarovsk Krai

Captain Franz Rostovsky wasn't a curious man by nature. Curiosity was detrimental to advancement in the Russian military, most particularly when his job sometimes required him to fly missions for the FSB. He knew some Russians, not to mention strangers on the far side of the world, believed the KGB had changed when it acquired a new name in the 1990s, but Rostovsky had his doubts.

With that in mind, he'd asked no questions when he was assigned to take his Mikoyan-Gurevich Foxbat on a second scouting mission over Khabarovsk Krai this morning. Again, he was assigned to find two people on a motorcycle traveling cross-country, eastward. He assumed they were the same two he'd been watching for last time, and wondered in the corner of his mind that harbored private thoughts how they had managed to evade the hunt this long.

If the FSB was hunting them in open country, on the Road of Bones, why were they still at large?

As last time, Captain Rostovsky began from the west and flew eastward, following the supposed path of his prey. His radar and IRST systems scanned the road and the surrounding woods for targets that satisfied his brief. So far, he'd seen a truck abandoned on the highway, with some bears nosing around it, and a smaller vehicle eastbound as he was, only moving at a fraction of his speed. Rostovsky drew no mental link between the two events, leaving assessment to the analysts who would review his data in a quiet room somewhere, secure from prying eyes and ears.

Or so they'd think.

But any Russian who had half a brain and hadn't fried that half with vodka ought to know that, even in a secret place, the walls had eyes and ears. In Rostovsky's view, the only secrets in the Russian Federation were the ones waiting to be exposed.

Too much philosophy for one day, he decided, concentrating on the quasi-wilderness below him. Once upon a time, he knew, legions of prisoners had labored long and hard to build the highway he was following—and Moscow, in its apathy toward anything outside the Central Federal District, had ignored it for the most part, since the road had been completed. Cash was always needed elsewhere, for some military project or construction of a dacha for a fat-cat politician's holidays.

Not that Rostovsky cared about the highway or its poor state of repair. Far from it. He would never be required to drive along its broken surface, ford its rivers or attempt to find the pavement where it vanished altogether. It was merely symptomatic of his homeland, where the little people never really mattered much, regardless of the slogans touted by their leaders.

So it had been from the days of czars, through revolution and dictatorship, into so-called democracy. So would it ever be, unless humanity itself was changed.

And what, Rostovsky wondered, were the odds of that?

A new blip on the Foxbat's radar drew him from his reverie. It was a vehicle much smaller than the last one he had overflown, another traveler to eastward. Could it be the pair of targets he was looking for?

Another moment, and his cameras confirmed it—or, at least, confirmed two riders on a motorcycle, far below the MiG. Captain Rostovsky couldn't say they were the right two motorcyclists, but they were approximately where he'd hoped to find them, headed in the right direction. Headquarters could ask no more than that.

He let the camera have them, snapping off three dozen photos and transmitting them in real time to a room where cybergeeks sat hunched over computers, tapping calculations on their keypads. They would judge the targets and decide what should be done with them.

For Captain Rostovsky, the job was done.

ANOTHER STREAM TO CROSS. Bolan had given up on counting them unless they qualified as rivers and required some special plan to get across. This one wasn't the worst he'd seen, by any means, but he still planned to stop and scout it first, for safety's sake.

More wasted time, but it beat being stranded on foot.

He coasted to a stop on the bank of the stream, where its course overran the highway. Bolan could still see bits and pieces of the pavement underwater, six or seven inches deep near shore. The only way to test it was to walk across and find out if the bottom dropped away when he got farther out.

If so, they'd need another place to cross.

Anuchin dismounted, then Bolan, an easier move than reversing the process. He'd switched off the bike, left it up on its kickstand while he examined the stream.

"We can make it, I think," Anuchin suggested.

"I hope so," Bolan said. "But I'll try it first to make sure it doesn't surprise us."

Bolan took his AK with him as he stepped into the stream, unwilling to be caught without it if they happened to encounter any unexpected company. Not likely, where they were, with half a mile of highway visible in each direction, but he wouldn't stake his life on what seemed probable.

Not in the wild lands of Siberia.

Cold water washed over his boots, climbed to his ankles as he made his slow way toward midstream. No rushing it at this stage, when a false step might wind up leaving him soaked. The broken pavement underfoot was slimed with algae, treacherous despite the lug soles on his boots, and Bolan raised one arm for balance, while the other kept his rifle snug against his side.

Halfway across, Bolan began to think of what would happen if he met another bear. Retreat would be a dicey proposition with his present footing, and if he was suddenly attacked, he'd have to hope the AK stopped the animal before it reached him.

There was no bear, and Bolan switched his full attention back to his appointed task. He reached the east bank of the stream with sodden trouser legs and socks, no way to stop the water getting in his boots once it topped ankle height. He thought the bike could make it, with some careful handling, and they'd be on their way.

The walk back took him half the time of crossing in the first place, Bolan now familiar with the path, translating in his mind how it would be for two-wheel traveling. Say, twenty yards, and they'd be clear, rolling on dry land once again.

"All right?" Anuchin asked as he joined her.

"Should be fine," Bolan replied. "You ready?"

She nodded, facing Bolan with her visor raised, and said, "Sooner is better, *da?*"

Oymyakonsky District

"I UNDERSTAND," Captain Pitirim Zelinsky said. "Yes, sir."

At once, dead air replaced Major Maxim Bucharin's voice, the tactical phone hissing softly in Zelinsky's ear to signal that the contact had been severed. No goodbye or anything resembling common courtesy.

Their targets had been sighted and were still proceeding eastward, last seen at a point around 140 miles west of Zelinsky's ambush site. Three hours, if they held a decent speed, but that was unpredictable with the terrain and poor condition of the highway.

Even if it took them twice that time, they should be in his sights before dusk fell. Zelinsky could be finished with his task this day, clean up the site and still be back in Tomtor for the airlift home by morning.

To await his due reward, assuming there was any to be had.

Zelinsky rose and stretched, enjoying it, and signaled his permission to the others for a break from lying in concealment. Petrov, the taller of the two, went through a brisk routine of exercise, bending to touch his toes, then twisting at the waist and crouching, working kinks out of his legs. Galitzin was more casual about it, pacing up and down the highway's shoulder while he swung his arms about and flexed his shoulders.

They were both professionals, stone killers, and Zelinsky knew they wouldn't fail him in a firefight. Given the advantage of surprise, he thought they should be able to dispose of their intended quarry without any difficulty, but he stopped short of permitting overconfidence to take root in his mind.

It was a critical mistake to underestimate an adversary when their capabilities were only known from second-hand reports. Planning was critical, but it could only go so far. A nearly endless list of variables could affect the outcome of a firefight, even when it seemed to be a sure thing.

Zelinsky sat on the highway's berm, then stretched out on his back and ran through a routine of leg lifts, followed by a rapid fifty sit-ups. When he felt that he had done his best to keep his joints and muscles limber, he lay back, glanced at his watch and gave himself another twenty minutes to relax.

Then they went back to hiding, waiting for the strangers they'd been sent to kill. Whatever the people had done to rate an ambush on the Road of Bones, Zelinsky hoped it had been satisfying. In a few more hours, when they lay in blood and gasped their dying breaths, would they be satisfied with whatever they had achieved?

And when his own turn came, as every soldier's did in time, how would *he* feel?

With any luck, Zelinsky thought, he wouldn't see it coming. Wouldn't hear the shot that killed him on some other battlefield. A quick, clean death was every warrior's secret and unspoken wish.

But not too soon.

Pitirim Zelinsky wasn't ready for the end just yet.

This day, it would be someone else's turn. He had come to deliver the message of death, not receive it.

Killing was Zelinsky's business.

And business was good.

Yakutsk

MAJOR STEPHAN LEVSHIN was proud of his ability to keep a civil tone with his superiors—with anyone, in fact, who could do harm to his career. It was a talent he had cultivated from his early days in uniform.

He informed his caller, "Sir, I understand how you must feel. Frustration is to be expected in a situation such as this one."

And the voice came back at him from Moscow, "So, you understand me, do you? Then you must know that I'm *not* frustrated, Major. I am *furious* at having this fiasco dragged out for so many days. I thought your people knew what they were doing?"

Levshin took a deep breath, trying to control his blood pressure. Grigory Rybakov might be a thug, but he was one who mattered. Fabulously wealthy, friendly with the prime minister, as well as top-ranked leaders of the FSB. That friendship was, in fact, the reason for their present dire predicament.

"Sir, if I may remind you," Levshin said, "the men involved are yours, as well."

"And they've been making progress," Rybakov replied, "while yours are getting shot out of the sky. You've heard from them by now, *da*? With the latest news?"

"Indeed, sir. I was gratified to hear that they've obtained word of the targets, but our overflight accomplished the same thing without a spectacle."

"You talk to me about a spectacle?" Rybakov sneered. "What do you call a military helicopter shot to hell, all hands on board? Your men can't even kill them from the air!"

Thankful that his line was scrambled, Levshin told the mobster, "We have other men in place, sir. Ready. Waiting. I assure you that the problem will be solved."

"I've heard this all before," Rybakov said. "You know the saying, 'If you want a job done right, do it yourself'?"

"I've heard it, yes, sir," Levshin answered. "But I really don't think I—"

"Not you!" the gangster interrupted with a snort of scornful laughter. "It's time for *me* to take a hand. I'm flying out to join my men within the hour. They have given me coordinates. I have their GPS."

"Sir, I don't think—"

"Perhaps that's for the best," Rybakov said. "Your thinking hasn't done much for us lately, has it?"

"Sir—"

"Goodbye, Major. I have a flight to catch."

The line went dead.

Levshin considered calling back, but thought it would only make him seem pathetic. But there *was* another call that Levshin had to make, and he was dreading it.

Colonel Marshak wouldn't be pleased to hear of Rybakov's decision. Logically, no blame attached to Levshin for the Moscow gangster's rash, impulsive move, but long experience had taught Levshin that logic played a relatively small role in the workings of the Russian government. In fact, sometimes he thought it played no role at all.

Perhaps, if he moved swiftly, Marshak could dissuade Rybakov from flying east to join the hunt himself. But if he failed, what difference did it really make?

Captain Zelinsky's ambush party was in place. If all went well, they should have solved the problem by the time Rybakov joined his men.

If all went well...

So far, Levshin admitted to himself, nothing had gone well on this mission. If he'd been a superstitious man, he might have thought that they were cursed.

Ridiculous!

He speed-dialed Marshak's private number, waiting

for the gruff voice to respond. Marshak would recognize his number and—

"What is it, Levshin?"

"Sir," the major said, "I'm afraid there's more bad news."

M56 Kolyma Highway

THE WEST BANK of the stream was steep enough that Anuchin clung to Cooper's waist more tightly than she would have, rolling over level pavement. When the BMW's front tire entered the water, she could feel her muscles clench involuntarily. She reminded herself to breathe, hoping her nervousness would not transfer itself to Cooper through her touch, or through the rigid posture of her body.

The bike felt wobbly now, with one wheel in the water, rolling over slimy, crumbling asphalt, and the other still on solid ground. Tatyana made an effort to distract herself, thinking about the science-fiction programs she had seen when she was younger, on the television, when the government relaxed its ban on Western programming. Most of them seemed absurd, but now she wished that they could beam themselves to Magadan by simply wishing for it, and get off the Road of Bones.

She tried, just for the hell of it.

No luck, of course.

The bike's rear tire was in the water now, shifting uncomfortably. Cooper tried to hold it steady, used a light hand on the throttle, but the water rushing past beneath them gave Tatyana a disorienting sense of sideways motion that was almost dizzying. She focused on their goal, the distant bank, as she might do if crossing a rope bridge, above a chasm.

No help there.

Her boots were wet now, and she wondered how much deeper they could go before the motorcycle's engine was affected. If they flooded it, could Cooper fix the problem, or would they be left to walk the last eight hundred miles to Magadan?

Each time that she allowed herself to hope, it seemed that hope was dashed by circumstances she could not control. There had been so much death and suffering since she decided to embark on her crusade—and all for what? To die here with a stranger in the wilderness?

Anuchin wished that there was someone else to blame for her predicament, but it came back to her. Her childish scruples telling her that someone had to rock the boat, for everybody's good. If she had only—

The FSB agent felt the BMW's back tire losing traction, slipping to her right, in the direction of the stream's flow. With a startled gasp, she tried to brace herself, one hand clutching at Cooper's waist, the other clenched beneath the pillion seat. She leaned away from the direction that the bike was sliding, hoped the shift in weight might help, felt Cooper fighting with the handlebars.

Too late.

The motorcycle's tail slid farther to the right and tilted sharply. Anuchin nearly put her left foot down, to brace herself, then realized that she could break her leg that way, maybe her hip, as well. She tried to ride it out, instead, then felt herself begin to fall.

She kicked free of the motorcycle at the last instant, afraid of being trapped beneath it. Water rushed to meet her, and the stream bed paved with stones. She landed on her left side, was submerged, then came up soaked and spluttering, chasing Matt Cooper and the bike downstream.

Moscow

IT WAS AN UNGODLY hour to be awake, much less disturbing those of higher rank, but Colonel Marshak had no time to waste. The word from Levshin in Yakutsk had set his teeth on edge, and if he failed to pass it on immediately, he might wind up shouldering the full responsibility for anything that happened next.

At least this way the burden would be shared.

A servant answered on the first ring, initially resisted waking up the second deputy director of the Ministry of the Interior, but finally absorbed the urgency of Marshak's tone. A moment later, Kliment Gabritschevsky's sleepy voice came on the line.

"What is it, Colonel?" he demanded.

"Sir, I'm sorry to disturb you, but I've had a call from Yakutsk."

"And?"

"It's Rybakov," Marshak said.

"What about him?"

"He's decided that he needs to take charge of the search himself. He's flying out tonight."

"Why don't you stop him?"

Marshak tossed the hot potato back to Gabritschevsky, asking, "How should I do that, sir?"

"Talk to him. Persuade him."

"I believe his mind's made up, sir. He was agitated when he spoke to Major Levshin."

"Agitated? All of us are *agitated,* Colonel. Make him understand that..." Gabritschevsky hesitated, running out of words, a rare condition for a lifelong politician.

"Yes, sir?"

"Never mind. I don't suppose you could arrest him?"

"Not for getting on a private plane, sir. And, in any

case, detaining him would cause more problems than it solves."

No further explanation was required. No mention of the prime minister or other men of influence who owed their present status to the godfather of the Izmaylovskaya Family. If Marshak ordered Rybakov's arrest, there would be hell to pay.

"We have to let him go, then, I suppose," Gabritschevsky said.

"I believe so, sir," Marshak agreed.

"And hope that nothing happens to him in Siberia."

"Yes, sir." Marshak frowned, trying to read the second deputy director's mind.

"It's dangerous out there, I understand," Gabritschevsky said.

"Without question, sir," Marshak agreed.

"A place where almost anything could happen."

"Yes."

"Already, there's been killing."

"That's correct, sir." Marshak thought he saw where this was going, but he couldn't risk a question that would clarify it.

"Thankfully, you have your Spetsnaz personnel in place," Gabritschevsky said.

"Yes, sir."

"Can you trust them to watch out for Rybakov?"

"They follow orders to the letter, sir," Marshak assured him.

"That's a comfort," Gabritschevsky said. "You'll give the necessary orders, then?"

"Of course, sir. Right away."

"And we can all rest easier," the second deputy director said before he cut the link.

Marshak switched off his telephone, laid it aside,

thoughts racing through his head. Unless he was hallucinating, Gabritschevsky had instructed him to execute the godfather of Moscow. Was there any chance of misinterpretation?

No.

Unless, of course, he'd meant Zelinsky's ambush team to serve as bodyguards for Rybakov. But why would Gabritschevsky order that, when Rybakov invariably traveled with an entourage of gunmen on his own payroll?

No, it was clear: the second deputy director of the Ministry of the Interior had passed a death sentence on Rybakov. And what would happen after it was carried out?

"That's not my problem," Marshak muttered to himself, and reached out for the sat phone on his desk.

CHAPTER NINETEEN

M56 Kolyma Highway

The bike slid thirty yards downstream before Bolan wrestled it to a halt, digging in with his boots and hauling back with every ounce of his strength on the handlebars. Even then, the stream's current gripped the rear end, pushing on the panniers and pillion bag, swinging the back wheel farther downstream than the rest.

Bolan was soaked through, shivering, but couldn't rise out of the water, couldn't surrender his tenuous grip on the bike without losing it. Two hundred pounds of flesh and bone against five hundred, give or take, and he was lucky that he'd been able to stop its downstream slide. Unless he got some help, and quickly, it was gone.

He tried to look around for Anuchin, but his neck would only crane so far while lying on his back, wearing a crash helmet. He couldn't spot her, thought of calling out to her for help, but felt the BMW slipping farther, and put his energy into restraining it.

Somewhere amid that wrangling, the motor died.

Flooded, he thought, and they would go no farther on the motorcycle if he couldn't fix it. First, of course, he had to get the damned thing upright, on dry land, which looked to be impossible.

A moment later, Anuchin was beside him, splashing water on his visor as she high-stepped over stones slick-

ened by moss. She passed Bolan and caught the rear end
of the motorcycle, kneeling in the cold water to block its
downstream progress with her body.

Progress.

"Can you hold it there while I get up?" he asked her.

He got a jerky nod in answer, and began the awkward
task of rolling over, struggling to his knees, then to his
feet, without relinquishing his death grip on the handlebars. He felt and saw the left-side mirror buckle, with
the turn signal, and didn't care. Unless they got the bike
ashore and running, mirrors and assorted warning lights
were meaningless.

Between them, straining painfully while fighting to
remain upright themselves, they got the BMW on its
wheels. Next came the task of steering it against the current, over slimy footing, to the eastern shore. It hadn't
looked that far away when they were riding, but it felt
like miles as they propelled the deadweight of the bike
by sheer brute force.

And then, the sloping bank.

While in the water, they'd been fighting current and
the constant tendency to lose their balance on a bed of
algae-coated stones. Emerging from the stream, they had
to battle gravity itself, rolling the heavy bike uphill. Instead of shifting rocks, now it was sliding sandy dirt beneath their boots, the BMW wobbling in their grip with
no support from water underneath it.

Bolan went ahead to pull the BMW. He dug in his
heels and put his broad back into it, tempted to laugh at
the idea of getting sidelined with a hernia when there
were miles to ride and battles still remaining to be fought.
Behind the motorcycle, Anuchin pushed and shoved,
twice slipping to her knees before they got it to the top
and put the kickstand on level ground.

The bike was dripping wet as Bolan settled on the driver's seat, but so was he. A breeze that might have felt warm, otherwise, raised goose bumps on his skin and made him shiver. They would have to change their clothes, if anything was dry enough to make a difference, but first, he had to try the bike.

He flicked the kill switch off, then on, engaged the clutch and pressed the start button.

Nothing.

"Okay, it's flooded," Bolan said.

"Now, what?" Anuchin asked.

"First, we change into dry clothes, if we still have any," he replied. "And then we go to work."

Khanty-Mansi Autonomous Okrug

GRIGORY RYBAKOV HADN'T been strictly honest when he spoke to Major Stephan Levshin of the FSB. First and foremost, he wasn't in Moscow when he answered Levshin's call. Nor did the latest news update from Yakutsk prompt him to fly east and join his soldiers on their hunt.

In fact, he had been airborne when his cell phone rang, with Levshin on the line, two hours out of Moscow in his private Learjet 60 at an altitude of forty thousand feet.

The flight from Moscow to Yakutsk spanned 3,038 miles, with a mandatory fueling stop at Bratsk, in Irkutsk Oblast. He had a good jump on the seven-hour journey by the time Levshin disturbed him, and a helicopter would be waiting for him on arrival in Yakutsk to take Rybakov the rest of the way. His order to Milescu's hunting party called for them to travel on as best they could, until he reached Yakutsk and signaled them to stop. They would supply him with coordinates at that point, for a rendezvous, and Rybakov would take the place of one who'd fallen.

He would lead them on to victory.

But first, he actually had to reach the scene.

His subterfuge had been designed to deal with any interference from the FSB or politicians who were glad to take his money, but who cringed when dirty work proved necessary. In their zeal to guard their own so-called good names, they might attempt to frustrate Rybakov's intentions. That would be a foolish move, but frightened men did foolish things.

Now, they were too late to obstruct him, even if they wanted to. Looked at in one light, Rybakov had saved them from themselves—or from his wrath, if they had dared to stand against him. He was on his way, with half a dozen of his soldiers as an escort, who would also join the hunt if it was feasible.

They couldn't fit into the vehicle Milescu's team had rented, obviously, and they would be useless to him if they found another SUV in Yakutsk, losing days of travel on the Road of Bones before they overtook the front-runners. Rybakov hoped, instead, to leave them with the helicopter, if it had sufficient fuel, to scout the road and help him find his targets.

Leaving Rybakov himself to make the kill.

All wishful thinking, for the moment, when he knew that many things could intervene. Colonel Marshak had put a Spetsnaz team in play, which might locate the targets first. Milescu and his men might overtake them before Rybakov landed at Yakutsk. It was even possible that the prey would crash their motorcycle, or be killed and eaten by the region's legendary bears.

The one outcome that Rybakov refused to contemplate

was their escape. He willed it not to happen, and in his world, as the godfather of Moscow, wishes did come true.

A wish of death, in this case, powered by his will alone.

M56 Kolyma Highway

THEY GOT LUCKY with the spare clothes, found them dry inside the latched panniers, and separated for a quick change with a nod toward modesty. When both of them were dry and dressed, still shivering, they cleaned and dried their several weapons, magazines included, to be sure that they would operate at need.

That done, Bolan began trying to resurrect the BMW.

First step: remove the spark plugs. In the motorcycle's tool kit, Bolan found the spark plug wrench and went to work, using it cautiously, avoiding damage to the plugs as he turned each one counterclockwise and removed it. All of them were wet, and he let Anuchin clean and dry them, taking special care with the electrodes, while he did his best to dry the sockets on the spark plug cables.

Next, Bolan turned off the fuel line and the choke that fed the carburetor. Anuchin helped him tilt the BMW toward the carburetor's side, draining a mixture of gasoline and water from the overflow tubes. After a quick wipe with the wet shirt he'd removed to clear the carburetor and adjacent bits of excess moisture, Bolan mounted up and gave the kick-starter a dozen kicks to dry out the compression cylinder.

All good, so far.

Before replacing the spark plugs in their sockets, Bolan found the gapping tool and tested each in turn, to satisfy himself that they would spark correctly. Each one had a snug fit, but he pushed the tool between electrodes several times, as recommended in the manual, to guarantee the proper spacing. That done, he replaced the plugs, attached their cables and was ready for another test.

"What if it doesn't work?" Anuchin asked, sounding anxious.

"Then I guess we're walking," Bolan answered. "I don't have the tools for stripping down the engine, even if I was a BMW-certified mechanic, which, you understand, I'm not."

"And if we're walking, then we're dead," she said.

"Not necessarily," Bolan replied, although he couldn't really see survival in their future if the motorcycle failed them now.

"All right, then. Try it," she encouraged him.

Mounted again, he left the fuel and choke turned off, held the hot-start button down and dropped his weight onto the kick-starter. The engine fired, and Bolan quickly turned the gas back on, feeding the carburetor while he twisted the accelerator, revving it. The engine's throat rumbled, music to his ears.

Anuchin uttered a prayer in Russian.

"Ready to go?" he asked.

"Ready."

Bolan pulled on his helmet, watching his companion do the same, then waited while she climbed aboard behind him. They'd lost precious time, maybe too much, but they were mobile once again, and Bolan meant to give their enemies a fair run for their money.

Quitting wasn't in his playbook. When the Executioner committed to a game, he finished it.

And God help anyone who stood between him and his goal.

Oymyakonsky District

CAPTAIN ZELINSKY felt his sat phone vibrate on his belt beneath the poncho that protected him from drizzling rain, and scowled while reaching in to answer it. At this point in his mission, it could only be bad news.

And worst of all, the word that his intended targets had been overtaken by another team, that he wouldn't be needed to complete the job.

Because no one of lesser rank would call him there, Zelinsky answered formally. *"Zdravstvujte!"*

"Captain." Stephan Levshin's voice. "I'm afraid I have bad news."

Of course.

"Yes, Major?"

"We've been informed that Grigory Rybakov plans to join his men in the field, headed your way. You know him?"

"By reputation, of course, sir."

"Which, essentially, is accurate," Levshin said. "Now, unfortunately, he injects himself into a situation that can only be made worse by his involvement."

That was disingenuous, Zelinsky realized. If not for Rybakov's involvement with the government, there would have been no hunt, no targets to be stalked along the Road of Bones. Grigory Rybakov, and others like him, were a large part of the reason Russia's government was so corrupt and inefficient—a kleptocracy, of sorts, with thieves and grafters in control.

Zelinsky harbored no illusions concerning that political reality, harbored no dream of changing things. He simply meant to do the best he could for himself, within the system that existed.

And so, he asked, "What should we do, sir?"

"We were unable to dissuade Rybakov from his plan," Levshin said. "In fact, it turns out that he left Moscow before telling anyone of his plan. He will be joining his men on the highway within a matter of hours."

"And then?" Zelinsky wasn't letting Levshin off the hook. He'd follow orders, but required them to be stated for the record.

"We realize the situation that you face is perilous," Levshin said. "Rybakov assumes all risk for his behavior in this matter. If some evil should befall him, well, it might be for the best, when all is said and done."

"No repercussions, then?" Zelinsky asked, speaking as plainly as he dared.

"We all have every confidence that you will rise to the occasion in this difficult circumstance," Levshin answered. "Understood, Captain?"

"Perfectly, Major."

"Good luck, then."

The line went dead. Zelinsky smiled, accepting the extension of his mission without question. He would have to brief Galitzin and Petrov, but it was best that they shouldn't be burdened with the full details. Enough for them to know that new targets had been appended to the first pair. If, in fact, it came to that.

There was a decent possibility that Rybakov would never reach them. His team was already behind the fugitives, and they would lose more time waiting for him to join them on the road. Another possibility: if they caught up with the two runners they were tracking, Rybakov and company might join those who'd been killed already.

If the pair could take down Spetsnaz troopers in a helicopter gunship, why should they be cowed by two-bit gangsters from Moscow?

But Zelinsky hoped that Rybakov *would* make it. He

enjoyed a challenge, and was looking forward to the credit he'd receive from solving one more problem for the FSB. Why not be happy with a golden opportunity?

Why not, indeed.

M56 Kolyma Highway

"WHY IS HE COMING out to join us?" Izvolsky asked.

"He doesn't trust us, obviously," Stolypin said, sprawled beside him in the backseat of the Lada Niva SUV.

"It isn't that, so much," Milescu told them.

"What, then?" Ryumin asked.

"He likes the action sometimes," Milescu replied. "You know that. And these two that we're hunting, they've embarrassed him. He wants to deal with them himself."

"Why is he more embarrassed now than when he sent us in the first place?" Stolypin asked with a note of challenge in his voice.

"Because it's gone on too long," Milescu said. "The first team lost them in Yakutsk, and we've been playing catch-up ever since. It looks bad for the Family."

"So, all our fault," Izvolsky said, half sneering.

"Did I say that?" Milescu asked.

"It comes down to the same thing," Izvolsky said. "Daddy comes to help his bumbling little children."

"If you see yourself that way," Milescu said, "feel free to tell him when he joins us."

"Don't go putting words into my mouth," Izvolsky said.

"How many others is he bringing?" Stolypin asked.

"I have no idea," Milescu answered truthfully.

His talk with Boris Struve had been abbreviated, short on details. Struve had told him their boss was coming to take charge, that he would fly from Yakutsk, meet them somewhere on the highway. And beyond that, nothing.

Having Rybakov preempt him was one thing, but if they were all replaced with other soldiers, it could be the kiss of death. Milescu wouldn't know how bad their situation really was until the boss arrived.

By which time it could be too late for him to save himself.

Strangely, he felt relaxed. There was no point in worrying about whatever happened next. If Rybakov intended to dispose of them, they were as good as dead.

The only way to salvage it, Milescu knew, was to locate and kill the fugitives before Rybakov met their team. They'd been delayed twice now, at the stockade and for a shorter time dealing with brother Leon, but the latest river and its fallen bridge were now behind them. They were still in hot pursuit.

Too late?

And how could Rybakov advance them, simply by assuming command of the team? Perhaps, if they could use the helicopter that was bearing him from Yakutsk...but the soldiers who had tried that didn't fare so well.

Press on, Milescu thought, and see what happens.

If it meant the end for all of them, by one means or another, he wouldn't go down without a fight.

IT WAS GOOD to be rolling again. The setback hadn't shaken Bolan's confidence, but it had reminded him—as if he needed the reminder—that another single slipup on the way to Magadan could be their last. The end of everything for both of them.

If they were caught, he'd likely have the easy out. Die fighting, as he'd always pictured it, against one adversary or another. He knew Anuchin would resist, as well, but their pursuers had a greater stake in grilling her before she died, learning how much she'd spilled already, and to whom.

So, what to do if they were cornered and it had a hopeless feel about it? Bolan knew he had it in him to dispatch a mercy round—had done it more than once, in fact, when friends were suffering with no hope of release—but it was never easy. Never any kind of first resort.

And then again, he might not have the option. Taken by surprise, an ambush or another flying gunship, something of that sort, he could be down and out before he even knew that battle had been joined.

They should have talked about it, but it wasn't something that you dropped into the average conversation, most particularly not with someone who'd already been kidnapped and tortured recently. *Hey, by the way, if things look bad, should I just go ahead and kill you?*

No.

It was the kind of moment people recognized, but couldn't quite anticipate. Something in human nature clung to hope with the tenacity of ants climbing a drainpipe in the rain. Hope springs eternal and all that, until it finally runs out.

Which hadn't happened yet.

The sat phone shivered under Bolan's coat. He brought the BMW to a standstill, pulled his helmet off, told Anuchin, "Someone's calling. This won't take a minute."

"Striker," Hal Brognola said, "there's something that you need to know, right now."

CHAPTER TWENTY

"I'm listening," Bolan said.

"Okay," Brognola said. "You know we're tracking you by satellite, as feasible."

"You mentioned that," Bolan replied. The silent message of his words: *Get to the freaking point.*

"All right. Sometimes we catch a break and get an eyeball on your opposition while we're at it," Brognola went on.

"That's handy," Bolan said.

"In this case, absolutely. You seem to have a team of hunters coming on behind you. No surprise, I guess. They got sidetracked awhile ago, some dustup with the locals, but they're making up for it."

"What kind of dustup with the locals?" Sudden urgency appeared in Bolan's tone.

"I couldn't give you the specifics," Brognola replied. "Looks like they hit some kind of residential compound, say a hundred-some-odd miles behind you. Then they hit a trucker, farther down the road."

"Survivors?"

"None apparent. Other than the shooters, that would be."

A curse from Bolan startled the big Fed. The warrior rarely used profanity in conversation. It was rare enough to be remarkable, in fact.

"Someone you knew?"

"It was," Bolan answered. "They were."

"Sorry." What else was there to say?

"Nothing you could've done about it," Bolan told him. "Nothing anybody could."

"I guess not. Anyway, that isn't why I called. There's something else. Ahead of you."

"Go on," Bolan instructed.

"Sixty miles or so downrange, before you hit the next town, Tomtor, there's an ambush waiting for you. Three men that we're sure of. Soldiers from the look of them, or maybe mercenaries. Anyway, in uniform and armed. They've got the road staked out."

There was a momentary silence on the other end, halfway around the world. Then Bolan said, "Okay. I appreciate the heads-up."

"Christ, if there was anything that I could do—"

"There isn't," Bolan said, letting the big Fed off the hook. "We'll deal with it."

"Okay. Your ride's in place and waiting when you get there. *Kansas City,* home and dry."

"Be looking forward to it," Bolan told him. "Thanks again for checking out the bird's-eye view."

"It isn't much, I know."

"Don't sell it short," Bolan replied. "I need to go now."

"Right. So long."

Brognola cut the link, cursing himself. He'd nearly said, "You're not alone in this," and what kind of bullshit was that? As he set the phone aside, he thought he knew how a spectator had to feel at the execution of an innocent man.

Bolan had always put himself in harm's way for the sake of others. Long before Brognola ever heard his name or met him in the flesh, it was the pattern of the warrior's life. But knowing it and *watching* it, damn right, were very different things.

Time for another call, this one to Stony Man. Brognola used his private line, bypassed the Justice switchboard, and got Aaron Kurtzman on the fourth short ring.

"Message delivered," he informed the computer wizard.

"All you could do," Kurtzman replied.

"Yeah, I keep hearing that," Brognola said. "It still doesn't help."

"We'll keep the eyes open," Kurtzman said. "Pass on anything we see."

"Regardless of the time."

"Sure thing."

How long would it take Bolan and his passenger to travel sixty miles? What would they do, now that they knew a trap was waiting for them on the highway? Hell, what *could* they do but forge ahead, when there was no alternative route?

Do or die. The same game Bolan always played.

And this time, Brognola was in the bleachers, waiting with his teeth clenched for the final gun to sound.

M56 Kolyma Highway

"AN AMBUSH," Anuchin said when he had briefed her on the news. "Soldiers."

"Men in uniform, at least," Bolan replied.

"Internal troops," she said. "Most likely Spetsnaz. Like the others in the helicopter."

"But only three," Bolan reminded her.

"Of course. I should feel great relief."

Sarcasm didn't faze him. She had every right to worry, but he couldn't let the warning paralyze her.

"We can deal with it," said Bolan.

"Yes, we can." She didn't sound convinced. "I'm sorry about Leon and the rest," she added.

Bolan nodded. He hadn't let it go, and never would, but he couldn't afford to focus on the friendly dead today. Their pain and trouble was behind them. His, and Anuchin's, had no end in sight.

"All right," she said. "What shall we do, then?"

"Shooters coming up behind us," Bolan said, "number unknown. Nothing back there to help us, even if we turn around and take them out. The only thing we *can* do is go on."

"Into the ambush."

"No. I didn't say that."

"What, then? If they watch the road, we must confront them," Anuchin said.

"'Confront' means stand in front of," Bolan answered. "As in face-to-face. I don't see that succeeding for us, in the circumstances."

"We can't fly and land behind them," she advised him.

"No. But we've got fifty-something miles before we need to make a move," Bolan replied. "I'll want to check out the terrain and see what we can make of it. Surprises have been known to backfire."

"You seem confident," Anuchin said.

He shrugged. "I never won a fight by thinking that I'd lose."

"You are an optimist," she said.

"I never looked at it that way," Bolan replied.

In school, he'd read *The Devil's Dictionary,* penned by Ambrose Bierce decades before the Executioner was born. It was satirical, but struck close to the mark. Bierce had called optimism an intellectual disorder, yielding to no treatment but death. An optimist he had defined as one who thought that black is white.

That wasn't Bolan. Wasn't even close.

He'd seen the worst that people did to one another, understood that selfishness was the default position for humanity, but the exceptions kept him battling on. If not for them, what was the point?

A soldier had to fight *for* something if he wanted to maintain at least a vestige of his soul. Without a cause of some kind, an ideal, it all came down to killing for the hell of it.

"You think we have a chance," Anuchin said, amending her last observation.

"A fair one, at least," Bolan said. "But we'll have to get bloody."

"No problem," she answered. "We already are."

Khabarovsk Krai

GRIGORY RYBAKOV was making good time. There'd been a tailwind for his flight from Moscow to Yakutsk, shaving the better part of thirty minutes from his journey, though he didn't claim to understand the physics of it. The helicopter had been waiting for him, a Sikorsky X2, the compound model with coaxial rotors that had exceeded 250 miles per hour during recent tests.

That was extreme, of course. This day, the X2 was flying Rybakov eastward at a mere 220 miles per hour, eating up the landscape as its GPS monitor homed on Nikolay Milescu's sat phone. His soldiers were somewhere behind him, traveling in a slower Mil Mi-14 helicopter, code-named "Haze" by NATO. They would catch up to their boss eventually, but this day Rybakov wanted to fly fast, and in style.

Milescu was expecting him, not pleased at being relieved of command, but wise enough to keep a civil tongue in his head. Rybakov demanded respect at all times. There was a heavy price to pay for those who challenged or insulted him.

The good news: most such foolish men would only pay it once.

It had to have seemed peculiar for Rybakov to leave the comfort and security of Moscow in pursuit of an informer and her bodyguard. In Russian terms, he was shooting sparrows with a cannon. But there were some things a man of respect had to do for himself, and that included settling scores with anyone who seriously threatened him.

And how serious was the threat posed by an FSB sergeant with stories to tell? In part, the answer to that question would depend on how much evidence she had to document her accusations. Generally speaking, though, Rybakov treated every threat as serious and dealt with each in turn aggressively.

For such a stunt as this, the penalty was death, as slow or swift as circumstances might require.

He didn't ask the pilot, seated straight in front of him, how much time remained on their flight. The chopper's LHT-801 turboshaft engine, packed into the slim fuselage behind him, was doing its best, and the bonus he'd offered the pilot ensured that the man did likewise. They would land as soon as possible, and fretting over it wouldn't advance the schedule one iota.

Ten minutes later, Rybakov heard and felt a change in the aircraft's speed. The pilot's voice was in his ears a moment later, saying, "Sir, we have your party just ahead. Two miles."

A minute or less to arrival. Rybakov smiled and willed

himself to relax. The handoff of command over the hunting party would be easily accomplished, and they would proceed to find his enemies, destroy them as he had so many others in the past.

No one escaped the godfather of the Izmaylovskaya clan.

"Prepare for landing," the pilot said, not that Rybakov had anything to do.

The helicopter circled once above a Lada Niva SUV, then descended in a cloud of dust whipped by its rotors. Rybakov kept the smile fixed firmly on his face and waited for the jolt of contact that would tell him he'd arrived, alive and in one piece.

Oymyakonsky District

HOW MUCH LONGER? Captain Zelinsky checked his watch, but knew the exercise was futile. He couldn't predict the targets' rate of speed, much less predict what obstacles might interrupt their journey to the point where he planned to annihilate them.

All in vain, until he saw them coming down the road and had them in his gunsights.

He resisted the impulse to check on Petrov and Galitzin once again. It would accomplish nothing more than to irritate them, impugning their ability to stay alert. Zelinsky had selected them specifically for their professionalism, and he had to trust them now.

When there were targets to be fired on, both would do their jobs with the efficiency he'd witnessed time and time again. Neither had failed him in the past, nor would they on the present mission.

He had placed Galitzin farthest forward, naturally, since his Saiga-12 had the shortest range among their several weapons. On Zelinsky's order, Galitzin would lay down a blizzard of buckshot in rapid fire, stopping the cycle and possibly killing its passengers outright. That wouldn't stop Zelinsky and Petrov from firing, however. Both would empty half a magazine or more into the fallen fugitives, to make sure both were well and truly dead. Zelinsky thought he might unload a high-explosive round from his grenade launcher, as well, just to be doubly certain.

It would be messy, but very effective. Zelinsky's trademark.

And after that?

He still might have to deal with Grigory Rybakov's gangsters, assuming they showed up in time. Zelinsky didn't plan to sit around and wait for them when there was still a risk of meeting the Militsiya. He had no way of knowing what instructions had been issued to protect his team, if any, and a firefight with police would not sit well with Stephan Levshin and the FSB.

But if the Moscow gangsters did turn up, Zelinsky and his men would deal with them. Galitzin seemed enthusiastic at the prospect, mentioning a friend of his who'd been addicted to cocaine and heroin, while Petrov took it all in stride. If anything had power to disturb the older man, Zelinsky hadn't seen it happen yet.

Zelinsky shifted his position slowly, cautiously, maintaining discipline despite the fact that there was no one in the neighborhood to see him, other than his two compatriots. Such painstaking precautions had become an ingrained part of him, through training and experience on battlefields where any slipup could mean sudden death— or worse, a slow and agonizing end in hostile hands.

Zelinsky was professional, and always would be. Even

if his orders did include killing the godfather of Moscow on a lonely highway in the middle of Siberia.

Another day, another challenge.

M56 Kolyma Highway

THE ROAD NEVER RAN straight for very long, and Bolan was relieved to find it snaking through another thickly wooded area as they approached the ambush site Brognola's satellite and Stony Man's tech crew had spotted for them. With a mile and change to go, he started looking for someplace to stash the bike off-road, while they proceeded by a shorter route on foot.

Spetsnaz was good, no doubt about it. In Russia's military universe, they were equivalent to U.S. Army Special Forces, Navy SEALs and the FBI's Hostage Rescue Team, all rolled up into one. Aside from their excellent training, when they were unleashed in the field, Spetsnaz troops enjoyed a freedom of action, unfettered by rules, that was foreign to troops in the States—and, indeed, to Western armies overall.

Bottom line: Spetsnaz fought dirty. And it wasn't only black-ops dirty on some foreign battlefield, where anything they did was classified beyond top secret. The outfit's *Vympel* unit—translated as "pennant"—had evolved from a Cold War-era KGB assassination squad, on par with the historic SMERSH. Its members were repeatedly accused of various atrocities in Chechnya, but none had ever gone to trial, as far as Bolan knew. Back home in Moscow, Spetsnaz had been sent to deal with the Islamic terrorists who seized the Nord-Ost theater in 2002. Their solution had killed thirty-odd gunmen, and four times that many unarmed civilians.

So Bolan expected some tough opposition, but he

wasn't worried, per se. Some wise man whose name he'd forgotten once said that worry was interest paid on disaster before the bill came due. Bolan preferred to plan, prepare and let his adversaries do the sweating while he worked on target acquisition for a kill.

Like now.

He found the bike stash he was looking for about three-quarters of a mile west of the ambush site. It was a gully, likely cut by flash floods sometime in the recent past, now choked with weeds. A clear sky overhead told Bolan that there wouldn't be another flood to steal his ride before he'd dealt with whoever was waiting up ahead.

Or they had dealt with him.

Anuchin dismounted before Bolan nosed their ride into the gully, feeling weeds and brambles plucking at his clothes, scraping the BMW's sides. He didn't care about the paint job, only that the motorcycle was concealed from prying eyes as they trekked overland to find the men who lay in wait for them.

It had occurred to Bolan that the ambush might be meant for someone else—another bandit gang lying in wait for anyone who came along, perhaps—but he'd rejected the idea. It trusted too much to coincidence.

"Ready?" he asked when he was satisfied with his concealment of the bike.

"Ready," Anuchin said, almost sounding like she meant it.

CAPTAIN ZELINSKY stubbornly refused to check his watch again. He wasted no time speculating on the countless mishaps, obstacles and incidents that could delay a pair of travelers on the Kolyma Highway. Those he waited for would either come, or they wouldn't. If dusk fell with no sign of them, he and his men all had night-vision gear at hand to keep up their surveillance.

They would wait, however long it took, until their targets were eliminated or word came from Stephan Levshin the runners had been intercepted by some other means. If that occurred, there still remained the question of Grigory Rybakov, whether they ought to wait for him, or pack their gear and double back to Tomtor. Zelinsky's reputation would remain untarnished, either way, but he admitted to himself that he would feel a certain disappointment if they turned and left without a shot fired in the field.

The blast surprised him, actually made Zelinsky jump, a small embarrassment forgotten instantly as his mind recognized the sound and shock wave of an antipersonnel grenade. Zelinsky saw the puff of smoke and dust rise from the point of detonation, near enough to where he'd placed Galitzin that his hand was gliding toward his two-way radio before he caught himself and froze.

He obviously didn't need to warn Galitzin or Petrov of danger now, and if Galitzin had been struck by the shrapnel from the blast, it was beyond Zelinsky's power to help him. He could only scan the roadside trees for moving targets and respond as soon as one appeared.

Remaining concealed, Zelinsky scanned the highway and its flanking woods over the sights of his Kalashnikov, trusting the enemy to show himself in time. His men were still observing good fire discipline, at least in Petrov's case. Zelinsky couldn't say for sure about Galitzin without checking in by radio. And he wasn't about to give himself away.

Not when the enemy had come this close, unseen.

It troubled him, that bit, with its suggestion of forewarning. He couldn't believe the fugitives had stopped each mile along their way to scout for enemies. If so, it would have taken months for them to drive the thousand miles from Nizhny Bestyakh to Magadan. Zelinsky hadn't heard their motorcycle, much less seen it, so they had to have stopped a mile or more away, proceeding through the woods on foot.

Or had they?

It occurred to him that he and his two soldiers might be facing someone else. But who? Grigory Rybakov? More traitors from inside the FSB?

Before Zelinsky had a chance to think it through, another blast echoed along the Road of Bones, this one erupting from his left, closer to his position. Petrov opened fire this time, and instantly Galitzin joined him, proving he was still alive, at least.

Then other guns were firing, and there was no time for strategy. It came down to survival, and an urge to kill the enemy before they found Zelinsky and eliminated him.

CHAPTER TWENTY-ONE

The Spetsnaz troops were good, as expected. They had concealed themselves so well that it took Bolan ten minutes to spot the first one, time that had to have left Anuchin's nerves strained to the snapping point as she lay back and waited for him to begin the action. Even then, after he'd worked out where the first shooter was hiding, Bolan couldn't reach him without crossing the highway on foot, couldn't signal Anuchin to warn her, because they had no walkie-talkies.

So, he'd had a choice to make: spray the sniper's position with autofire from his AKS-74U, thereby giving his own position away to the others, or take his chances with a frag grenade. Unfortunately, where the Russian soldier lay concealed, Bolan's grenade would either have to bounce precisely off the highway's berm and roll into his nest, or drop down pinball-style through the sheltering branches of a tall Siberian pine.

Not great choices.

He'd picked the grenade and the tree, lobbed it high and long across the Road of Bones, counting the seconds until detonation in his head. The high-explosive egg went in all right, then hit a branch some sixty feet above ground level, wobbled on it for a precious second and a half, then plummeted to detonate an estimated twenty feet above the target.

That was close enough to wound or kill, but Bolan

thought the pine's trunk might have shielded his intended mark from some of the shrapnel, at least. No time to wait and check it, either, as another member of the ambush team cut loose with automatic fire, raking the south side of the road.

That was the wrong side, as it happened, for the Executioner, but he'd sent Anuchin over there—a pincers movement—and he hoped that she would keep her head well down below the Spetsnaz soldier's probing fire.

Bolan refrained from firing, primed a second frag grenade instead and pitched it overhand toward the second shooter's position. Again, the soldier had taken good advantage of the landscape and natural cover, protecting his flanks with stout trees and boulders. Bolan couldn't drop the grenade in his lap, but he could make some noise and obscure the soldier's field of vision long enough to make a move.

Mission accomplished as the blast threw up a cloud of smoke, soil and evergreen needles, obscuring the second shooter's field of fire. Bolan was on his feet and moving in an instant, not directly toward the enemy, but gaining ground with every stride, while keeping trees between the two of them for cover.

Vital cover, as it happened, when the third soldier cut loose with automatic fire from farther back and higher up the sloping ground on Anuchin's side. He'd spotted Bolan racing through the woods, but missed him with the first two bursts from his Kalashnikov.

Bolan pitched headlong onto the forest floor and started crawling, still in motion as the third soldier corrected his initial aim and put the next burst closer. It was still too high, but he was obviously skilled and bent on finishing the job as quickly as he could.

Same here, Bolan thought, knowing it was time that Anuchin joined the killing game.

In spite of everything, she'd kept her head and hadn't fired her SMG, still waiting for the first rounds out of Bolan's weapon that would signal her to do her part. He fired that signal now, a 3-round burst with little hope of injuring the sniper who was tracking him.

But it was good enough. Across the road, another automatic weapon chimed into the fight, dividing the attention of their enemies while Bolan did his best to stay alive.

ZELINSKY WASTED NO BREATH cursing when his first rounds missed the moving target in the woods. He absorbed the information that his enemies had managed to anticipate the trap—or that his team had been betrayed somehow—and then dismissed it for the moment.

He was fighting for his reputation and his life.

Investigation and revenge could wait.

The first shock of surprise might have unnerved a lesser soldier, but Zelinsky managed to recover almost instantly. Likewise, his failure to bring down the runner with his first rounds didn't faze him. Spetsnaz studies showed that several hundred rounds were wasted for each one that found its mark in combat, so he wasn't doing badly.

Yet.

Zelinsky saw the runner drop, then lost him in the undergrowth. It was a gamble, guessing whether he would move backward or forward, but Zelinsky didn't think that he was one to simply hide and hope the fight would pass him by.

Forward or back?

Zelinsky didn't know his man, but thought he would

advance. What did he have to lose, except his life? And turning back meant certain death, with all the hunters coming on behind him.

Having made his choice, Zelinsky sighted quickly with his 40 mm launcher and fired a VOG-25 fragmentation grenade across the highway and into the trees. It struck a spruce's trunk and detonated on impact, spewing razor-edged shrapnel with a twenty-foot kill radius, but Zelinsky knew most of those projectiles would be spent on trees and undergrowth. Still, he needed only two or three to find their mark in order for his enemy to be disabled, maybe killed.

Watching for movement over there, Zelinsky missed the entry of a new combatant to the contest. When it came, the higher pitch of automatic fire from a 9 mm weapon told him that a shooter had approached on his side of the highway and had closed to fighting range. Zelinsky couldn't tell the weapon's model, and it made no difference. He and Petrov had better range and stopping power with their twin Kalashnikovs—but only if they scored a hit.

Zelinsky had expected two targets and an easy kill. Now, instead, he had combatants carrying the fight to him on foot, concealed, and he was still uncertain that he'd stopped the first with his grenade.

Ten second later, as he turned to track the submachine gun's sound, that doubt resolved itself into a certainty. A burst of AK fire peppered the trees above Zelinsky's head, spraying his scalp with shards of wood and bark. He ducked, unable to contain the curse this time, his anger barely mollified by hearing Petrov's shotgun roar.

Both of his men were still alive and ready to defend themselves. Now, it remained to see how long they would stay that way, whether they could defeat an unseen enemy, or if they'd leave their flesh to fertilize the Road of Bones.

GRIGORY RYBAKOV DIDN'T shake hands with Nikolay Milescu or the other members of his team. He'd come to take command, not fraternize with underlings. He made no pretense of equality, which would demean him, even while insulting their intelligence.

"You made good time," Milescu said, stating the obvious.

"And we have none to waste," Rybakov replied. "You're ready to proceed?"

"Yes, sir!"

"Let's go, then," Rybakov commanded. "I will ride in front."

Milescu naturally raised no protest over his demotion from the shotgun seat to riding in the back. If ordered to, he'd run beside the Lada Niva and pretend to like it, showing his godfather all due respect. It was a fact of life, well understood between them, uncontested.

By the time his door was shut, the Niva's engine rumbling, Rybakov's helicopter was airborne and hurtling eastward, following the highway in search of prey. He had issued orders before they landed, made sure that the chopper would scout ahead of them, reporting back by radio.

He had considered staying with the aircraft, but decided it was better if he joined the ground team, took command of it and led the hunt that way. His soldiers in the helicopter had instructions not to kill the fugitives if they could possibly avoid it, but to halt their progress until Rybakov could reach the scene and take charge of the enemy himself.

It would be a fitting resolution to the embarrassment

he'd suffered, thanks to negligence among his so-called allies with the FSB and in the government, but Rybakov wouldn't be satisfied with wiping out two gnats who had annoyed him. Someone was responsible for letting matters go this far, and when he finished with them, there would be more vacancies in Moscow.

Anyone who thought they could play fast and loose with Rybakov, or take his bribes for granted, was a suicidal fool.

The road was rougher than he had imagined, slower traveling, but it was too late now to reconsider his decision, call the helicopter back. Rybakov hated seeming indecisive, had a reputation for examining tough situations and reacting swiftly. Always coming out on top. The day he lost that edge would be the day that he lost everything.

The day he died.

Rybakov cleared his mind, deciding that he ought to treat the hunt as a vacation—no, as a safari. Soon enough, he would be back in Moscow, dealing with the daily drudgery of business, measuring his enemies for coffins. This experience reminded him of younger days, although he'd never been a country boy.

The quest was everything, in life and business, as in hunting. When enthusiasm failed, the man was on his way to obsolescence. And in Rybakov's profession, that meant being on the fast track to extinction.

Now, he had a chance to teach his underlings and all the upstarts of the world a lesson they wouldn't forget.

School was in session.

The professor was prepared to educate.

TATYANA ANUCHIN TRIED to be silent as she scuttled through the woods, slipping and sliding on a layer of fallen leaves and pine needles. It wasn't easy, but the gunfire crackling along the highway below her helped cover any noise she made.

She had already joined the fight, as planned. Waiting for Cooper's signal—gunfire from the hillside opposite, not the grenades he'd planned to use at first—she had quickly discovered one potentially fatal disadvantage in her choice of weapons.

It wasn't the Bizon SMG's power that worried her. She was close enough to hit her targets with its 9 mm Parabellum rounds, and firing downhill helped, as well. It was the weapon's *sound* that had betrayed her. Cooper and two of the three Spetsnaz troopers were using Kalashnikov rifles, which made the same rattletrap commotion regardless of caliber, while the fourth man was armed with a 12-gauge shotgun. Her weapon had a higher pitch, which helped her adversaries find her by its sound alone.

Too late to switch, she thought, unless I kill one of these bastards and take his.

It would be easier if she could hate them. They'd been sent to execute her, and she was angry and would kill them if she could, but hatred didn't factor into it. Anuchin knew that they were soldiers following the orders they received, as she had done for years before deciding she had to take a stand for honesty. It seemed ridiculous, now that she thought of it, but there could be no turning back.

The shotgunner was nearby, blasting holes in shrubbery where Anuchin had been crouching when she fired her first short bursts to join the fight. He'd obviously lost her, but it wouldn't take him long to reacquire his target, once she fired again.

The next burst had to count. It had to put him down.

His gun was almost certainly a Saiga-12, which had a maximum capacity of thirty rounds if using a drum magazine. The drums were awkward, bulky, rarely used, in fact, suggesting that her enemy was likely loading 8- or 10-round detachable box magazines. Either way, one hit from the Saiga would disembowel her, maybe shatter a limb, but she had to eliminate him if she meant to proceed.

The dull *pop* of a grenade launcher, farther ahead and on her own side of the road, told Anuchin where the third man was. To reach him, she had to first eliminate his friend.

She was dangerously close now, near enough to see dead leaves raised by the Saiga's muzzle-blasts. Her motorcycle helmet helped to shield her ears from the percussive noise, but it still had an impact on her nerves.

One blast to gut her would leave her dying on the ground, helpless, while he came to stand above her, leveling the shotgun at her screaming face.

Anuchin chose her moment, waited for the Spetsnaz trooper to change magazines, then hosed him with her Bizon, burning half a magazine to finish him. Before the last bright brass touched down, she was already scrambling higher up the hillside, knowing that the closer rifleman would certainly react.

A second later, she heard AK fire flaying the trees below her, chipping bark and raising foot-high spurts of leaf mold, missing her. She almost cackled with relief, but knew it would be foolish hubris.

One man down, and one to go for her part of the fight. Unless the second bastard killed her first.

ZELINSKY HEARD Galitzin die. He didn't witness it, since he was searching for a target on the far side of the highway, and the forest would have screened his view in any case. He recognized the submachine gun's sound, however, and the cry of pain Galitzin uttered as the bullets ripped into his flesh. He knew that the wounds were mortal, from that sound.

He spun and raked the closer hillside with his AK-103, not really thinking he could score a hit so easily. There were such things as lucky shots, but counting on them was an idiotic approach.

Still, he had ample ammunition, and he had to try.

Between the runners they'd been waiting for, Zelinsky hoped it was the man who'd killed Galitzin. Dead was dead, but he imagined Konstantin's embarrassment, if he was looking up from hell and saw that he'd been finished by a woman. How he'd be swearing now!

Zelinsky heard Kalashnikovs exchanging fire across the highway, but he left Petrov to handle it alone. The enemy on his side of the road was closer, obviously dangerous and should be coming for him any moment now.

His mind's eye framed a photo of the woman they were tracking, no face for the man who'd been escorting her. No matter. Anyone approaching through the forest was his enemy and would be killed on sight, without a heartbeat's hesitation. Then, if Petrov hadn't stopped the other one…

If the stalker was approaching, he—or she—had to be somewhere between the gully where Galitzin died and Zelinsky's position. There were limits to how far off-track his enemy could wander, counting on a submachine gun for the kill. Too far upslope, and he'd be out of range, with trees obstructing any field of fire. Too close, and the approach would be so obvious Zelinsky couldn't miss.

The compromise left ample room for movement, most of it obscured by woods and undergrowth, but that didn't mean that Zelinsky was helpless, forced to simply sit and wait for an assault. Moving was perilous, but he could still make life more difficult for his intended executioner—and maybe score a hit while he was at it.

Smiling in anticipation of the showdown, Zelinsky reloaded his GP-25 launcher. This time, he chose a VOG-25P round, a "bouncing" grenade equipped with a small impact charge in its nose, which caused the grenade to leap upward from three to six feet before detonation, creating an air-burst for greater effect.

A little something to surprise his crafty enemy.

Without a target visible, he calculated roughly where the hunter ought to be, if advancing by the path of least resistance. The captain aimed, squeezed off and sent the 40 mm package lofting through the trees. He heard the first explosion, like a muffled pistol shot, immediately followed by a louder blast, the whickering of airborne shrapnel.

Hunkered down, he waited for a scream.

BOLAN WAS SHIELDED from the first grenade blast by a line of Siberian fir trees, their trunks and branches absorbing the shards meant for him. The next blast, when it came, was on the far side of the highway, following a burst from Anuchin's SMG and strangled cries of pain that told him she had found her mark.

The Executioner pushed on, trusting the lady to look out for number one. He could only handle his side of the fight, and she had known that, going in.

Some thirty yards in front of him, an AK stuttered, spitting bullets toward the far side of the highway, seeking Anuchin over there. Bolan took full advantage of the moment, sprinting toward the sound of automatic fire, boots digging in for traction on the littered slope.

He'd covered half the distance when his adversary got his mind back in the game and swung around to cover

Bolan, triggering a burst that might have nailed him if the Executioner had been a second slower. As it was, he saw the move coming and let the forest floor slide out from underneath him, thumping down on layers of leaves and needles piled up over decades.

Bolan slithered twenty feet downslope before his boot soles came to rest against the rough bark of a Russian larch that stopped his slide. By then, the big American was already firing, locked on to the soldier who'd half risen from his hiding place, stitching a line of spouting holes across his chest. The guy went over backward, finger frozen on his AK's trigger as he fell, his bullets clipping limbs that fell around and over him, a green and aromatic shroud.

Two guns accounted for, and Brognola had told him that the ambush party was a trio. Anuchin was across the highway, with the third man, and to help her—if he *could* help—Bolan had to show himself.

There was no telling where the final shooter was, exactly. Bolan hadn't spotted him, but there was one way to unmask him and perhaps to give Anuchin her shot.

The plan was all he had, and Bolan didn't hesitate. Rising, he kept on going down the slope, skidding a little on his heels but staying upright now. The risk would come when he had cleared the tree line and reached the open road. From there on, it was down to speed and instinct, dodging for his life, since no one could outrun a swarm of slugs from a Kalashnikov.

One second, he was covered by the trees; the next, he was exposed and running over grass, toward fractured asphalt, shoulders hunched, already weaving like a quarterback with half of the opposing team in front of him, the other half behind and closing in to drag him down.

The first rounds struck a foot or so to Bolan's right,

before he heard the shots. The AK-103's 7.62 mm projectiles traveled at speeds between 2,100 and 2,400 feet per second, depending on weight, roughly doubling the speed of sound in either case.

Soldiers liked to say you never hear the shot that killed you, but that only counted with a quick, clean kill. If you were gut-shot, say, or had your legs shot out from under you, you would hear everything. Feel everything.

The Executioner ducked, slid through a shoulder roll and came up firing toward the hillside. He heard another weapon now, Anuchin's SMG, and then the AK fire swung back in her direction. Bolan took advantage of the moment, saw his target as a man-size shadow in the forest fifty feet above him and lined up the shot.

He'd never know, in retrospect, which of them brought the Spetsnaz soldier down. When he stood over him, a moment later, the man bore hits from Bolan's AKS and Anuchin's SMG. No difference once he'd received them, blank eyes staring at the treetops and the distant sky beyond.

"You're hit," Bolan said, noticing the blood on one of his companion's sleeves.

"A shrapnel graze," she said. "I'm fine."

"I'll put a bandage on it when we get back to the bike," he told her.

"*Da*. Okay. More riding, then."

"A lot more," Bolan said. "We've still got seven hundred miles or more to go."

"I'm sick of this," she said.

"Sick means you're still alive," he answered back. "Let's keep it that way, if we can."

CHAPTER TWENTY-TWO

Hal Brognola was working late, from home. He had been catching catnaps when and where he could since Bolan started two-wheeling across Siberia, but the fatigue was catching up with him, reminding Hal that he wasn't a young field agent fresh from Quantico these days.

Turns out Mick Jagger had it right from the beginning. Getting old was one infuriating drag.

He dialed the Moscow number, listened to the ringing start and calculated times. It would be 7:25 tomorrow morning in the Russian capital, 2:25 tomorrow afternoon wherever Bolan and his passenger might be after surviving the Spetsnaz ambush. That was a not-so-minor miracle itself, and the big Fed felt a degree of pardonable pride that he'd contributed to their survival with the information Stony Man had gleaned from Big Bird orbiting the planet with all-seeing eyes.

All-seeing *sleepless* eyes, Brognola thought. Like his, in that regard.

"Allô!" the now-familiar, French-tinged voice responded, midway through the second ring.

"It's Justice calling," Brognola told Gerard Delorme, omitting any mention of his name.

"Ah, yes. And is there news?"

"There is," the big Fed said. "Your package passed another checkpoint, hopefully undamaged."

"But you can't be certain?" Delorme inquired, a note of worry in his voice.

"It's still in motion," Brognola advised him, "so it can't be damaged badly, if at all."

"It is nerve-racking business, eh?" Delorme said.

"Less for the two of us than them," Hal said.

"*Mais oui*. Of course. I only meant to say—"

"No problem," the big Fed said, interrupting him. "I do the same thing all the time. You can't be there to help, no matter how you wish for it."

After a moment's silence, Delorme asked, "You've had communication from the East?"

"Not recently," Brognola replied.

"Then how…?"

"My people watched it on TV. Eyes in the sky."

"*Bien sûr*. I understand. Does that make waiting easier?"

"I wouldn't go that far. Sometimes the opposite, in fact. In the old days, waiting meant you hung around until a phone call told you everyone's okay, or not. Watching the action happen…it can send your blood pressure to Mars."

"Our budget offers no allowance for such marvels," Delorme explained. "But then what would we do with them in any case? We chase no one, arrest no one. I am what you would call a paper-pusher."

"I prefer 'facilitator,'" Brognola replied. "It makes me feel like I contribute something. Anyway, it's what we do. The paper's there. Somebody has to push it."

"Or propel young men and women into danger," said the man from Interpol.

"My courier's a volunteer," Brognola said. "Did someone drag yours into this against her will?"

"The young always believe that they can change the

world," Delorme said. "In May of 1968, I manned the barricades in Paris, stoning the *gendarmes*. Was I an idiot, or simply an idealist?"

"I've given up on judging anyone except myself," Brognola said. In fact, he judged his fellow humans every day—and sentenced some of them to die. It was a burden that he'd carried for so long, he sometimes felt that he'd collapse if it was lifted from his shoulders.

"In any case, I thank you for the news," Delorme said. Half joking then, he added, "Do you think a prayer might help?"

"It couldn't hurt," Brognola said, and cut the link, thinking that if he remembered how to pray, he might try it himself.

M56 Kolyma Highway

ANUCHIN HAD SCUFFED both knees through her jeans, and had sustained a grazing wound across her left biceps. Bolan stopped the bleeding with a dose of clotting powder, then applied a sterile bandage to the arm before they left the ambush site.

It was lost time, but if the Spetsnaz team had any backup waiting in the wings, the trap would have been sprung before he could retrieve the BMW. The enemy had gambled on a three-man crew and lost. Any reaction, he supposed, would be delayed while someone back at headquarters—in Yakutsk, Magadan or Moscow—waited for a sitrep from the field.

If there were scheduled contact times, the next would pass with no word from the team, then someone from control would reach out to the officer in charge, on-site. Failure to reach him might initiate some prearranged reaction, but with any luck, the targets would be miles away by then.

And if there was no mandatory check-in time, what then? Headquarters might sit waiting through the night for word of a successful ambush. Bolan knew he couldn't count on that best-case scenario, but either way, they'd bought some travel time.

Bolan supposed that when the reinforcements came they would be coming from the east. He'd nearly reached the halfway point between Yakutsk and Magadan, where sending troops to hunt him from the west would take more time and effort than his adversaries could afford. He should expect another ambush, then, or possibly a move in force to block the highway and prevent him reaching Magadan with Tatyana.

That, in turn, made Bolan think about their ride home to the States, already waiting off the coast, submerged and doubtless locked into radio silence. Making it to Magadan alive was only half the battle, if he couldn't find a way to reach the submarine and get aboard with his charge.

Could the FSB bring Russian naval forces into play? He guessed that it would only take a confirmation of the *Kansas City* lurking close to shore—a provocation, at the very least, and some might say an act of war. When Bolan thought about the crew, close to 150 now at risk, he wondered whether any of it could be worth the risk involved.

That train of thought led nowhere, and he quickly squelched it. Soldiers on the firing line gained nothing from excessive rumination over abstract points of policy. He trusted Brognola to judge whether a job was worth pursuing, just as the big Fed trusted the Executioner to know if it could be accomplished.

They were still alive. The troops sent by their enemy to bring them down were not.

GRIGORY RYBAKOV was tiring of the hunt already. On the flight from Moscow, he had managed to convince himself that simply by arriving on the scene, he could produce results that had eluded Nikolay Milescu and his men. Now that he felt the Lada Niva lurching under him, swerving to dodge the larger potholes, now forsaking pavement altogether, he began to see the error in his thinking.

Frustrated, he radioed the helicopter once again—five minutes since the last time—to demand an update on their scouting. There was no news to report, and it required a force of will for Rybakov to hold off cursing at the pilots for their failure to produce targets by magic.

He peered out through his mud-flecked window, scanning trees, then blinked and asked, "Is that a bear?"

"Could be," Milescu said. "I didn't see it."

"Right there! Just around—"

But they were past the point already, leaving Rybakov with nothing but a mental image of a hulking shadow in the forest, watching him roll past.

"How far from here to Magadan?" he asked.

One of his soldiers snickered in the backseat, then thought better of it, turned the sound into a hacking cough.

"Approximately seven hundred miles," Milescu answered. "Two days, more or less, with sleep."

"Two days, for seven hundred miles? Son of a bitch!" Rybakov snarled. "We'll drive on through the night, no stopping. Take turns at the wheel. This travesty has already gone on long enough."

None of the others dared to contradict him. Even now, alone with four armed men who might resent him, Rybakov commanded by the force of personality, and by his reputation for suppressing any opposition ruthlessly.

He would prevail because he always had, because a different outcome was intolerable. Rybakov's competitors had always failed because they flinched at the last moment, or because they were too stupid to think through the consequences of rash actions. Neither weakness plagued the godfather of Moscow. He was more than a survivor.

Rybakov, at least in his mind, was a modern emperor.

How else could he describe his global operations, other than an empire? And when emperors were threatened anywhere, at any time, they struck with crushing force. They buried the pygmies who believed that they could duel with giants and emerge triumphant, when they had been born to serve their betters, nothing more.

The hunt across Siberia might be monotonous, but it would strengthen Rybakov's already fearsome reputation, proving him a warlord who accomplished what the Russian government itself couldn't. And who would dare oppose him then? The prime minister? His deputies? The Minister of Justice or Internal Affairs?

Not one would have the balls to stand against him after this. Aside from all the bribes he'd paid them, and the information he possessed that could unseat them overnight, they would be forced to grant the fact of Rybakov's personal courage. His propensity for violence.

They would fear him.

What else mattered in the final scheme of things?

Yakutsk

STEPHAN LEVSHIN WAS nervous and hated the feeling. Long accustomed to wielding his authority as a scalpel or bludgeon, whichever a situation required, he hadn't been prepared for a loss of control with a problem he'd planned to solve quickly. It embarrassed and infuriated him.

And he was frightened, too.

Failure was tolerable in small doses at FSB headquarters, though it always stalled promotion and might sidetrack a career for good. A failure on the level he was now experiencing, though, might wind up killing more than his career.

Levshin had lost track of his running tally for the dead, but three more had been added to the list. The latest air force overflight between Yakutsk and Tomtor had confirmed the worst: Captain Zelinsky's Spetsnaz team had been eliminated by the fugitives, who, in their turn, seemed to be indestructible.

Levshin suspected Colonel Marshak had to have heard the news himself by now, but that didn't relieve Levshin of his responsibility to call, deliver the announcement and absorb whatever verbal punishment ensued. Rank had its privileges, and one of them was the occasional selection of a delegated whipping boy.

Levshin could play that role as well as anyone, but he didn't enjoy it, and when he was forced to suffer an indignity, Levshin always sought opportunities to pass it on. His first impulse had been to call and vent his wrath on Nikolay Milescu's hunting party, but Grigory Rybakov's assumption of command removed that option.

Raging at the godfather of Moscow could destroy whatever still remained of Levshin's FSB career, and with annihilation of Zelinsky's team, Levshin had lost his best chance of eliminating Rybakov.

Levshin had no clear grasp of how his life had suddenly gone sour in the past few days. This time last week, he'd been blissfully ignorant of Tatyana Anuchin's existence. This day, she was a comet hurtling toward fatal collision with his world, and every effort to avoid the crash thus far had failed. As for the stranger who escorted and protected her, Levshin had yet to even learn the name of his relentless nemesis.

No matter.

Levshin meant to plant him in an unmarked grave, so any name he used in Russia was irrelevant. It would be useful to identify his sponsors and superiors for payback at some later time, but Levshin couldn't think that far ahead. His focus at the moment was survival first, then maintenance of his position in the FSB. Unless he lived and kept his rank, thoughts of revenge would be superfluous.

Indeed, without the FSB behind him, it would likely be impossible.

Priorities.

First, he had to somehow find a way to intercept the FSB's rogue agent and her bodyguard before Grigory Rybakov could do the job. Second, if feasible, he had to fulfill Colonel Marshak's command to make sure Rybakov didn't return alive from his Siberian safari. Then, and only then—when he had proved himself a winner who defied all odds—could Levshin plan a wider war.

But where would he find soldiers to assist him now?

Tomtor, Sakha Republic

THE TOWN ALMOST TOOK Bolan by surprise. He'd been expecting it, of course, knew it was there, and kept a sharp eye on the bike's odometer. Still, after all that they'd been through this day, and after all the empty miles that lay behind them, it was startling to see a hamlet rise out of the taiga, crouched upon the highway in their path.

Bolan considered what he knew about the village. It was twenty-some-odd miles southeast of Oymyakon, which claimed to be the coldest spot on Earth with permanent inhabitants—and which was otherwise irrelevant to Bolan. Tomtor had a small airport, but Bolan and Anuchin couldn't use it. Worse, it might prove dangerous if it had been the access point for the late Spetsnaz ambush squad.

Had they left other men in town as backup, just in case they dropped the ball? Would Tomtor's villagers be on alert for Bolan and Anuchin, possibly inspired by a reward for trapping them?

That seemed unlikely in the circumstances of a covert operation, but he couldn't rule it out completely. On the other hand, as they approached Tomtor, Bolan was wondering if there might be a way to turn the Spetsnaz presence to his own advantage.

Dicey, but if there was any chance at all…

He thought about the airfield, wondered if the soldiers might have transport waiting for them there. If so, and none of them had been the pilot, could he hitch a ride at gunpoint for himself and Anuchin?

Possible, but risky to the max. A military aircraft could be tracked by GPS, as well as radar, and the Russian air force might be willing to destroy it in midair if they suspected Anuchin was on board. Still, wings would carry them to Magadan within a fraction of the time they'd need to drive 650 miles.

He stopped a quarter mile outside of town to hide his AK and his companion's Bizon SMG, still handy for emergencies, but tucked away from prying eyes as they rolled into Tomtor. Villagers slowed or stopped dead in their tracks to watch the motorcycle pass, and there were gawkers idling about when Bolan stopped to fill the BMW's tank at Tomtor's only gas station.

The airfield wasn't hard to find, but it revealed no plane or chopper waiting for the Spetsnaz troopers to return. Bolan supposed that they'd been ferried in from somewhere, and their ride had gone back home to wait for word that they had done their job.

No joy.

A little restaurant downtown produced some tempting smells, but Bolan knew that they couldn't afford the luxury of sitting down to hot food on a plate, with napkins, silverware and coffee on the side. Time wasted now could cost them dearly on the highway, so he cut their losses and moved on.

Goodbye to Tomtor. Next stop, Oymyakon, but they were only stopping there if it had gasoline to sell. At this point in their journey, Bolan would seize any opportunity to fill the BMW's tank, as long as no one in the village raised his hackles with the threat of ambush.

And if anything went wrong, they would blast through it, right. Or go down fighting.

Either way, he didn't plan to linger on the Road of Bones.

CHAPTER TWENTY-THREE

Grigory Rybakov was seething, an internal stew of fury and frustration, when the walkie-talkie crackled and his pilot's voice came to him, as if screened through sandpaper.

"Falcon to Wolfhound. Calling Wolfhound. Over."

Rybakov picked up the two-way radio and thumbed the button to transmit. "Wolfhound!" he snapped. "Where are you, Falcon?"

"Topping off with fuel in Tomtor, Wolfhound," came the pilot's answer. "While they're working on it, I've been asking questions."

"Well?" the godfather replied, snarling between clenched teeth. "Is this a guessing game?"

"No, sir." The pilot sounded worried now, as well he should. "There was a couple here, riding a motorcycle. Well, two people, anyway. They didn't take their helmets off, but one was smaller, like a woman. They were looking at the airport."

"*Looking* at the airport?" Rybakov echoed. "What does that mean?"

He almost heard the pilot shrug before responding. "I don't know, sir. It's what the locals said. Two people on a bike came up, sat looking all around, then left."

A narrow ray of hope shot through the thunderclouds of Rybakov's internal rage. He leaned into the two-way radio and asked, "Are they still there?"

"No, sir. We checked first thing, before I called."

The light went out. He ground his teeth until his jaw ached, clutched the radio so tightly that he thought it bound to shatter any second. Somehow, when he replied, Rybakov kept his voice pitched low and calm.

"So, you've just called to tell me they were there, some time ago," he said, "and they've moved on?"

"Yes, sir," the pilot answered. "Heading east."

The godfather exploded, bellowing, "We knew that when we started, idiot!"

His driver cringed from the ensuing obscenity shouted into the radio. Behind him, Rybakov could almost feel the other soldiers cringing, carefully averting their eyes. The pilot muttered something, but the ringing in his ears prevented Rybakov from understanding him.

"What's that?" he growled.

"I said, 'I'm sorry, sir!' They bought some gasoline for the bike and left. There's no more information to be had."

As always, when a gale of rage passed over him, Rybakov felt a sudden letdown. It was physical, as if someone had pulled the plug and drained the roiling anger from his body. It was better when he got to smash something, or hurt someone, but he felt better for the outburst, even so.

"All right," he told the pilot. "Finish with your business and get after them. Call me immediately if you spot them."

"Yes, sir! Of course, sir! Falcon out."

The very instant they were disconnected, Rybakov remembered that he hadn't asked how long ago the targets were in Tomtor. How far behind was he now? Could the helicopter catch them? And if so, could Rybakov hope to arrive before they'd battled to the death?

He meant to have a hand in finishing the gnats who had bedeviled him, but even the godfather of Moscow had limitations. Time-travel was beyond him. He couldn't convert the Lada Niva to a rocket sled and hurtle down the Road of Bones at speeds flaunting the laws of physics. He couldn't be in two places at once, or strangle two opponents with a single pair of hands.

Too bad.

But he could motivate his driver. That was definitely possible.

"Come on!" he said. "We haven't got all night! Speed up! Or would you rather walk back to your little Moscow flat from here, without kneecaps?"

Aboard the USS Kansas City

COMMANDER HOUSTON GREENE had trespassed into Russian waters twice before, helming the *Kansas City,* but his present mission was the first that had required him to remain there, sitting like a practice target for the enemy to fire on as they pleased. And truth be told, he didn't like it.

Of course, the Russians weren't supposed to be his enemies these days. The Cold War was a fading memory for those who'd served in it, and most of Greene's crewmen had joined the U.S. Navy long after America and Russia had declared themselves the best of friends—or whatever they were, in fact, with all the tension crackling back and forth between them in these times of "peace" and "understanding."

All bullshit, as far as Greene could tell.

He liked his missions simple, cut and dried. Not like this job, where he was told to sneak in, then remain on station with no end in sight, until two strangers no one would identify showed up and made themselves available to come aboard. Greene figured they were spooks—none of his business, if the brass thought otherwise—but waiting in a hostile zone for two could cost 143 lives.

Hiding the *Kansas City* was no easy task. It was 362 feet long, well past the end zone of a football field, and would have tipped the scales at something close to seven thousand tons, if scales that size existed. Even idling as it was, eight hundred feet below the surface, it could be detected by the other side.

And then what?

They could run, at twenty knots—or thirty-three miles per hour, for landlubbers—and hope that Russian destroyers managed to miss them somehow. If fired upon, they could fight, but what happened then? Were two unknowns worth lighting a fuse to a global catastrophe?

The bottom line: Greene had his orders, and he'd follow them. It helped to understand what his superiors were planning, but understanding was nonessential. The brass expected Greene to follow through, and he had never let them down.

So far.

Lieutenant Commander Charles Jackson approached and addressed Greene, tight-lipped. "Still no word, sir," he said. "If we're waiting—"

"We're waiting," Greene told him. "They won't be in Magadan yet if they went overland. Maybe sometime tomorrow."

"Permission to speak freely, sir?"

"There's no need, Mr. Jackson," Greene replied. "I've thought of everything you want to say, and I don't like this any more than you do."

"Yes, sir. But—"

"We have our orders, Chuck. We're bound to follow them."

"Yes, sir. Of course, sir."

"You've read the poem, I assume? *The Charge of the Light Brigade?*"

"Yes, sir."

"'Theirs not to reason why.'"

"I never liked the next bit, sir."

Theirs but to do and die, Greene thought. He said, "It shouldn't come to that. We're on a taxi run, that's all."

"Yes, sir."

A taxi run through hostile waters, with two fares the Russkies obviously didn't want to lose.

Simple? Not even close.

Theirs but to do and die, Green thought again, and cursed under his breath.

Oymyakon, Sakha Republic

THE DRIVE FROM Tomtor to Oymyakon took longer than Bolan had planned. Cruising at sixty miles per hour on a normal highway, covering a mile a minute, he should have reached the second town in under half an hour. Then again, the Road of Bones was anything but normal.

They'd been forced to cross another stream, managed it better than the last one, but it still took time. Then they'd run out of pavement for the umpteenth time since leaving Yakutsk and were forced to creep along at walking pace for something like two miles, before the vanished blacktop reappeared. No bears, at least, but Bolan had dodged an ungodly heap of feces four miles past the stream, hoping they didn't meet whatever dropped it there.

We're in it deep enough, as is, he thought, and almost smiled.

In Oymyakon they bought more fuel, and Bolan did

the highway math. Six hundred forty miles to Magadan from where they stood, beside the village's one gas pump. No one had a choice of octane in a town that small, that isolated. You bought Lukoil's EKTO brand or nothing, at a price that had to have kept most peasants traveling on foot or via bicycle. Anuchin did the talking and paid cash, the shriveled-up pump jockey preening for her, like he thought he had a chance of scoring.

Bolan sometimes wondered how people got along from day to day. The answer: many didn't.

Was it worse here in Siberia than in the wilds of Appalachia? Colder, of course. But did the poverty and government indifference hurt any more, or less? Was crime a more oppressive problem here than in the Tex-Mex border towns? From what he'd seen firsthand, Bolan believed that suffering was more or less the same. A universal leveler.

And there was little he could do about it—thin the ranks of predators as opportunity allowed, perhaps strike random blows for decency along the way and hope that someone else picked up the torch when he was forced to lay it down. The tale of human history was written in a simple two-word epitaph: *They tried.*

And if at first you don't succeed...

A thrumming sounded in the air above him, distant but approaching at high altitude, and drew Bolan's concentration from the road. He slowed, looked up and back to see a speck above him in the dusk, hastening eastward. It sounded like a helicopter, but if it was hunting him, it made no move to swoop and strike.

He filed it, something else to think about, knowing it stood to reason that there had to be air traffic above Siberia on any normal day. No reason to believe the chopper carried soldiers sent to silence Anuchin.

But it might.

Refocused on the highway, Bolan fed the bike more gas and rolled on with the sunset at his back, determined not to waste the daylight he had left.

NIKOLAY MILESCU felt the waves of anger radiating from his godfather, as if a space heater the size and shape of Rybakov were sitting in the Lada Niva's shotgun seat, turned up full blast. The man couldn't sit still, was muttering incessantly, his nervous fingers fiddling with the submachine gun resting in his lap.

Milescu wondered if the boss had lost his mind.

Leaving his lair in Moscow, hell-bent to participate in what had started as an ordinary murder contract, had been strange enough. Milescu understood that Rybakov had suffered some embarrassment—and part of it was Milescu's fault—but there was no reason for him to fly halfway across Russia, clearly in a rage that he couldn't suppress, to prove himself a man.

Or was there?

Milescu cherished no inflated view of himself or his place in the Family. He was a soldier, possibly a sergeant if you looked at it a certain way, but nothing more. He would never be a boss, never hoped to be—except, perhaps, in alcoholic dreams. But he could see when one of his superiors was running off the rails.

Like now.

Good news: the helicopter Rybakov had brought with him might actually spot the fugitives and bring this whole farce to an end, at last. The key word: *might*. Milescu, for his part, wasn't convinced and wouldn't be, until he stood over their bleeding corpses on the road.

Milescu watched the gray trees flit past his window, rolling with the punches as the SUV hit one pothole after another. With Stolypin at the wheel, cowed by the fury of his front-seat passenger, they jolted over every bump and crevice in the pavement, where there *was* pavement. When it ran out, Stolypin did his best to keep them out of mudholes and prevent them bogging down in streams, but otherwise he went for speed and let his riders bear the punishment.

Another sign that Rybakov wasn't himself: he didn't seem to mind the rocky road at all. Milescu had been present, in the city, when the godfather had chastised drivers for taking a corner too fast, rippling the vodka or champagne that he was drinking in his limousine. This day, he didn't seem to mind it, even when his skull came close to rapping on the Lada's ceiling.

Hungry for revenge? Or frightened that the runners posed some danger to him personally?

Could they bring him down somehow?

Milescu knew the woman was an agent of the FSB. Make that "had been"; he guessed her contract would be canceled after this. She had to know something that could damage Rybakov, or why else would he even care if she escaped? But to go through all this…

And he was trapped now, with a madman who would sacrifice the lot of them—even himself, it seemed—without a second thought.

"Falcon calling Wolfhound! Falcon calling Wolfhound, over!"

Rybakov answered the radio, his voice an anxious rasp. "Wolfhound! What is it, Falcon!"

"We have visual contact," the helicopter pilot said. "They're just below us now. Seeking instructions, Wolfhound."

"Pass them by," Rybakov ordered. "Find a place somewhere ahead and land there. Block the highway. Hold them there until we reach you."

"Understood, Wolfhound," the pilot's voice came back. "Give me your location, Falcon."

Hearing it, Milescu wondered whether they could reach the spot in time. Or would the fugitives destroy a second helicopter, leave them in the dust again?

If that happened, he reckoned Rybakov would lose all touch with sanity. Might even turn on his own men, enraged.

If that happened, Milescu didn't plan to be a sacrificial lamb. He would defend himself.

Even if that meant killing his godfather.

VITUS BYKOVSKY WORRIED if they would find a place to land the helicopter, but their pilot simply set down in the middle of the highway. It required a place where trees wouldn't snap off the tips of his four rotor blades, each twenty-two feet long, but moments after getting his instructions from the godfather, their pilot found a clearing on the highway where the trees had either fallen in a storm, or else been cut and left to rot.

Siberians.

Bykovsky didn't understand them, and he wasn't about to try. In his opinion, all their brains were frozen from enduring ten months of winter every year, and pickled with the vodka they swilled down to ward off chills.

To hell with them. At least it would be warmer there.

As soon as they were on the ground, Bykovsky jumped down from the chopper, barking orders at his men. He had four guns to back him up, handpicked by Rybakov to join the hunting party, but he planned to take full credit for whatever they achieved.

His flunkies would expect no less.

Not that he meant to kill the targets personally. Rybakov had stressed the point that they were his alone—unless, perhaps, it seemed they might escape before he reached the ambush site. Given the helicopter's speed and range, that was entirely possible. The SUV with Rybakov still had to clear the stinking burg of Oymyakon, then catch up to them on the Road of Bones.

A stretch, but not impossible.

Bykovsky wouldn't openly defy the godfather—he loved his relatively carefree life too much for that—but it would be an even worse mistake to let the targets slip away from him, for fear of using deadly force. If he allowed them to escape, Bykovsky knew he was as good as dead.

So, a dilemma. And Bykovsky thought that he had a solution.

He would have his soldiers hold their fire initially, permitting him to take the first shots. Those would be directed at the motorcycle, rather than its passengers, to stop the bike for good and leave its riders dazed from tumbling on the pavement. Swarm them as they tried to rise and reach their weapons. Hold them for the boss.

Of course, Bykovsky saw the weakness in his own best-case scenario. The targets might turn back or veer into the woods at first sight of the helicopter. They might charge it, firing as they came, in hope of blasting through the roadblock. Having killed a dozen men or more already, they'd be damned unlikely to surrender and accept whatever fate Rybakov had in mind for them.

In fact, that was a fantasy.

But if he *could* bring down the motorcycle, at the very least, they would be left to fight or flee on foot. That gave his team a great advantage with their warbird, while the godfather rolled up behind them in his SUV.

Bykovsky smiled as he deployed his men, made sure they understood their orders. He could win this yet, and earn himself a fat reward.

All it required now was a clear eye and a steady hand.

FATIGUE WAS CRAMPING Bolan's muscles as the purple hues of dusk descended, bringing on another night. He had begun to feel as if there was no end running, understood how generals throughout recorded history had underestimated Russia's size and let themselves be lured to destruction.

Not my game, he thought, and tried to shake it off. He didn't plan to conquer Russia or the smallest part of it. He simply wanted out, with Anuchin safe and sound.

And that was proving difficult enough.

She tapped his shoulder, leaned in close and shouted from behind the visor of her crash helmet, "You saw the helicopter, yes?"

Bolan responded with a nod, which failed to satisfy her.

"Well?" she asked. "What do we do about it?"

Bolan braked to turn and speak with her. The last thing that he needed, at the moment, was to drop the bike and maybe damage something that he couldn't fix with their small tool kit.

"What we do is watch our step," he said. "The same as we've been doing all along. The chopper may be nothing."

"Or another ambush," she replied.

He nodded, agreeing with the woman. "Could be," he acknowledged. "But unless you've picked up psychic powers somewhere in the past few miles, the only way to find out is to go and see. Regardless, we're still heading east."

He couldn't see her face behind the tinted plastic bubble, but he pictured her frowning, recognizing their dilemma. It was rock-and-hard-place time, no turning back from where they stood, and something very close to certainty that they would find more shooters waiting on the road ahead of them.

They'd been running a gauntlet since they left Yakutsk, and they wouldn't escape it until they were clear of Russian soil, aboard the *Kansas City.* As to how they'd manage that, well, Bolan hadn't worked that out as yet.

"You ready?" he asked.

Anuchin hesitated, then nodded. He turned back toward the highway, gave the bike some gas and they were on their way.

Toward trouble, right.

No matter what the helicopter signified, that much was guaranteed. The men who wanted Tatyana Anuchin dead weren't giving up because they'd suffered one more setback. Each curve on the Road of Bones potentially concealed another trap. No secret there. No real surprise.

The Executioner was ready as he'd ever be.

CHAPTER TWENTY-FOUR

"They should be here by now," Karl Dokuchaev said. "So, where are they?"

Vitus Bykovsky scowled and answered, "How would I know? Anything can happen in this godforsaken place. You saw the bears."

"You think bears ate them?" Yuly Koltsov asked.

"I didn't say that. All I'm saying is, a hundred different things might slow them down."

"They should have been here," Dokuchaev repeated.

"Just remember what I told you," growled Bykovsky. "When they get here, no one fires but me, unless I give the order. Right?"

The others muttered confirmation of his order, clearly disappointed that they might not have an opportunity to kill someone this day. Bykovsky knew they thought he wanted all the glory for himself, and that was partly true. But he was also well aware of how their boss might punish anyone who killed the couple they were hunting before Rybakov himself could do the job.

And Rybakov would want to take his time.

"I saw the godfather working on an informer once," Koltsov said.

It was easy to imagine. No one asked for details, but Koltsov kept talking. "He had these big tongs and a welding torch. When he—"

"Enough," Bykovsky interrupted him. "We're here to do a job, not reminisce around a campfire."

"Now you mention it, a fire would help," Dokuchaev said. "The sun is going down, and we'll soon be freezing."

"No fire," Bykovsky said. "They could see it."

"Damn!" Koltsov said. "There go my balls."

"So what?" Dokuchaev replied. "You never use them, anyway."

"That's not your mother's story," Koltsov told him, grinning.

"Stop going on like children," Bykovsky commanded. "Pay attention to your jobs and watch for headlights once the sun's down."

"We can use the spotlight on the helicopter," Koltsov said.

"*After* we spot them," Bykovsky said. "Not before. We're hoping for surprise, remember."

"With this fat cow sitting in the middle of the highway?" Dokuchaev asked him, nodding toward the fifty-one-foot helicopter, fifteen feet in height, long rotors drooping. "There's no hiding that."

"And by the time they see it," Bykovsky said, "they'll be on the straightaway. I'll have a clean shot at the motorcycle."

"Better hope so," Koltsov said. "You mess it up, there may be tongs and torches in your future."

"Never mind," Bykovsky said. "I mess up nothing."

But he'd thought about the consequences if he failed, and they were grim. A long and lousy way to die.

IT WAS NEAR DARK, and Bolan had begun to look for somewhere they could park the BMW off the highway, pitch a cold camp for the night and start over tomorrow at first light. He'd been thinking about the helicopter that had overflown them, still uncertain what it meant to him and Anuchin, when he rounded one more curve and there it was.

"Hold on!" he barked, and hoped that Anuchin heard him, or at least that she had seen the chopper squatting in the middle of the highway like some giant dragonfly. Men were ranged in front of it, guns raised as if they'd hear the motorcycle coming, and there was no time to think about the next move Bolan made.

He swung the bike hard left, gunned it off-road and climbed the hillside, spraying soil behind them, his companion clinging to him for dear life. And that was what it came down to as someone by the helicopter fired a single shot, then ripped an autoburst into the trees. Bolan could hear the bullets striking here and there around him, felt the branches whipping past with force enough to blind him if he hadn't worn a helmet with a visor, then the gunfire sputtered out and he was sliding, switching off the BMW's engine, laying down the bike.

They scrambled clear of it and crouched in shadows, seeing to their weapons as a spotlight flared below them from the helicopter and began to sweep the wooded hillside. Spotting them would be a problem for the shooters if they didn't move, but Bolan *had* to move.

"I've got a plan," he said. "If it works out, we've got a faster ride to Magadan."

"And if it doesn't?" Tatyana asked.

He shrugged. Nothing to say, because the answer should be obvious.

"*Da, da,*" she said. "What is this plan?"

"Take out the shooters," he replied. "Try not to hit the pilot or the chopper."

"Ah." She raised the visor on her helmet. Smiled. "It's worth a try."

Bolan had counted four armed men before he took the BMW off-road, which didn't mean that there were only four. They'd have to watch it, going in, and most particularly, they would have to dodge the searchlight, if they could.

"As quiet as you can," he cautioned Anuchin, and began to make his way downslope to meet the enemy.

ANUCHIN TRIED TO FOLLOW Cooper's footsteps as they crept downhill, not using him to shield herself, but rather noting where he stepped and how he moved, barely producing any sound. She marveled at the way a man his size could slink through clinging undergrowth without making enough noise to wake up the dead.

Below them, from the highway, she heard angry voices arguing. One man was shouting down the others, who complained about his marksmanship. The loudest seemed to be the leader, which she'd often found to be the case in situations where a leader was required. Now he was barking at the others, telling them to fan out on the hillside and begin a search, reminding them that since they couldn't hear the motorcycle any longer, their intended prey had to be on foot.

But he expected them to run away, and that might be his last mistake.

In front of her, Cooper froze. Anuchin stopped dead in her tracks, clutching her Bizon submachine gun with a force that made her knuckles ache. She consciously relaxed her grip and listened for the sound of men climbing the hillside, hunting her.

As she was hunting them.

The trick was waiting until Cooper fired the first

shots, and she had to have a target, even then. It took more nerve to crouch and wait, she thought, than to go charging headlong through the trees, making the kind of racket that would bring them under fire and likely kill them within seconds flat.

But waiting hurt. It set her nerves on edge and made her muscles burn from clenching in frustration, made her teeth ache as she kept her mouth clamped shut. Even her eyes burned, straining to pick out a man-shape in the dusk that cloaked the hillside, darker than it should have been in contrast to the helicopter's probing searchlight. When it swept across them, Anuchin closed her eyes. Considered pulling down the tinted visor on her helmet, but it would have spoiled her vision when the light moved on.

She waited, down on one knee to relieve the trembling in her legs, the Bizon braced against her hip. Someone was coming up the hillside now, hasty and loud, never considering a trap might lie in store for him.

A moment later, it took shape. A man, holding some kind of automatic weapon in his right hand, while the left reached out ahead of him, clutching at trees and bushes as he pulled himself uphill.

When Cooper fired, off to her left, Anuchin stroked the Bizon's trigger, rattling off a burst. Downrange, the lurching man-shape screamed.

Oymyakon, Sakha Republic

THE WALKIE-TALKIE SURPRISED Rybakov with its crackling sound while one of his men was filling the Niva's fuel tank. Excited nearly to the point of panic, a voice called out to him.

"Wolfhound? Please answer Falcon! Over!"

Rybakov snatched up the radio. "Falcon, it's Wolf-hound. Go ahead."

"They're here, Wolfhound. We've found them, but it's all gone wrong. Over."

"Explain yourself!" Rybakov snapped. He spit out "Over!" as an afterthought.

"They saw us…drove into the forest…now there's shooting all around me. Over."

"Shooting? Who is shooting?" Rybakov demanded. "Over!"

"I can't tell, sir. First, your men followed the motor-cycle, then the gunfire started. Over."

Teeth clenched in frustration, Rybakov inquired, "What kinds of weapons, Falcon? Are they ours? Over!"

"I can't see anyone," the pilot answered. "And the guns all sound alike to me. They're getting closer! Hurry!"

Then the line—or would it be the air?—went dead. No matter how Rybakov snarled or shouted at the walkie-talkie, sitting hunched inside the SUV, he could raise no response.

At last he gave it up, bolted and told his soldier on the gas pump, "Finish that! We have to go, right now!"

"But, sir—"

"Finish it, I said!" the godfather raged. "The rest of you, get in the damned car!"

From the gas pump, timidly, his soldier said, "But, sir, we have to pay for this."

Rybakov cursed and ripped a wad of notes—one thousand rubles each—from his pants pocket. Wadding up a dozen in his fist, he hurled them at the stunned attendant standing near the pump.

"That covers it!" Rybakov rasped. "Now, everyone get in the fucking car, before I leave you here!"

They piled aboard without further delay, Milescu at

the wheel this time. He gunned the Lada Niva from the station, onto Oymyakon's portion of the highway, swiftly gaining speed. After a mile or so, he dared to ask, "What is it, sir? What's happened?"

"What? They've sprung the trap without us," Rybakov replied, still seething at the news. "And now it's going sour on them. Hurry up, before we miss our chance again!"

M56 Kolyma Highway

BOLAN WONDERED if it could be true that only four gunmen were stalking them. The helicopter he had seen, if he recalled correctly, carried up to sixteen soldiers, with two pilots on the crew. If there were eighteen guns circling around them in the forest, it could definitely be a problem, but if there were only four…

He had a chance to find out when the first appeared before him, laboring upslope against the pull of gravity, boots sliding on loose soil and fallen leaves. Somewhere behind Bolan and to his right, he knew Anuchin waited for his signal, wise enough to keep her finger off the trigger of her SMG until he got the party started.

Like right now.

He stitched the climbing gunman with a 3-round burst across his meaty chest and blew him backward, airborne for an instant as he tumbled down the hillside. Anuchin's stuttergun kicked in immediately, and another target squealed with pain, then went down thrashing in the undergrowth.

If there were only four men ranged against them, they'd just cut the odds by half to make it one-on-one. If there were more, they'd simply tipped the enemy to their positions in the woods and might regret it very soon.

As if to prove that point, incoming fire ripped through the forest, bullets slapping into tree trunks, clipping branches, rattling shrubbery. The helicopter's searchlight swept across the hillside, seeking targets, finding none. That meant at least one man had stayed back with the chopper—say one of the pilots—but did that affect the odds?

No way to answer that as Bolan started down the slope, looking for targets of his own. Someone had sent the helicopter hunting for them, and he knew it had a radio. Each moment he delayed from that point on increased the threat of reinforcements showing up to tip the scales against him.

On the other hand, if he could carry out the hasty plan he had explained in brief to Anuchin...

It was dangerous, of course, and might get them killed, but he could say the same for every move they'd made since meeting.

Moving toward their one big change, the Executioner struck off downhill.

VITUS BYKOVSKY heard gunfire, followed by a cry of mortal pain. He couldn't recognize the voice, strained as it was and cut off in a gargling kind of sound, but it was certainly a man's. Four gunmen on the hillside made it three-to-one that it was one of his, the woman unaccounted for.

Bykovsky hesitated at the tree line, worried about going in to join the fight, more worried about what might happen if he didn't. He'd already screwed up as it was, missing his shot before the targets went off-road. If he allowed them to escape entirely, then he might as well sit down and put the muzzle of his own gun in his mouth.

At least that would be quick and merciful.

Unlike his godfather.

No choice, then.

Cursing silently, Bykovsky edged into the dark woods, barely able to pick out the trees in front of him. A second later, when the helicopter's searchlight found him, he was blinded by its glare—and made an instant target for whatever enemies were lurking farther up the hillside.

Furious, he rounded on the gunship, bellowing at its two crewmen, "Move the fucking light, you idiots!"

It moved, in jerky fits and starts, but was the damage done? Bykovsky's night vision would take time to recover, but he couldn't linger where he was, in case he had been seen. Lurching uphill, half-blind, he clutched at saplings with his free hand for support, felt that he might fall down with every step.

He was caught in a nightmare, and for what? To stop some FSB hack from announcing that her boss took money from the Mafiya? Who didn't in the New Russia? What else was the big surprise? Was it worth dying for?

It was too late to think about that now, when he was into it beyond the point of no return.

Say, one man down—or maybe two, since he had heard a submachine gun firing on the hillside—but Bykovsky reckoned he could pull it off regardless. All he needed was a lucky shot or two to finish it. Dead soldiers would alleviate some of his godfather's anger if he killed the fugitives instead of taking them alive.

And if he had to shoot a couple of his own men just to make it work, why not?

ANUCHIN DUCKED beneath the searchlight's sweeping beam and lost her footing, slid a dozen yards downhill before she jammed one foot against a tree and stopped herself. It wrenched her left hip painfully, but saved her life at the same time, as bullets ripped across the ground in front of her, inches from where she lay.

Falling, she'd nearly dropped the Bizon SMG but saved it at the final instant. Now, returning fire without a target, Anuchin rolled and scrambled to her left, behind the tree, willing herself to power through the pain and find cover. The next incoming burst flayed rough bark from the tree that sheltered her, but couldn't reach her through its trunk.

At least, not yet.

She heard the gunman circling, tried to pin down his position, but her ears were ringing from the gunfire. Did the crunching footsteps come from right or left? Which side would he attack from when he came?

She knew only one way to cover both flanks simultaneously. The Bizon weighed five pounds, more or less, and could be fired one-handed, though it compromised the weapon's accuracy. With the submachine gun in her right hand, Anuchin drew her double-action semiauto pistol with her left and thumbed off its ambidextrous safety. Rising stiffly with her back against the tree trunk, she stood waiting for the enemy to show himself.

Which side? She held both weapons ready, index fingers on their triggers, tacking up the last bare ounce of slack. She was ready to kill again, because she didn't want to die this way. Not here. Not now.

He came at Anuchin from the left, growling like some kind of demented animal as he attacked, his automatic weapon swinging toward her face. She shot him with the Grach first, two rounds aimed at center mass, then ripped him with the Bizon for a chaser, heard the bullets smacking into flesh, a couple of them ringing off the gunman's AK as they tore it from his hands.

Then he was down and thrashing in the leaves, heels

drumming for a moment as if he might rise to fight again. His life ran out before Anuchin had to waste more bullets on him, and she limped around his body in the sudden stillness, waiting for the next trap to reveal itself.

How many adversaries still remained between herself and Cooper's goal? If they survived to reach the helicopter, would he find a pilot waiting? Was the man they needed already among the dead?

Unwilling to consider that, she made her painful way downhill, obeying Cooper's last instructions. Hoping that they wouldn't get her killed.

BOLAN MET THE LAST man on his way down to the chopper, still not certain that he *was* the final soldier. It was over in a heartbeat.

One moment, Bolan had the helicopter in his view; the next, a man loomed up in front of him, huffing from the exertion of his climb. The shooter wasn't ready with his weapon when he met the target he'd been tracking.

Bolan was.

His AKS carbine stuttered and put the big man down, stone dead before he hit the ground and started slithering downhill. Bolan pursued him, with no need to finish it, intent on getting to the chopper now and clearing any soldiers who'd been left behind.

None was.

The pilots huddled by their aircraft, cringing in the dark as he approached. They weren't armed, nor did they seem particularly anxious to resist. He called back up the hill for Anuchin, and she joined him in another moment, limping when she reached the level roadway.

"Are you hit?" he asked.

"No," she said. "I fell. Something about my hip. Not broken, but it hurts."

"Okay. Translate for these two, will you? My Russian is a little rusty."

"Yes."

"Ask how they stand for fuel."

Anuchin posed the question, listened, then told Bolan, "Nearly full. They stopped at Oymyakon."

"What kind of range, with that?"

Another back-and-forth. "About 350 miles."

A little under half of what they needed, bound for Magadan. "Is there another place en route where they can stop for fuel?" Bolan asked.

Anuchin spoke, listened and told him, "Seymchan. It's a settlement two hundred miles from Magadan."

"That's it, then," Bolan said. "Will they cooperate, or do I leave them like the others?"

Both men nodded eagerly. Anuchin made it official. "They'll fly us wherever we want them to go." More conversation, then she said, "They'd like to leave before the godfather arrives."

"Godfather?" Bolan raised an eyebrow. "Where is he coming from? When?"

"The west," Anuchin translated. "And soon."

"Sounds like there's hunting to be done," Bolan replied, "before we leave."

CHAPTER TWENTY-FIVE

Flying felt like magic after days of jolting over broken pavement and no pavement on the BMW. Before they lifted off, Bolan had checked the Kamov Ka-60's armament and found a Kord heavy machine gun laid by for emergencies. There was a pintle mount on standby, but the weapon hadn't been attached to it, so Bolan did the job.

The Kord 6P49 weighed close to sixty pounds and fired 12.7 mm rounds, the Russian equivalent of NATO .50-calibers. Belt-fed, it spit an average 650 rounds per minute, and the ammo boxes left for Bolan had been filled with armor-piercing rounds. It was a bit much for a moose hunt, but ideal for stalking human jackals in an SUV.

While he prepared the weapon, Anuchin had another heart-to-heart discussion with their crew. She made the pilots understand that she had no life left in Russia; nothing but a long scream into darkness waiting if her enemies should capture her alive. In short, she would do *anything* to get away, by any means. If that meant bringing down the chopper with herself inside, so be it.

They believed.

Bolan was painfully aware of passing time, troubled that the godfather of Moscow, Grigory Rybakov, and company might catch them on the ground, perhaps disable the Ka-60, but they lifted off with no sign of the enemy so far.

And headed west.

It went against the grain, big-time, with Magadan receding in their rearview, but the Executioner was bent on taking care of business. Dealing with the Moscow hunting party now should help to clear their eastward path— or, at the very least, prevent a radio alert that they were flying instead of traveling by motorcycle.

One more benefit: it would reduce the list of Anuchin's enemies. Whoever followed Rybakov as Moscow's godfather might hate her, even want to see her dead, but by the time the power vacuum had been filled, Anuchin would have testified. Pursuing her could prove to be a costly waste of time.

That left the FSB, but there was nothing Bolan could do about officials with a penchant for revenge. He *could* stop Grigory Rybakov and do the world a favor in the bargain.

Bolan didn't know how far the hunters were behind their flying scouts. The pilots, under questioning, quite naturally couldn't say how fast the SUV was traveling behind them, overland. At last contact, the trackers had been gassing up in Oymyakon, some eighty miles from where Bolan had left their point men scattered in the forest, meat for wolves and bears. The KA-60 cruised around 170 miles per hour, meaning they could be back at Oymyakon themselves in half an hour. Somewhere in between those points, his enemies were rushing up to meet him.

And he meant to find them.

Any minute now.

GRIGORY RYBAKOV WAS fairly vibrating with nervousness, not that he felt his enemies might be within his grasp.

Worse, though, was the oppressive fear that they might kill his scouts and slip away before he came to grips with them.

His mind raced, trying to remember anyone he knew in Magadan who could assist him, raise a troop of soldiers on short notice, price be damned. He had no clue who might be waiting for the fugitives when they ran out of highway, what provisions had been made for their escape, but Rybakov wouldn't allow it. If it cost him his last ruble, he would know the pleasure of his fingers wrapped around their throats.

When they were cold and dead, he could—

"They're coming back!" Milescu blurted out.

Rybakov turned to him, his temples throbbing. "What? Who's coming where?"

Milescu pointed through the windshield. "There! The helicopter's coming back!"

Rybakov saw it then, blinked at the aircraft racing toward them from the east, flying a hundred feet or less above the highway. He felt something deep inside him snap, unleashing waves of pent-up fury.

"Idiots! Are they insane?"

Rybakov snatched the walkie-talkie, mashed the Transmit button with sufficient force to crush it as he snarled into the microphone.

"What are you doing here?" he raged. "I ordered you—"

Milescu swerved the SUV just then, flung Rybakov against his door with force enough to make him drop the two-way radio. Blind with rage, the godfather of Moscow reached out for his driver, might have strangled the man despite the danger to himself, except Milescu squealed, "They're shooting at us!"

Disbelieving, Rybakov turned back in time to see a

stream of bullets ripping into asphalt, gouging divots in the highway as they blazed a trail to intercept the Lada Niva. Any vestige of coherent thought fled from his mind within that fraction of a second, Rybakov unable to conceive a reason why his own men should be firing at him.

When the first rounds struck the Niva's right-front fender, his side of the SUV, Rybakov raised his feet, knees pressed against his chest, as if the vehicle had plunged into a river and he was afraid to get his feet wet. Stupid, but it was instinctive. Nothing else to do, before—

The heavy slugs veered to the left, from Rybakov's perspective, ripped the Niva's hood like a huge can opener, then found the windshield on Milescu's side and blasted it to powder. Somewhere in the midst of all that noise, Milescu may have screamed, but then his blood and brains were sprayed over Rybakov, drenching his cheek, his shirt, his pants, and there was only silence from the driver's seat.

The SUV surged forward, with a dead foot jammed on the accelerator, no hands on the wheel. Rybakov lunged across the console, tried to steer it, but he was too late. A ditch at roadside proved to be no obstacle. The vehicle simply soared across it to the forest on the north side of the highway, ricocheted from glancing impact with a tree, then continued on its way, with two tires in the ditch and two up on the hillside, running tilted at an angle close to forty-five degrees.

Rybakov's soldiers in the backseat bellowed curses, tried to wipe Milescu's fluids from their faces while they clutched their weapons, waiting for a chance to use them. In the shotgun seat, Rybakov braced himself against the dashboard, wondering how long the SUV could go on with a corpse behind the wheel.

The answer came with rending metal as they crashed

into a large, half-buried boulder and rebounded, spewing vapor from the ruptured radiator. Underneath the mutilated hood, finally, the vehicle's engine died.

"GO BACK. I NEED another pass," Bolan said, letting Anuchin handle the translation for their pilots.

Standing in the chopper's open door, behind the Kord machine gun, Bolan felt the Ka-60 bank and turn, its rotors slashing at the air while trees blurred past them. He had seen the SUV swerve off-road, crash and stall, but men were leaping out of it as the helicopter soared out of range.

No good.

He hadn't sacrificed this vital time to put Grigory Rybakov afoot and make him hitchhike. If the Russian godfather survived this meeting, it meant more danger for Anuchin going on indefinitely. While he had a chance to end it here, he meant to take advantage of the opportunity.

Another pass, and Bolan saw his targets scattering into the trees. Four runners had their backs turned toward him, and he couldn't tell which one was Rybakov. He knew dropping all of them would be his one and only means of making sure none radioed ahead to warn another welcoming committee on the road.

Framing the first man in the Kord's iron sights, Bolan squeezed off a burst of slugs designed to penetrate light armor. Each projectile weighed fifty-two grams and traveled at 2,740 feet per second, powered by twenty percent more powder than a Browning .50-caliber cartridge. They struck the runner like a heavy-metal hurricane and virtually shredded him between one long stride and the next. A crimson mist enveloped him as he went down.

The second runner heard death coming for him and

half turned to meet it, triggering a wild burst from his short assault rifle. It might've done the job, if he had taken time to aim, but as it was he missed his killer and the roaring helicopter altogether. Rounds and effort wasted absolutely.

Bolan fired again, with near-identical results. The only difference: this time, his bullets plucked the Russian off his feet and held him briefly airborne, twitching like a rag doll as the armor-piercing slugs ripped flesh and bone to bloody tatters. When he fell, the dead man landed with the impact of a loaded duffel bag dropped from a second-story height.

And that left two.

"Another pass!" he called to Anuchin as they swept by the last two runners. She translated, and the Ka-60 came around to make another strafing run.

Fish in a barrel, Bolan thought. Except that these fish were piranhas, and they still had the ability to kill, if he gave them a fighting chance.

No mercy, then.

I AM THE LAST MAN standing, Grigory Rybakov thought, and nearly laughed out loud at the idea. For years, since rising to command the Moscow underworld, he'd been surrounded by a private army and protected by authorities who wanted the illicit payments they received to keep on flowing without interruption.

Now, most of his army was at home, or scattered over outposts where they did no earthly good for him at all, and those with him were dead. Obliterated, really, by machine-gun fire from his own helicopter.

That was funny, in itself. Rybakov didn't know how his intended victims had hijacked the aircraft, but he had to give them credit for it. And, if he survived this mess—

which seemed unlikely at the moment—he would have to kill the pilots for surrendering their ship. They should have died defending it, protecting *him*.

Rybakov slumped against a tree trunk, breathing heavily, his heart pounding like a jackhammer against his ribs. He had gained weight the past few years, and cut back on his workouts in the home gymnasium he'd built at great expense. Too late, he realized that he didn't possess the stamina required for playing hide-and-seek with airborne killers in the backwoods of Siberia.

The helicopter thundered overhead once more, and this time gunfire came along with it. He ducked and dodged as heavy slugs cut through the treetops, searching for him. When his feet flew out from under him, dropping him on his backside, there was nothing he could do but slide downhill, leaving a broad skidmark behind him all the way.

He wound up near the bottom of the slope, within a few yards of the highway, his clothing soiled, expensive shoes covered with muck, leaf litter in his hair. The sheer indignity of his position was enough to make him bellow fury at the sky.

There was only so much that a man with any self-respect could bear. Cursing nonstop, Rybakov struggled to his feet, using his automatic rifle as a crutch until he gained his balance. Once he'd managed to accomplish that, he checked the weapon, brushing off the dirt that coated it, and pulled the magazine to check its load.

Still full, since there had been no opportunity for him to fire it yet. But he would change that in a moment.

Pausing one last time, Rybakov wondered whether anyone would ever know that he had gone down fighting. Would they care, or would they all be too damned busy picking over his remains, dividing up his territory and possessions to consider how a legendary godfather had died?

No matter.

He would know, while he was roasting in the fires of hell. Or, if there was no hell, as he suspected—nothing but an endless void beyond this transitory life—then nothing mattered, anyhow.

Resolved to die as he had lived, defiant to the end, Rybakov put a broad smile on his face and stepped from cover to confront his enemies.

"You bastards! Here I am!" he shouted, blazing at the giant insect overhead with his Kalashnikov.

And when it came, he barely felt the killing rain.

EPILOGUE

Seymchan Airport, Magadan Oblast

The airport bearing Seymchan's name stood one mile southeast of the town itself. Ten thousand people occupied Seymchan, mostly employed at timber-cutting or food-processing. A spur of the Kolyma Highway linked the town to Magadan, but Bolan didn't plan on driving any farther in Siberia.

Refueling at the airport was a snap. One of the pilots had a credit card supplied by Rybakov, and there was no traffic ahead of them. In fact, it looked to Bolan as if traffic had been light for years. He and his three companions had the place all to themselves.

Within an hour after touchdown, they were airborne once again. Bolan had used his time at Seymchan to touch base with Stony Man and had the call sign for the *Kansas City,* if they made it to the coast. He hadn't ruled out fighter interception yet, but saw no reason why the Russian air force ought to be aware that they'd appropriated Rybakov's helicopter.

Three hundred miles and change to Magadan from liftoff at the rural airport. Call it two hours in the air, plus time over the water while they radioed the *Kansas City,* waited for it to respond, then made connections.

How?

Their Ka-60 didn't have pontoons to land at sea, and

even though it stretched beyond a football field in length, the submarine had no facility for choppers landing on its deck. That narrowed Bolan's choices down to two: jump from the helicopter at a height that wouldn't further damage Anuchin's hip, or ditch the bird at sea and try to swim for it, assuming that they weren't killed or disabled in the crash.

Bolan spent their flight time with the Kord machine gun, watching out for any hostile aircraft that might suddenly appear. Anuchin watched the pilots, making sure that neither of them touched the Ka-60's radio until they cleared the coastline and were ready to make contact with the sub. In fact, the crewmen both seemed glad to be alive, and no planes showed up in their wake.

Approaching Magadan, they had to watch it, skirting wide around the city and ignoring radio feelers from Sokol Airport's control tower. If the operators were alarmed, they might contact Dolinsk-Sokol airbase, home to the Sukhoi Su-15 fighters that shot down Korean Air Lines Flight 007 in September 1983. By that time, though, the chopper should be well offshore and close to contact with the *Kansas City*.

Unless something had gone wrong.

That was always a possibility, but as they cleared the coast and Anuchin started sending out their coded message to the submarine, Bolan stayed focused on the positive. He would do everything within his power, while they lived, to carry out his mission as required.

She got an answer on her third attempt to hail the *Kansas City*—code name "Narwhal," for the Arctic whale that boasts a ten-foot spiral tusk atop its snout. The callback came through loud and clear, together with a homing signal for the chopper's GPS device.

Five minutes later, they were on target and hovering, the great form of the sub rising beneath them like a whale itself, foam breaking on its deck and conning tower. Anuchin kept the pilots covered, had them bring the Ka-60 down to ten feet above the surface, almost skimming the wavetops, then joined Bolan in the open starboard bay.

"Ready for this?" he asked her.

"Long past ready," she replied.

The chopper had no life jackets aboard, but Anuchin had assured him she could swim. After squeezing Bolan's hand, she waited for his signal, then leaped into space.

Before the pilots could try anything, he followed Anuchin down, dropping feetfirst into the roiling Sea of Okhotsk. Minutes in that frigid water could be lethal, but the *Kansas City*'s crew was scrambling to retrieve them, hauling both aboard and down belowdecks by the time the Ka-60 was a dwindling spot on the horizon.

Commander Houston Greene was waiting for them on the bridge, greeting the new arrivals with a tight-lipped smile. He kept them waiting while he issued orders for a dive and hard run eastward, out of Russian territorial waters.

That done, he turned to Anuchin first, saying, "I see you're injured, ma'am."

"It's nothing," she assured him.

"I'd prefer to let our doctor be the judge of that, if you don't mind," Greene said. "I'm tasked to make delivery of you in A-one shape, if possible."

"I'd like some dry clothes first," she answered.

Greene nodded. "That's job one, for both of you. Hot showers likely wouldn't hurt you, either. While you're getting squared away, I need to put some mileage between us and Mother Russia. And about those sidearms that you're carrying..."

"You're welcome to them," Bolan said. "We shouldn't need them here."

Greene frowned at that, said, "If you do, my next post will be swabbing out the bilges on a trawler in the Bering Sea. You're safe now, people. Next stop, San Diego, U.S.A."

Where Bolan's younger brother lived, at least part-time. He might call Johnny while he was in town. Maybe they'd get together, catch a game if he could manage some downtime.

Until the next time out. New faces on the same old enemies.

Names changed, along with ideologies, but Evil stayed the same. It was relentless and insatiable. It never slept. It couldn't be defeated in the long run.

But this day, right now, it had been bruised a bit.

Forced to retreat a little, from the Executioner.

* * * * *

TAKE 'EM FREE
2 action-packed novels plus a mystery bonus

NO RISK
NO OBLIGATION TO BUY

Don Pendleton
CLOSE QUARTERS
Violent extremists spark hellfire in the Middle East.

When Peace Corp volunteers working in Paraguay are kidnapped and brutalized by a mysterious new Islamic terrorist group, Stony Man gets the call. His dual mission: an under-the-radar jungle rescue and a hunt through the backstreets of Tehran for the terrorist masterminds. Surrounded and outgunned, is Stony Man willing to make the ultimate sacrifice to complete the assignment?

STONY MAN®

Available June wherever books are sold.